Random Tendencies

Random Tendencies

By

David Goldstein

Print ISBN-13: 9798989166435

1

It was late afternoon as Mabel Belkin was walking along a cliff edge path that ran along the western border of Olivia Cleaver's women's hippy commune. She was responding to an invitation from Olivia, her boss, (who was the publicly much beloved founder of Havanna Bandana Cannabis products). No other details had been provided about the upcoming meeting which had left Mabel wondering what was up.

Directly in front of her was Olivia herself, toting a leather crossbody satchel as she led the way to an outcrop that provided a striking vista of the Pacific ocean that included a distant view of the Golden Gate bridge.

Portions of the path skirted the cliff edge, bordered by a wooden guard rail, which had been erected two decades back when Olivia first acquired the property.

When they arrived at their destination, Mabel noted that Olivia had authorized an eight foot long park bench to be installed for people to be able to sit and enjoy the frequent colorful sunsets— the woman was always doing things like this for the commune members.

For her part, Mabel considered it a big waste of money as she was not fond of the commune concept as well as many of the women inhabitants. She was self-focused only on wealth acquisition. It was one of the many things the two women did not agree on.

Mabel had been hired twelve years earlier based on her previous successful record of accomplishments at other companies, (though not enough had been done to confirm the truth of what was in Mabel's resume at that time). She had convinced Olivia that she could help guide her through the Wall Street wilderness of big money, but time and again, Olivia would seek her counsel, then did something completely opposite, and each time, Olivia's plan worked. She had often felt like a bystander as Olivia patiently developed her company's signature cannabis product. The upshot of which left Mabel increasingly resentful over time, even though she enjoyed the rewards of a good salary, a generous yearly bonus and benefits. So here they were today, to discuss something that Mabel assumed would piss her off by the end of the conversation.

Olivia sat down on the bench and signaled for Mabel to take a seat on the other end. Mabel had known Olivia long enough to realize the woman was struggling with what she was wanting to talk about. This raised alarms in her head as she again began to speculate—it crossed her mind that she had been making entries in the company's financial ledgers that led to donations to a fake charity she had set up for herself to improve her financial portfolio. Her pulse began to race as she pondered if Olivia had finally caught on to her shenanigans after a recent audit.

Sighing, Olivia opened with, "Mabel, I wanted to let you know I am looking at retiring. I intend to spend more time with my daughter, Elizabeth, and set her on a more proper course with her life."

Mabel nodded but said nothing.

Olivia continued, "Work is too much of a distraction these days for me to continue. Also, I have transferred my stock and all my other assets as well as the commune property into a non-profit foundation. Elizabeth will be in charge of that, with my guidance at first, then later, all on her own."

Exercising all the control Mabel could muster, she said, "So where does that leave me?"

Olivia nodded and said, "That's the other thing we need to talk about. Listen, you have been a… good employee and for all your efforts, I want to recognize that. The severance package I am providing is more than fair and the stock options I am giving you, along with the cash should be quite helpful in enabling you to look for new opportunities."

Mabel felt a spike of adrenalin, driven by rage. After all her time helping this ungrateful woman, she realized she was being let go— her recent embezzlement activity never crossed her mind. "So, you're dumping my ass?"

"Please don't think of it that way Mabel. It's more of a… corporate rightsizing that my accountants say we need to do. Especially after they took a serious look at the company's books." She paused to let that sink in with Mabel, then continued, "And, as I said, you will find HBC has been more than generous in this severance package."

Olivia then reached into her satchel and handed over a thick envelope containing the paperwork prepared by HBC's human resources department. She said, "The second copy is yours."

Mabel narrowed her eyes as she accepted it, but her rage was escalating as she flipped through the documents, even though it was obviously a substantial severance. Finally, she looked up and said, "So, you are getting great pleasure out of all of this, aren't you."

Olivia tilted her head, now expressionless and said, "No, not at all. In fact, I brought you here to do this in private because I wanted you to know there is nothing personal about this even despite all the times we have had disagreements. Now… I need you to sign that last page so we can both move on."

Sensing a lack of sincerity in Olivia's demeanor while suddenly thinking about her own embezzlement behavior, Mabel sighed, scribbled her signature and handed back the paperwork, which Olivia accepted and placed back in the satchel. Mabel then said, "Well, Olivia, I do have animosity. Years of it in fact."

The expression on Olivia's face was undisguised contempt as she said, "Is that why you have been cooking the books lately?"

Mabel realized the woman knew everything. Now fearful as well as boiling mad, she leapt to her feet, (best she could anyway, she was not particularly athletic) and attempted to attack her boss.

The ground, however, was uneven and she tripped over a rock projecting out of the soil in front of the bench, fell to her knees, scraping one badly, so the assault was pretty much negated.

Olivia hopped to her feet, grabbed her satchel as she shouted, "You're a thief! I know about all the money you stole, you... embezzler! I am calling the cops now!" She then began running back towards the commune.

Mabel struggled to her feet and chased after her, screaming like a banshee. She caught up with Olivia at the old wooden guard rail and pinned the woman against it, screaming at her "I should murder you!"

Olivia looked terrified and said, "You're fucking nuts! I always knew it! So yes, consider your ass fired! Now get off of me!" Olivia then took a swing and hit Mabel in the right eye, making her yelp.

Which led to Mabel shoving her shoulder into Olivia's chest and pushing as hard as she could. The old wooden plank that Olivia was up against bent outward and then snapped. Olivia screamed as she fell off the cliff and to her death.

Mabel almost went with her, instead she sprawled forward onto her knees at the cliff edge. Her fury evaporated, now replaced by abject fear for what she had just done as she reluctantly peered over the cliff's edge. Below was Olivia's lifeless body jellying up the shoreline boulders.

Panicked, Mabel high tailed it back to her car and as calmly as she could to not attract attention, drove out of the commune and headed back to her apartment. Looking in her bath mirror, she saw her black eye from Olivia's parting blow, swollen shut and bruised. After her brief examination, she started ruminating about every sort of scenario that would lead her to a life sentence or likely her own execution.

Several days later the police dropped by her apartment to question her whereabouts on the day of the death of Olivia Cleaver, which was now in the papers and on the daily news shows. She claimed she had been out of town on vacation at the time as the cops made notes. She played dumb, asked sincere questions and appeared somewhat bereft.

She later read in the paper that once Olivia's body had been found after her fall, and being an unattended death, suicide was a possibility, though according to the article, the circumstances were still under investigation. Mabel breathed a sigh of relief, thinking she might be in the clear.

However, all was not perfect. A week later, she heard from Elizabeth Cleaver, Olivia's spoiled rotten daughter, who said she was now in charge of HBC until they got a new CEO. Also, Mabel was terminated for an unexcused absence, having not shown up for work for the last two weeks and that Mabel needed to meet immediately with HBC human resources as she was part of a downsizing list of one that Liz pointedly declared had been found in her mother's last notes.

Mabel shook her fist at the heavens, raging again about how Cleaver women were diabolical. Then, to add insult to injury, day after day, the local TV news played stories about the great Elizabeth Cleaver and how she was leading the Cleaver Foundation into the future of modern dental care and that the police were thinking the death of her mother was now a tragic accident.

2

A decade later after Olivia's mysterious death, and Elizabeth's rise to power, fortunes had flipped, leading to the current situation where Elizabeth had been demoted from emperor to peasant status. Liz, as she was known to friends and enemies alike, had lost everything—her lover, her vast fortune and especially, her illusions of grandeur driven by her elevated position in life. Her forced departure earlier that morning from her palatial estate and her old life had only added insult to her injured psyche.

The drive down from Santa Del Lola to San Francisco was absolute misery. Under a vigilant escort, she was first taken to a spartan, low income apartment where she was handed a set of worn keys and told to dump off her two suitcases of belongings. Without being given time to unpack, she was then shuttled to a free dental clinic where she would be required to actually work and for which she would receive a monthly beggarly stipend, (paid in arrears of course). And she now desperately needed the stipend because the money was her sole source of income.

One of the older women providing the unwanted taxi service was a former member of her mother's old commune that Olivia had ejected due to bad behavior, as was the driver. Liz only vaguely remembered the incident involving the pair. The woman climbed out of their sedan and opened the door for Liz as she growled, "Welcome to your new destination… your majesty." She then pointed to the clinic entrance and smiled, offering a display of some really dingy, badly maintained teeth.

As Liz climbed out of the car, she grimaced at the brownout she was viewing and unable to resist, said, "Looks like you need to be here a lot worse than me." The other woman that had been driving walked up behind Liz and snapped, "Shut your yap woman!" as she propelled Liz from behind with a big shove—Liz stumbled forward, barely avoiding a fall. She was now walking towards her new day-to-day hell with zero positive thoughts.

Bad teeth woman now shuffled past Liz to the clinic counter and asked for Dr. Adams, the dentist in charge. When he arrived, the woman said, "Liz Cleaver, reporting for duty. Make her fucking miserable." Dr. Adams laughed and replied, "No problem!"

3

Billy Fuller grunted in frustration as he reset the circuit breaker on the dishwasher for the third time, (it immediately tripped in response to each effort). There were dirty dishes everywhere, piled high and deep on a stainless steel wrap-around table situated in the back of an old, tiled wall diner kitchen filled with steamy air and funky odors. The ancient dishwashing machine was belly up. Bus boy Patrick, a somewhat juvenile delinquent teenager, was continuing to deliver more plateware needing to be cleaned by the minute, and now everything was in a full, manual operation with the diner's manager looking around the corner every couple of minutes to check on Billy's progress.

Staring at the mess in front of him, he sagged. This had been another shit day of many similar days since his previous high tech employer, Pearly Whites, went bust, leaving him jobless, benefitless, and when his meager unemployment had run out, forcing him to take the only position he could find. For some reason, having been a laboratory assistant at a genetic tooth laboratory never got him far on his resume in Santa De Lola but his post high school background in restaurant kitchen work had managed to secure this job.

Heaving a sigh, he ran his tongue around the inside front of his mouth, grimacing and again noting his four missing teeth, another unfriendly reminder of his experiences at his previous employer.

Jerome, his partner, rode Billy's ass all the time about that fiasco. He would say things like, "Why did you decide to volunteer to have four front teeth replaced at *once?*" Billy could hear the implied, "moron" at the end of that sentence, even though Jerome never actually said it. Then a month ago, his erstwhile partner quit his own low paying job from the local "Whatah' Chicken" fast food joint and with his meager savings, had departed, saying he needed a break and would be spending extended time with his relatives in Hicksville, Mississippi.

Returning to the present, Billy watched as the diner's manager, Veronica, approached, a stern expression on her face. She said, "So, the repair folk should be here in about an hour or two. Need you to pick up the pace though Billy. Perky Petite's diner is a true historic destination in this town and we gotta deliver. Which means, we need plateware now!"

Billy nodded, his mood transitioning from depressed to annoyed. What the fuck did Veronica think he was doing? Polishing the silverware at Perky fucking Petite's? Still, he simply mumbled, "Sure Veronica, sure."

She frowned, apparently trying to make out the muffled reply. Which was normal because ever since Billy had decided to have his defective genetically grown teeth removed and having run over his own temporary prosthetic teeth in an embarrassing screwup, indistinct speech patterns were his trademark.

Veronica said, "Uh, I hope that was a yes. Listen, we've got customers waiting. Chop-Chop Billy." She then turned and scurried back to the cash register where he could hear her bantering with some regulars paying their bill.

For his part, instead of stepping up the pace, Billy stepped out the back door into the alley to get some fresh air where he spotted what looked like a bum rummaging through the trash. Something about this person looked familiar. Billy said, "Hey there!" He received no response, then shrugged to himself, not needing to find out at that moment what the familiarity was. He stepped back in and washed a few dishes while keeping an eye out for the boss.

*

More than a little put out, Agent Jade Miller was sitting in the office of her grouchy boss, Supervisory Special Agent In Charge, Matt Salton. Her summoning had happened while she was on vacation, trying to complete a second photo shoot with her French boyfriend, Jean-André for their series of racy images entitled Mocha & Alabaster. The regularity of her day job interfering with her hobby seemed almost premeditated in nature.

Salton had a grim expression on his face, oblivious to her hostile expression as he peered at the computer screen in front of him and sighed. Actually, he rarely considered his agent's attitudes, as his days were typically consumed with his superiors crawling up his own rear for detailed inspections, demanding results on various cases.

Plus, he was used to agents with attitudes, since he typically pressured them the same way he was pressured. All one big happy federal family. He sighed again and rolled his chair back from his screen, steepled his fingers, shifted his glum gaze to Miller and said, "So, your Pearly Whites investigation. About wrapped up?"

Miller nodded and pointedly said, "Yes sir, in fact it was some weeks back. That was why I was on *vacation*." Salton nodded, ignoring the sarcasm. He said, "Well Miller, you're getting a promotion. You are now a special agent. Your pay is getting bumped as well."

Miller brightened, suddenly feeling a bit less annoyed.

Salton continued, "Along with that raise, got a new assignment for ya. Sort of an extension of your old assignment. International in scope. Highest priority." Miller, now realizing the worm dangling in front of her was on a hook, said, "And what would that be boss?"

"The AG wants to investigate a lot of the shenanigans around the bunch that funded the company Pearly Whites. The investment firm that Martin Crosswaithe runs. Apparently, the stock debacle got the SEC and then the AG's attention."

It was Miller's turn to sigh and shake her head. She said, "You're referring to Sand Harvest Investments."

"That's my special agent! See why you got promoted? And along with that, it seems there is some sort of relationship between S.H.I. and the Cleaver foundation. It's shady, out of country, off the books sort of stuff as best I understand it. Should keep you busy for a while now that you are promoted!"

The last comment made Miller realize that Salton had used the "sandwich" technique on her. First good news, then bad news, then good news. However, he had used the first good news for the second good news. She saw that as a lack of imagination. Miller said, "So, I need a psychiatrist to go back and start interviewing some of the Pearly Whites folks for deep background."

"Fresh out of shrinks Miller."

Expecting that comeback, Miller replied, "I have someone in mind. Dr. Borders, the psychiatrist that was involved with the previous investigation. The woman knows her stuff and we need her insights about the various people that were involved in that situation. We could contract with her instead of starting from scratch and we still got plenty of discretionary money we could use."

Salton leaned back, eyebrows raised, then shrugged, "Sure, sure, whatever you need to get this ball rolling." He then turned back to his computer and sighed.

Realizing the session was over, Miller stood and left, heading to her office. Upon arrival, she logged into her laptop and brought up the notes on the Pearly Whites' case. She got to the profile on Martin Crosswaithe—the man had an extensive profile of making lots of money via shady investments. She clicked her pen a few times, then started writing some notes.

An hour later, she called Dr. Borders and set up a lunch appointment to discuss bringing her onboard to build some in-depth profiles of specific members of the former Pearly Whites senior staff. The doctor suggested they try Bartholomew's Broccoli Bistro, the latest all vegan destination in Santa De Lola, to which Miller agreed.

Finally, Miller called Jean-André to let to tell him about her promotion, which was her not so subtle way of letting him know vacation was on hold due to her new assignment. He cursed in French, and said, "Jade, this FBI thing. It is interfering with the building of my career! You must consider quitting."

Miller gave up on trying her own sandwich attempt on the guy and replied, "Listen dude, it's your career, my hobby. When I met you, you were living with four other male "models" going nowhere. Now you live with me, use *my* personal car, and get to live a high life while *I* work as you pursue *your career*! So, take a powder."

Jean-André sniffed and said, "You don't have to be so aggressive. Sometimes it's sexy, but right now, it makes me limp."

Miller rolled her eyes and ended the call with, "Boohoo. Now, I have got to actually work, so see you whenever I get in. And fill up the damn car for a change."

An hour later, she arrived at Bartholomew's. Dr Border's was already there. They shook hands as they were seated at a table for two situated on a deck overlooking the busy street below.

Dr. Borders led with "Thank you Special Agent Miller for giving me a call. So, what are we thinking here?"

Miller said, "Don't be so formal Doc." She smiled and continued, "Call me Miller."

Dr. Borders shrugged and said, "Terrific. Call me Borders."

"I probably would anyway after a while."

"Okay then, Miller, that's settled. What's the drama here?"

Miller outlined her plan, "I need to build a case against some criminally inclined international players in the investment world. I can't tell you a lot more until I get your formal background investigation completed, but I think you will be invaluable in helping the FBI develop a deeper understanding and insight of some of the senior members of Pearly Whites you previously encountered, along with their relationships with the criminal suspects I am looking into."

Borders nodded, and replied, "Sounds like fun, so, I am in. Let's talk money."

"Excellent! The FBI can pay you $200 per hour with a $10k upfront retainer."

Borders nodded and said, "Sounds better than talkin' to nuts in the ER that just attempted to stab their uncle but got their own thigh." She then provided basic information for Miller to get started on her background including her professional and educational history.

Miller looked up from her note taking and said, "Harvard? Wow."

Borders shrugged, "Grew up in Boston."

Their lunch arrived and as the meal progressed, Miller said, "You don't have much of an accent."

"Ah, you mean, like Hahvahd Yahd? I got tired of being made fun of when I moved out west, so I've worked to suppress it."

Miller shrugged, "Makes you sound tough. You should use your accent in the interviews. By the way, this food sucks."

Borders nodded in agreement and let her accent flow, "I'm renamin' the dump to Bahts Bahf Bistro!" They both laughed, shoved their plates aside, and continued their chat.

4

Agent Miller parked her car outside the FBI office, then sat for a moment contemplating her next steps in this investigation. Werner Brandt, the disgraced former CEO of Pearly Whites had finally made a deal to hand over a large chunk of his cash to settle his criminal charges. Miller had gotten approval that the money would finance the way forward in her investigation.

The man had been a hardass about forking over his money that was cached offshore. She guessed she could not blame him, except for the part where he had broken the law, though it did seem he had been pretty clueless about the act when he did it. Not that the AG even cared when deciding to prosecute—which had led to Brandt's deal, as he preferred his mansion over a prison cell. She sighed happily as she exited her vehicle and headed on into the building. Sitting down at her desk a few moments later, she began perusing some administrivia emails Salton had sent out.

Borders wandered in and sat down next to her after placing two cups of coffee on the table. She sipped hers while Miller gave a quizzical look and finally said, "What's up?"

"Well, I've been doing what you are paying me to do. I noticed a few interesting things as I have gone through my background work on apparent relationships Pearly Whites had with Martin Crosswaithe and the Cleaver foundation. Psychologically, weird shit. Financially, however? Fascinating."

"Oh? Sounds intriguing, please continue."

"Elizabeth Cleaver. Did you ever meet her?"

"Liz Cleaver as I recall from all the media press?" Borders nodded. Miller continued, "Nope, never did. Isn't she the one that resigned from her mom's old foundation?"

"Resigned might not be the right word. In fact, Ms. Cleaver seems to have been very absorbed in running her foundation and the joys of being wealthy. I suspect a dose of narcissism in her makeup. At any rate, I asked some of your folks to check up on her. Interestingly enough, she is working for one of the dental clinics she was so proud of, though apparently living on some meager salary. Not at all her style."

Miller sat up in her chair and said, "Now, that is damn peculiar."

Borders nodded and continued, "It appears that she may have been railroaded. The current chairperson is Mabel Belkin according to some recent court filings. Now, this is where it gets a bit wonky, but I wanted to provide you detail that came back as we dug in deeper." She then dove into the past history of Liz's mom, Olivia Cleaver, and the old hippie commune she had once founded and maintained. The most interesting aspect to this part of the saga was Mabel Belkin was formerly employed by HBC and had been fired by Liz Cleaver shortly after the mysterious death of Olivia.

Pausing to let all that sink in, she concluded her analysis, "Also, when Liz took over, she shut down the commune and built her opulent estate on top of it. Now, why in the world would the woman walk away after all the things she'd done and all the wealth she had? And how did Belkin suddenly become the one running things, if previously she was fired?"

Miller nodded as she looked at Borders expectant expression, "There's something else?"

"Your agents have discovered that Mabel Belkin is talking with Martin Crosswaithe, and apparently those talks began taking place even before Mabel took charge. What I wonder is—what would that working relationship be?"

Miller raised an eyebrow, nodded and said, "I think we need to meet with this Liz Cleaver." With a smile, Borders nodded.

Liz Cleaver was reflecting on her always being perched on the precipice of wanting to either burn or murder someone, (and on a regular basis). By her definition of regular, this could be daily, hourly or due to more recent events, even minute to minute. Now a mere two weeks into her new reality, Liz found working for a subsistence wage to be vile and demeaning.

She was positive that she was better than this hovel-like existence, having been told repeatedly how special he was by her beloved late mother, Olivia. Plus, she knew what it was to live a life of no limits, (especially financially).

Liz also spent plenty of time recently focusing on her new nemesis, the wicked old witch, Mabel Belkin, who had taken everything that mattered from her. Once the shock had worn off of being forced into this indentured servitude-like position, Liz became determined to make a comeback and avenge the wrongs perpetrated on her. Yet so far, the path forward had eluded her. However, she was determined not to give up. In her mind, Mabel was in deep shit. She just did not know it yet.

Her boiling hot reverie was disturbed by Dr. Adams as he said, "Liz, we need you to go pick up our lunch order over at China Pantry. Please get a move on, the rest of the crew is hungry." Dr. Adams, Liz had learned, had been assigned to this clinic at the same time that she had. He was an old associate, as it turned out, with Mabel Belkin.

She replied, "Dr. Adams, that's on the other side of town! Why not just get it delivered?"

He shrugged, "Foundation pressure to conserve money. You know, delivery fees, tips, that sort of thing."

"Really? So, is everything okay?"

Obviously annoyed at her questions, he sharply replied, "That is no longer your concern. Is it? Now, you need to get your rear in gear." He then turned and left.

Liz got to her feet, flipped off the man's receding figure then walked to the front desk of the clinic to get the keys to an old panel van as she considered locating some lighter fluid and matches so she could toast Dr. Adams testes.

Moments later she was at the wheel, wangling through traffic to China Pantry. She picked up the order, placed it on the passenger side floorboard of the van then walked around to the driver's side. As she began to open her door, from behind her she heard, "Liz Cleaver, I need a few moments of your time." Liz immediately thought this was some further harassment on Mabel's part and spun around ready for a confrontation. Instead, she found Special Agent Miller standing there holding out her credentials.

Liz stepped forward, glanced at the ID, then said, "What in the world do you want with me?"

Miller smiled, "Thought you might want to talk about your relationship with Mabel Belkin."

Tersely, Liz said, "I wouldn't call it a relationship."

"I know. Which is why we need to talk. Do you remember Martin Crosswaithe?"

Liz was suddenly curious, though she was still feeling cautious. This was an FBI agent after all. She said, "Uh, why are you asking me these questions?"

Miller replied, "I hear he might have done some shady stuff… once upon a time."

Liz's reservation about talking to Miller fell to the wayside as she said, "Okay, I do know him. What do you need from me?"

"I am working on a case and can't give you much detail at this point, but it involves both the people I mentioned. I can tell you more, but only after you formally decide you want to work with the FBI. If you do, we need to meet up very soon. Here is my number, call me if you want to be involved." She handed over a folded piece of paper.

Liz accepted the note, and after a moment said, "I'll be in touch."

*

Robert Oppenheimer, (he preferred being called "Bob"), was sandwiched sideways in the passenger seat of his once prized corvette, legs draped over the console and into the driver seat. He was trying to sleep and as usual, a car designed for performance made a poor substitute for a bed.

Things had gone particularly poorly for Bob since losing his job. His main problem: he had almost no cash resources, having spent extravagantly during his previous employment period at Pearly Whites. His stock had tanked before he could sell any. He had managed to recover a Mercedes he had bought for his ex-girlfriend Helga and sold it off to a used car lot operated by pirates, for a third of what it had cost new. That cash was running thin, so he had moved out of his econo-midget apartment and into his car to conserve what little money he had left. His formerly well-dressed and coifed persona was now transformed into a t-shirt, shabby jeans, and a nearly shaved head motif to keep living costs down to zero. Finally, Bob kept the vette and his right foot in econo-mode and tried to walk more than drive if possible.

Job interviews had been tough. He had been circulating his resume via a computer at the public library with no success. Recently, he had removed his references to his position at Pearly Whites—the head librarian had suggested that to him when she was peering over his shoulder helping him with his mediocre spelling skills, joking that it was like advertising as the former designer of the Titanic. The editing changes didn't make any difference. Any paying positions in the corporate world were currently beyond his reach. He had recently begun to consider changing his last name since Oppenheimer was associated with a lot of negative thoughts about nuclear weapons on the one hand and financial disaster with heavy stock losses on the other.

Tonight was chilly, with a pacific breeze blowing in from the northwest. He had been rummaging in an alley outside a nearby diner earlier as sometimes food that came out of the dumpster was otherwise untouched but still edible. However, somebody had stepped out the back door and spooked him. He decided to slip back over in a bit as the place slowed down a lot late in the evening, then try to get a few hours rest in the vette.

Back when he initially lost his job, he was drug and alcohol addled and had for a time gone social media nuts, today rarely recalling what he had posted about. He had also been texting a few fellow ex-employees hoping to get some help. Some had kept wishing him good luck if they replied at all.

He had tried to hook up with Sally Dinklestern, one of the few people who had managed to retain her wealth out of that debacle. She texted back with a nasty "Fuck off loser and quit texting me." Her hostility was a mystery to Bob as he had never done anything but complement her looks and offer sage advice.

He was ultimately in denial over his own complicity in what had happened at his old job at Pearly Whites. He tried not to think about it most of the time, as he would get so upset it made him have to pee. In fact, having thought about it, he now had to do just that. It was around nine in the evening, so he decided to take care of his bladder and appetite, hopefully in one trip.

Clambering out of the vette, he wandered the back alley just short of Perky Petite's where he unzipped and relieved himself in the dark, away from nearby streetlamps, (nothing like explaining taking a public leak to a cop). He then slipped over to the diner to begin rummaging.

Standing in the front of the dumpster on a couple of concrete blocks he kept situated nearby, he was about halfway into the scattered trash when a voice said, "Watsh ya doin' mishter? Thatsh private property!"

Startled, Bob jerked his head up and banged it into the overhanging metal lid of the container. The world whirled as he tried to steady himself, but the knock to his brain was too hard. He stumbled off the blocks, fell backwards and hit the pavement with a thump.

As his discombobulation cleared, he found somebody leaning over him, looking vaguely concerned and very familiar. It then hit his still addled brain—his former Pearly Whites admin assistant, Billy Fuller, was bent over, looking down at him, frowning. The man was dressed oddly, Bob thought, for someone that worked as a lab rat and then secretary.

"Billy, what's with the apron? Did you see who hit me? What time is the conference call? His bewildered brain spun like a roulette wheel and stopped on, "Oh, and when did trash dumpsters become private property?"

*

Billy stood over Bob, realizing this was the same character he had seen earlier during the failed dishwasher episode that had led him to step outside to calm down. He peered quizzically at Bob, saying nothing, wondering if he ought to just go back into the restaurant.

Bob closed his eyes. When he opened them, Billy was still pondering what to do. Bob asked, "Please?"

Billy sighed, extended his hand to Bob, and unceremoniously pulled the man to his feet. He said, "Follow me."

Back on his feet, Bob temporarily used the side of the dumpster for support, then wobbled forward, trailing behind Billy, who led him to an old chair near the dishwasher area in the diner.

The place smelled fantastic to Bob. His stomach growled. Billy, expressionless, could hear the gut noise. He wandered off and came back after a few minutes with a grilled ham and cheese sandwich along with some fries. He simply said, "Eat."

Bob gave a lopsided smile as he dug in with gusto. Billy walked a few steps and pulled a final rack of dishes out of the now repaired machine. He stacked them, then shut the line down for the night. The fry cook, Miranda, walked over and smiled at him. Billy said, "Thansh for fishing Bob the sandwish." Miranda affectionately rubbed Billy on the back and said, "Your welcome Billy. Is this your friend?"

Billy grimaced as he shook his head in a vigorous no. Miranda just nodded, walked off and said, "See you later young man. I'm locking up in ten minutes." Billy watched his friend walk away. He then looked at Bob and said, "So…where are you shtaying?"

Bob said, "Uh, in the vette."

Billy rolled his eyes and said, "Follow me," as he took off his apron and hung it on a hook by the backdoor.

Once outside, they went down the alley past where Bob had urinated earlier and based on the stench level, apparently quite often. Billy's nose wrinkled as he sniffed the foul odor.

Continuing on, they arrived where Billy had parked his poorly maintained Chevy Vega. The car was another rather squalid reminder of his genetic implant tooth debacle as well as an inadequate replacement of his beloved, though now totaled Pinto. It beat walking, though the old beater's oil consumption was absurd, burning nearly as much oil as it did gas. He drove Bob to his car, and again said, "Follow me."

Once Bob was in his car, he dropped in behind Billy, getting a good dose of exhaust smoke and partially cooked hydrocarbons which made him sneeze repeatedly. They wound up in a tired part of town at an old rundown single story apartment complex sporting a totally dry swimming pool. Once parked, Billy again nodded for Bob to follow him. In the apartment, Billy pointed to the couch, "Shleep there!"

Bob said, "Where's Jerome? Will he mind?"

Billy, expressionless, said, "Jerome's in Mishishipi again. Don't worry."

Bob said, "Okay. Thanks, dude. You won't be sorry you did this." Billy rolled his eyes and headed to the kitchenette. Bob grinned to himself, sat down on the sofa, rolled on his side, thinking, *Just like old times!* He was asleep in about twenty seconds.

5

The next morning was a day off for Billy. He strolled into his kitchenette to eat some jelly donuts at five in the morning, maintaining his normal work schedule. Formerly a serious weightlifting fanatic that exercised religiously, he had let himself go since Pearly Whites had augered in, putting on a few pounds, mostly around his midsection. Buffness, at least for now, seemed like a pain in the ass. Sitting forlornly stuffing the pastries in his mouth he stared at Bob, who was snoring peacefully on the sofa.

Billy was still trying to divine why in the world he had decided to show mercy and bring Bob back to his apartment. He shrugged as he maneuvered the current bite to the side of his mouth so he could chew it—thinking about his own behavior of late was more effort than he liked to expend.

Bob suddenly snorted awake, saying, "I didn't do it!"

Billy said, "Didn't do what?"

Bob sat up, put his feet on the floor, and shook his head. He said, "That was a doozy of a dream."

"Nightmare?"

"No, not really. I dreamt we got you some new front teeth."

"Ah, and where did we go for that? Teeth are ush? Tooth fairy? We shtick up a dentish?"

Bob appeared in deep thought, snapped his fingers and said, "You know what, I do know where we can go."

"Where?"

"The free dental clinic down in San Francisco!"

"They have one in Shan Franchishco? We never got the one here in town that Cleaver bunsh promished."

"They do! And we can get you there in the vette via the new highway extension that runs from Santa De Lola right by the Cleaver bunch's estate to get to San Francisco faster than ever."

"You would do that?"

"If you pay for the gas."

Billy nodded cynically, "Of coursh."

So that day, Bob and Billy set out to restore Billy to full toothness. When they arrived, the normal line outside the clinic was non-existent. Finding a place to park the vette, Bob told Billy he was going to stay with the car, the area looked iffy, and he could not afford to lose any components or the car itself.

Billy said, "Iffy. Uh, like where I live now? Jeesh." He then turned and headed over to the office. A few moments later when he walked in the front door, the receptionist took his information and had him sit, saying a technician would be right with him. Which they were, an hour later.

Billy was almost dozing when he got a tap on his shoulder. Looking up, now startled, he thought he was seeing one of his arch enemies. The woman looked just like Liz Cleaver but in a dental tech outfit. The two ideas did not compute.

The woman gaped wide eyed at him. He realized it actually was Liz! He jumped to his feet and said, "Ish thish a joke? You and Bob in on thish together?"

Liz dropped her eyes and said, "No Billy, this is now where I work every single day. I… got demoted so to speak."

"What? Pleash!"

"Billy, I live in squalor now. My fortune stolen, my girlfriend lost, my dreams for cheap dental care for people like you dashed on the rocks of misfortune and corruption."

Billy realized Liz was telling the truth. At least she thought it was the truth, but hey, he was not one to judge.

Liz continued, "Come with me Billy. I know how much you have suffered. I think we can help today." And with that bit of encouragement, Billy went back to the dental chair where he got a temporary bridge and an appointment with an oral surgeon for permanent implants.

When he was leaving, he found he could enunciate a lot better and as he walked to the door with Liz next to him, he said, "It seems this clinic is actually doing what you said it would."

Liz nodded and said, "Well, sort of. I was defrauded out of my foundation by former commune members seeking revenge, led by Mabel Belkin. Remember that name Billy! They stole it, and to keep up appearances as they squander that fortune, they keep this place open."

"Commune? When did this happen?"

"Just as we were about to build the Pearly Whites production plant in Santa De Lola," Liz lied, since she had been the principal person holding back the money for that project.

Billy was livid. He said, "So these ex-commune people, they stole your foundation? How the fuck does somebody do that anyway?"

"Treachery Billy. Bloody treachery! Liz was now trembling violently, and the tone of her voice had gone up a few octaves as well as in volume. Billy began to blanch, and the receptionist said, "Cool it Liz. We don't need a scene like we had last week with the cops showing up."

With what appeared to be great effort, Liz regained most of her control as she focused on her recent conversation with Miller and that helped remind her of her new mission in life.

Billy walked out into the parking lot, with Liz by his side. He said, "Liz, I truthfully didn't know any of what you just told me. Let's stay in touch." He then nodded towards the corvette and added, "Bob Oppenheimer brought me down here, believe it or not. I found him scrounging food out of a dumpster where I work. Don't know why I decided to help him, but here I am today, I meet you, and I get an appointment for new teeth. Maybe we should all team up to get our lives restarted. Here is my phone number."

Liz pulled out her own phone and added it to her contacts, then gazed into Billy's eyes, and said, "Karma. It seems to be going around today. Believe me, I will be in touch."

With that, Billy returned to the vette and woke up a snoozing Bob. A couple of moments later, they headed back to Santa De Lola. As they headed north, Billy explained what happened at the clinic, running into Liz, his appointment, and the commune story she had laid on him.

Bob, still a bit vague on memories from all the drugs and alcohol he had consumed that ended when Pearly Whites went broke, started to build his own narrative in his mind about what happened. He exclaimed, "Rigged! The whole thing was rigged! Poor Liz! Poor Helga! Poor…" no other names came to mind at that point. "Anyway, we need to get our money back! We need to go after those communists Liz told you about!"

Billy said, "Ex-commune Bob. Though now they sound more like the mafia."

"Ex-communists? Wow! All I know, is we are putting the band back together!"

"Uh, yeah. Whatever."

*

Liz watched as the two men drove off, smiling to herself as they vanished from sight. In less than two days, her luck appeared to have begun to turn around.

That evening she texted Special Agent Miller and they agreed to a meeting. She went to her shabby apartment, changed out of her work outfit to something more appropriate, then per Miller's instructions, took a taxi across town to meet up with the FBI agent and someone Miller had referred to as Dr. Borders.

Once they were together, Miller walked her through the process of what they needed her to do as a confidential government informant, and that she would agree to cooperate with any aspect required in the investigation, (Liz noted that their conversation was being recorded on Borders phone).

Liz said yes to the arrangement, so Miller bought her dinner, reimbursed her both ways for her cab fees and made her aware of their next steps. Liz nodded and said, "This is great. And thank you for reaching out to me. I really thought I was totally on my own."

Miller nodded and said, "No worries, Liz. And here is some extra cash to help with what we need you to do. We can pay you occasionally to help you operate. Be careful as shit how you spend it, you do not want to arouse any suspicions with the clinic or Mabel."

Liz smiled, nodded, took the envelope and a few moments later was in a cab on her way back to her apartment.

6

On the other side of the Atlantic in the Mayfair district of London, at seven P.M. on the dot UK time, a large computer screen came online as Martin Crosswaithe entered the room from behind a sliding wood panel. He strode to his chair located behind a massive French oak desk that dominated the study.

On the screen was Mabel Belkin and two other elderly women who sat flanking her on each side. To Martin, they were quite attractive if a bit older.

Several weeks earlier, Martin had wangled a tentative alliance with Mabel since the press release that announced her taking over the Cleaver foundation. In Martin's world, that meant they might forge a fruitful relationship for additional wealth generation. This initial meeting was hopefully the first step.

Martin began, "I wanted to discuss the resurrection of TeeGentics, aka, Pearly Whites. I hate that name by the way."

Mabel smiled and said, "Yes, well, there are bigger matters than a name, but continue."

Martin smiled tightly and said, "I suppose you are right. Well then. Today we restart our efforts. I was thinking PhoenixGen. Rising from the ashes and all that sort of thing."

Mabel smirked and said, "A wonderful name. No more Pearly Whites then!"

Martin's response was again a grimace at the mention of the former company's name. He then dove into his favorite topic, money. "Now, about our spending. What is your commitment to this project? We will have expenses in bringing this endeavor back to life."

Mabel said, "I thought you had a lot of bucks."

Martin's eyes went wide at her comment. She smiled and said, "I kid. We can… assist in some of the costs."

Martin wondered for a moment at her remark—from what he knew about Mabel's temper, he decided to change his approach and not press too hard on the subject of financial support. He replied, "Excellent."

Mabel grinned and said, "Ok, that's settled. Well, Martin, I think we are nearly done here. So, do you think we should be able to get the plant into production in no more than three months? Who is going to spin that up?"

Feeling he had to be assertive. Martin said, "We have someone in mind. And then, the fortunes will flow. This will be a fortuitous arrangement for both of us." While he had answered her quickly, Martin knew he was riffing, as he was not at all sure who would run the facility operation at this point.

Mabel gave a wry grin and added, "We shall milk it dry. Well then, we must be off."

Martin nodded and said, "Have a wonderful day." He breathed an internal sigh of relief; his quick reply had worked. The screen went blank.

His butler Nigel entered the room. Martin sighed as he looked at the man and said, "I truly hope this alliance with this foundation is as awash in cash as we hope. The firm is quite deep into this one with what we spent on TeeGentics."

Nigel nodded and said, "Our due diligence has been thorough. We know the foundation's leadership proclivities as well. We can control them, whether they know it or not."

Martin sighed. He said, "Always good to know in these sorts of financial arrangements. I do have concerns about the way the original inheritor of the foundation was so skillfully displaced by Mabel Belkin, but the paperwork checked out with our U.S. legal team. Also, I have not cared for the way this Belkin woman tries to lord the foundations money and power as something superior to what we have accomplished with our firm. It shows disrespect and

I will not tolerate it in the long run." He nodded to himself, then continued, "We will prevail in the world of vast fortunes."

Nigel bowed in agreement and said, "One other important matter my lord, the one you have been waiting to have resolved." Martin's eyes widened and he said, "Our man has succeeded in his mission?"

Nigel nodded and replied, "And he is here to brief you." He then stepped to the doorway and said, "You may enter now Albert."

Martin stood and smiled to himself—Albert Schoonover was an old and trusted source of intelligence gathering as well as someone with an engineering background. Martin had learned to utilize these abilities in creative ways for his financial endeavors. As Albert entered the room, Martin pointed to the chair across from his desk. Albert nodded, proceeded to his spot and waited to be seated until Martin sat back down.

Martin said, "So, Albert, please elaborate."

Albert nodded, "I obtained the last code update from the former Pearly Whites programmer, Samuel Heneky and the geneticist, Fiona Kendle. I met with them in Paris where they had been burning through their own credit cards waiting to hear from us. They were rather distressed at their current dilemma and lack of financial resources."

Martin smiled and said, "I assume over the misfortunes of their… former benefactor, Elizabeth Cleaver."

"Yes sir. Plus being stranded and due to their own lack of funds, they were willing to negotiate away their final fix for a reasonable sum of money."

Martin said, "Nothing extravagant I hope."

"No sir, reasonable for us, though they were not particularly happy with the… settlement. Yet, as I told them, it was better than being dead broke in Paris."

"Excellent! Well, stay in touch, we have another mission for you in the not too distant future. Just need to get the wheels in motion." Martin then stood, which indicated the meeting was over.

Albert nodded and was escorted out of the room by Nigel. Moments later the old butler returned. Martin, in a cheery mood now declared, "Well, let's get ready for dinner with the firm's partners!" Nigel bowed and said, "This way my lord. All is prepared."

*

As the sun rose, Sally Dinklestern yawned, stretched sensuously, and from her south bedroom she embraced the morning as a gentle warm breeze wafted through the window of her villa overlooking the Spanish Mediterranean.

Carlos, her butler/chef entered with her breakfast and with a wave of her hand, she dismissed him as he sat her tray down. Carlos bowed as he backed out of the room.

She had to admit, Carlos came in handy on a lot of fronts, but she kept this relationship purely professional—a habit she had acquired after her near tragic and borderline criminal relationship with Werner Brandt. Least to her it was nearly tragi-criminal. And she was quite aware that in a last moment stroke of enlightened decision making, also known as saving her own ass, she had rescued herself and her small fortune by working a deal with the FBI. The decision—keeping that same small fortune or go down with Werner Brandt, as agent Miller had articulated in gritty detail and in no uncertain terms in the kitchen of her ex-lover/boss's home the day of his arrest. In hindsight, she knew she had made a tough but wise decision.

Sally was now a wealthy woman and had decided in her first months in Spain to become a savvy investor. The savvy—she had found a particularly aggressive and nasty hedge fund that kept her coffers overflowing with returns.

Nibbling on some toast from her tray, she reached to her left and retrieved the small laptop she habitually kept nearby to see what was happening with her financial portfolio at Zinger Wealth Management. Feeling a brief spike of adrenalin, she saw she was up a quarter million for the quarter. She flipped the lid shut, finished breakfast, and headed to her pool just outside the villa where she shed her nightgown so she could sun for a bit as she was determined to get rid of the last of her tan lines.

Near evening, she was preparing for a special dinner event with a wealthy couple she had met in the village when her phone rang. Picking it up, she noted it was from FBI Agent Miller. Wondering what the woman could possibly want, she answered, "Hello?"

Miller replied, "Hey there Sally. Got a minute?" Sally, annoyed, said, "Actually no, I am getting ready to go to a dinner party."

"Boohoo. I really wasn't asking Dinklestern. Now listen up. Get your ass packed. Tomorrow, dark thirty early, you are headed back to Santa De Lola." Sally held the phone at arm's length and stared at it. Putting it back to her ear she said, "What for?"

"Oh, love of country, doing something besides tanning in the nude, you know, that sort of thing."

"How do you know I tan in the nude?"

"Well, we are the FBI after all. Let's just say we know you spend most of your time in the buff around the old villa. Now, do you need an escort to the airport, or can you get your own well-tanned ass down there for your flight?" Sally sighed, "Yes Agent Miller."

The call ended abruptly with, "Wonderful! We've got an assignment for you! And these days, it's Special Agent Miller to you Dinklestern."

In a bad mood the next day, Sally found that her return to Santa de Lola was a bumpy, turbulent flight, making her spend half the trip in the airplane lavatory heaving out her guts. She decided she hated flying, along with Special Agent Miller.

At the airport, an FBI agent assigned to transport her was late and in a foul mood. When he arrived, she and her luggage were loaded up in a van that looked like it had been through World War III. The grumpy agent's name was Benowitz, who complained the whole trip about how he had been fucked over by Special Agent Miller and that it happened all the time as he was always delegated to these sorts of concierge level assignments.

Sally valiantly tried to tune the whiny man out. Plus, the van smelled so bad inside Sally wondered if somebody had died in it, which was certainly not aiding her in recovering from her flight sickness. All this left Sally with the feeling she was not about to have a good time on this "return to service".

At the FBI office, she was met by Miller and escorted to a conference room.

Miller had Sally sit down, then said, "So here is the deal. You are going to take a trip to London, show Martin Crosswaithe that you have a shitload of money that he needs to get the old TeeGentics back up and running."

Suddenly suspicious, Sally queried, "Money?"

Miller nodded and said, "Yep. Not yours so don't panic." She slid the convicted former CEO Werner Brandt's plea deal across the table. Sally read for a bit then said, "So Werner is funding this?"

Miller's sardonic grin was not lost on Sally as the agent replied. "Technically the FBI is, but this deal gets him on with his life and us moving forward with our little operation."

Sally nodded slowly. The briefing continued with an explanation Sally would use on Martin Crosswaithe about how she acquired the funds and that she wished to be CEO in exchange.

Miller concluded, "Basically, you got the money from Brandt and had offshored it before things went south so it looks like your cash. Also, we've got you into a nice condominium over by the old company headquarters, and you will pay for it out of your salary that this new company will provide. Here is the address."

She slipped a folded piece of paper across the table. She continued, "We got you a car as well, so have fun playing the part of CEO." Miller stood and indicated for Sally to follow her out. When they arrived at the car, Miller handed Sally the keys. It was a dark silver Mercedes AMG coupe.

Miller said, "You have to look the part, so just don't wreck the stupid thing. Your luggage is in the trunk. Now, best of luck and contact me if anything goes sideways or you need more detail."

Cynically, Sally thought to herself, *Right. Like what would go sideways?*

7

The next morning, Sally caught an Uber to the airport and boarded her second international flight for the week after Miller had confirmed that Martin Crosswaithe was currently at his London estate. This time, the flight was better, and she was able to get some rest on the way. When she arrived At Heathrow, a limo under her name transported her in proper style to the estate entrance. The footmen/security guards checked her over, called Nigel, who gave the clearance for her to be escorted to the front door. Sally climbed out of the limo as Nigel walked up and smiled cynically at her. The old butler said, "I'm sorry Ms. Dinklestern, are you lost?"

"So, you know who I am? Wonderful! I am here to speak with Martin Crosswaithe. He will want to see me."

Nigel snickered, "Oh, I rather doubt that Ms. Dinklestern."

Sally said, "Well…that is unfortunate. I really thought two hundred million dollars would interest your boss, but hey, what do I know?" She began to turn back to her limo as Nigel's snooty demeanor vanished and he said, "Now that is an interesting introduction Ms. Dinklestern. Give me but a moment."

The next thing she knew, she was in Martin's study admiring the fancy wood décor of an earlier era. A moment later, Martin came in through his secret door and stood in front of her, looking suspicious. He said, "Ms. Dinklestern, why are you here? Be quick about it, I have much to do."

Sally said, "I have only one thing to say. I want to repay a big chunk of the money you lost on Pearly Whites."

Martin raised an eyebrow and said, "And how do you propose to do that."

Sally said, "Transfer two hundred million into the account of your choice."

Martin scoffed, "And where would that sort of money come from?"

Sally said, "Indirectly? From the old CEO Werner Brandt. It is part of the proceeds from the massive stock sale that got him arrested and, I should add, that he entrusted me with."

Martin, eyebrows raised, asked, "And how, Ms. Dinklestern, do you happen to have his money?"

Without a twitch of nervousness, Sally said, "My ex-lover gave it to me as part of hiding his money before the FBI finally caught up with him. They actually never caught on to that particular transfer and feel free to verify what I am telling you. As for myself, since I had no prior history of criminal behavior, I think they assumed I was just plain naïve and stupid in selling my own stock based on Werner's advice, so they did not look that closely at what had transpired. Frankly, their opinion of me at the time was pretty much a spot on assessment. Flipping Brandt to the FBI got me off the hook and it left me moderately wealthy from my own stock sale, free to do what I want with my life. Which is why I am here."

Martin leaned back in his chair and eyed Sally. After a moment he said, "Why would you want back in Ms. Dinklestern?"

Crossing her shapely tanned legs, which caught Martin's attention, she leaned forward and said, "Please, just call me Sally."

Martin smiled, and said, "Sally then. Yes, call me Martin. And please, continue with this tale."

Sally nodded and began spinning the story she had been rehearsing in her head, "I loved TeeGentics and over time, I learned everything about how the company ran as I worked directly for the CEO. Things got out of control, as we all know, due to your grandson, Trace Orbaugh, the miscreant."

Martin sniffed a grimace at the mention of his grandson as she continued, "But we were so close to success. I want to make this product work, and I realize as much as anyone that it is not an easy path." Then, from her purse, she removed the wire information for the cash transfer and extended the paper to him.

Martin smiled and accepted the document. After a moment, he leaned back, then said, "Well, I admire your determination. Let's get the particulars of the cash transfer worked out. We also have to, as I am sure you understand, confirm your story. If all is well, tomorrow we will continue this conversation."

Sally smiled as he then pressed a button next to his desktop computer monitor. A moment later, Nigel arrived, and Martin instructed him to escort Sally to her car. Martin then turned to her and said, "There is a very nice hotel a short distance from here, Claridge's. Nigel will see to getting you settled in. We should be able to meet for lunch tomorrow."

Sally said, "I look forward to it." Martin beamed and said, "Very well! Have a nice evening and until we meet again." He stood and left.

Nigel gave a butler sort of nod and said, "We have arranged for one of our own limousines to take you to the hotel. I had your luggage transferred and secured lodging at Claridge's. It is a superb lodging I must say. I believe you will find it… more than adequate."

Sally said, "Most gracious of you Nigel."

Once at the hotel, she was in fact, dazzled. The place *was* palatial. After a luxury dinner in the Foyer and Reading room restaurant, she spent the evening in a bar listening to an outstanding performance by a woman playing a piano while she drank expensive Bordeaux. Tipsy at the end, she weaved her way to her room.

The next morning after a superb breakfast, a limo arrived for Sally whereupon she returned to the estate and was allowed to tour the grounds at her leisure. When the appointed time for lunch arrived, she was escorted back to the great dining hall where Martin was waiting for her.

After an exchange of pleasantries, Martin said, "After carefully considering your proposal, I believe you will be more than capable of performing the task of CEO of this new endeavor, so I had our legal staff prepare an offer letter and compensation package for you that I think you will find quite adequate. I also think you will agree, we best begin by restarting the old facility in Santa Del Lola. Oh and, we have changed the company name to PhoenixGen, and that will be reflected in the documentation you receive. For now, here is a printed copy of the offer letter. Finally, there is another aspect to this endeavor we need to discuss."

Sally accepted the letter, smiled as she read it and said, "This is certainly quite fair Martin. What other aspect are you talking about?"

He sighed dramatically and said, "We need to really press forward on FDA certification. We have arranged for a man from that very agency to be assigned to... ensure things proceed smoothly."

"I see. And who would that be?" Sally asked, her curiosity perked.

Martin said, "Reuben Corpenny. He understands that his job is to move things along and he will be well compensated for his efforts in that regard. So please greet him with...open arms."

Sally nodded. "I look forward to meeting this Mr. Corpenny." She could tell that Martin was relieved, presumably from this fortuitous turn of events. She was, however, aware of the man's predatory nature when it came to the world of finance and knew she would have to maintain her own vigilance in her dealings with him.

Martin said, "Excellent! I must say, I truly look forward to our working together. I think this should surge ahead to full production, the monetary dimensions of which should be substantial!" Again, Nigel arrived as Martin stood, "Nigel, please see to it that Sally is transported in style back to Heathrow. As the two rose to their feet, Martin concluded with, "Well, until we meet again. I must go now, important business as you might imagine."

Sally nodded and said, "Enjoyed the visit, Martin! And I will make you proud of letting me be CEO."

Martin smiled glibly, nodded, then left. Nigel became busy directing two of his footmen loading Sally's luggage into the limousine waiting at curbside. Task completed, Sally climbed aboard and waved goodbye. Everything seemed to be moving right along per Special Agent Miller's plan. Sally placed a call once at the airport and gave the woman an update. She then added the part about Reuben Corpenny.

Miller asked, "So this Corpenny person. FDA official that has been bribed?"

Sally said, "Sounds like it. I never met him before, but my understanding was he was somewhat involved higher up in the FDA back during the previous certification effort."

Miller sounded pleased for a change as she ended the call with, "Excellent update Dinklestern. See you soon."

8

A couple of days later, Liz called Miller, but instead got the woman's voicemail. She left a short message that she had some intel. Miller texted back that she was in a meeting and would provide a location for them to get together later that day.

When they later met up at an unused FBI safe house, Miller brought her up to date that her plan was moving forward, and that Sally Dinklestern would be one of her insiders at the newly funded PhoenixGen. Borders was taking her usual notes.

Liz leaned back in her chair, nodded and said, "So, I remember from things that happened in the past that Sally often exhibited an… interest in Billy Fuller. Plus, I think Billy is okay with me these days after he came into the clinic needing dental help and he and I talked. I'd really like to get in close with what is going on there. I am supposed to go with Bob and Billy to a meetup with my former girlfriend, Frieda Hansen and Helga Krantz this evening."

Miller nodded and said, "Interesting tidbit. It would be quite useful to have you working in the company headquarters rather than the clinic. Let me look into that and keep me posted how the meeting goes with your old flame."

"I am actually pretty nervous on this one. It did not end well when things went to shit." From what Liz had seen earlier, Miller was not one to provide much comfort.

Miller reinforced that opinion as she said, "Well, all I can say is you have a job to do Cleaver. I have confidence you will succeed."

Liz let out a sigh and said, "Uh, I imagine I will, just wanted to give you a heads up."

"Maybe I can get you some therapy time with Borders."

Liz shrugged and replied, "Thanks for the offer. I think I can manage." The fact was the last thing she wanted to do was talk to an FBI shrink since Liz was developing own strategy to achieve her personal goals. She decided in the future to keep her feelings to herself.

Miller, sounding distracted as she looked at a recent text message on her phone, said, "That's my girl. Well, gotta go!"

*

Frieda Hansen stared down from her seated position, across the raised service counter at the elderly woman on a walker that was hassling her about a leaking almond milk container she had bought a day earlier. Behind the old woman were several other customers. It was less than an hour till they closed at midnight but that was looking problematic at the moment.

The old woman said, "This stuff is stale! And it leaks!"

Frieda said, "Did you put it in the fridge when you got home last night?"

The old woman looked offended and said, "What, yah think I'm senile you little hussy? Let me tell you what. In my day, nobody asked customers questions like that. They just issued refunds."

Frieda pointed to the sign that was directly behind her that said, "Bruce's Discount FoodnStuff has a no return, no refund policy."

The woman huffed and said, "I don't give a shit. The damn milk is bad. It tastes weird."

"Yep, that's almond milk for yah."

The old woman looked confused and said, "Almond milk? I bought regular milk."

Frieda looked at the leaky container on the counter and said, "Uh, not according to that prominently displayed label."

The old woman picked it up and stared as she moved it forward and backward from her eyes, apparently trying to get the label in focus. She started and said, "It is almond milk! You all trying to poison me? What is this, bait and switch?"

Frieda pointed to the nondairy aisle and said, "Did you get it from there."

"Hell yes, where else would I get it from."

Frieda pointed to the other side of the store and said, "Um, the dairy aisle. That is where the good old cow milk is at. You bought the wrong thing lady. Now, are we done here?" Frieda could tell the customer behind the old woman was getting fidgety and several others had bailed out a few minutes earlier. The old woman said, "No, I am not. I want to talk to the manager."

Frieda said, "That would be me. Now, please move aside so I can take care of the gentleman behind you." She realized the "gentleman" label was a gross exaggeration, the dude looked like a Hell's Angel on steroids.

The old woman glanced over her shoulder and did a double take. She said, "Randy, is that you?" The biker dude looked uncomfortable and said, "Yes Mrs. Pinkston."

The now identified Mrs. Pinkston said, "Then make this woman give me a goddamn refund!"

Randy, the biker, looked sheepishly at Frieda who shook her head "no" before he even said anything. He said, "Uh, Mrs. Pinkston, let me get you a container of milk. It will be faster, and I can get my own business taken care of. Two birds, one stone sort of thing."

The old woman hemhaw'd but was out of gas. She said, "I will meet you out front. I am not spending another minute in this dump." She then pushed off, shuffling along with her walker.

Frieda watched the old woman with a wry expression, then looked at Randy and said, "Why did you do that?"

Randy said, "Uh, her son, Wolfang, is the leader of our little... club."

With a wry expression Frieda said, "The man's name is Wolfang? Pinkston? Really?"

Randy nodded affirmative, "We call him Pinky."

Sighing, she continued, "I see. Raised by an alpha female with spelling problems sounds like."

Changing the subject, Randy said, "So, I need to turn in this change I've been... collecting...if I could. Get some cash for it."

Frieda looked at the bulging sack and said, "How the fuck much coin you got there Randy?" She figured as she gaged the size of the sack, that Randy had been busy vacating the local parking meters.

Randy looked sheepish again, but got to the point, "How much you want of this to convert it to twenties?"

Frieda smiled and said, "Fifteen percent."

Randy barely pondered before he nodded that it was a deal. Frieda hollered, "Helga, get your rear up here. Got to run this *transaction* for this gentleman."

Helga Krantz came strolling up and looked at the sack. She sighed and indicated for Randy to follow her. After the coins to bills conversion was done, Randy got Mrs. Pinkston's cow milk and the two departed.

Watching the pair leave, Helga said, "Well, that was a quick fifty bucks."

Frieda stood and stretched, then shrugged, "What can I say. We persevere."

Helga stepped over and put an arm around Frieda's waist then said, "I'd like to get my PhD. Then we could persevere with my practice billing rich people at three hundred an hour."

"I'd like to get my foot up Liz Cleaver's ass!" Frieda exclaimed. They both laughed.

Frieda continued, "Actually, Liz is less of a pisser for me than that damn Mabel Belkin that took over the foundation. There has got to be a way to get to that woman."

Helga added, "And get the Cleaver foundation to live up to what I was told they would do—pay for my degree!" Frieda smiled, pecked Helga on the cheek, and said, "That's my angry girl."

Helga suddenly frowned as she was looking out the front window of the store. Frieda, noting the reaction, said, "What?"

"I swear, I think I just saw Billy and Bob drive by in that atrocious corvette!" She stepped away from Frieda and jogged to the front of the store, and exclaimed, "Shit!"

Frieda said, "What?"

"The Pearly Whites gang! It is them!"

"Really?"

Helga turned to Frieda and said, "What the fuck should we do? Call the cops?"

Frieda giggled and said, "For Billy and Bob? Hell no. This oughta be good."

A moment later, the two men came through the entrance together like a couple of gunslingers walking through the swinging doors of an old saloon. They tried anyway. Bob got smushed— Billy's bulk exceeded his as they came through the single door entrance. That elicited an "Ouch, goddamn it!" and Bob was sucking on a wounded thumb that got pinched in the door.

Frieda looked at Helga and said, "See what I mean?"

Billy glanced over his shoulder and said, "Dude, you alright?"

Bob grimaced while still sucking his thumb. Billy rolled his eyes and kept going. He stopped in front of the service desk, looking up at Frieda and Helga with an expectant grin. Bob finally dropped his thumb from his mouth, but stared at his feet, clearly uncomfortable to be back in front of Helga, his ex-girlfriend and Frieda who never much liked him anyway after she had gotten to know him.

Frieda, with a cynical smile, finally broke the ice with, "Well?"

Billy took a deep breath, then went into his spiel, "Hi you two. Listen, we wanted to reach out to you about the foundation and Pearly Whites and all of that stuff they did to all of us."

Frieda looked at Helga, shrugged, then back to Billy. She said, "Okay, go on."

Bob managed to summon his voice and said, "We're putting the band back together."

Helga looked at Bob, then Frieda, then back to Bob and said, "Band? What the hell are you babbling about Bob?" Billy glanced at Bob as he said, "Uh, it's an old expression. We want to team up with folks like yourselves and Liz Cleaver to go after the people that wronged us."

Frieda bristled and said, "Liz Cleaver? That psycho witch? She attacked me after I had done so much to recover the money she had blown building mansions and freakin' patios out the ass."

Bob said, "Yeah, but I know for a fact you helped blow a lot of that money."

Billy raised an eyebrow as he looked at Bob then the two women.

Frieda glared at Bob, then said, "And how the hell would you know that?"

Bob, looking at his feet again, said, "Uh, the source of that intel is standing next to you, your highness."

Frieda glanced at Helga who looked suddenly red faced. Frieda said, "Well?"

Helga, in an attempt to cover her early relationship with Bob, said, "Why would I do that. And what exactly do you mean Bob?"

Bob said, "You told me all about the wonderful multi-million dollar estate that Liz and Frieda had built. Then you mentioned the cars and helicopters. Oh, and the staff, the parties, the food. It was one night when you got back from a trip to visit them after they hired you and you were prying info out of me about the tooth problems with sexual inuendo, but no sex. Thinking about it as I got sober, I figured Liz and Frieda were embezzling money. Seems like a good guess from the way Frieda is reacting."

Frieda sighed and said, "So, Bob. This is your idea of putting the band back together? Well, fuck off."

Billy said, "Please, Frieda, wait up. What Bob just said is not why we came and frankly, is in the past and he has a big mouth. Listen. I ran into Liz. She is not living a high life. She works at one of the free dental clinics that is kept operating for show by Mabel Belkin, the woman currently controlling the foundation. She lives in squalor."

Frieda said, "Squalor? Good. Join the club, Liz Cleaver!"

Billy said, "I understand from what little I know that she regret's blaming you the day everything blew up at the estate. She would like to apologize."

Frieda said, "Kinda of late for that. I literally had to run for my life the day everything came tumbling down."

Billy said, "And Liz knows she was wrong, feels awful about it. After you left that day from the estate, she had her own ass handed to her by Mabel Belkin. Would you like to hear the story?"

While Billy was talking, Bob was on his phone. He looked up and said, "She's here."

The front door to the small store opened and Liz stood there in her scrubs, having come directly from the clinic. She walked quietly up to the service desk and stood between Bob and Billy.

Frieda looked at Liz, then Helga, who was tearing up. She sighed and said, "Hello Liz."

With a sincere expression on her face, Liz said, "Hello girls. Sorry we have to meet like this." She took a deep breath, then continued, "First off, Frieda, I found out a lot about what Mabel had been doing after we … broke up. And I only found it out the day it all went south. I never saw it coming and so much of what happened was entirely my fault." Liz sniffled and dabbed back some tears during her admission of guilt.

Frieda was not sure what to think, not having ever seen Liz in a humbled state before today, but Billy was smiling at her expectantly, so she said, "What?" She then started weeping and next thing, Billy, Liz, Helga and Frieda were in a big group hug, crying, talking about revenge on the foundation, getting their money back somehow, and finally, where they might all go out to eat Chinese together at this late hour.

Frieda, however, was holding Bob away from the group at arm's length. Billy gave Frieda another expectant look, and she rolled her eyes and patted Bob on the shoulder.

Bob grinned and said, "So! The band is definitely back!"

9

Sally sighed contentedly as she climbed in her Mercedes just as Miller pulled up alongside. Seeing the agent, Sally sighed again, her mood now soured, wondering what was up.

Miller got right to the point, "I need daily check ins on activity and prompt updates if anything significant happens. Don't screw around, we need to be on top of this deal. Now, do your job." She then drove off.

Sally shook her head as she headed over to Perky Petites—part of the current chore Miller had assigned her. Entering the diner, she sat at the counter. A server quickly took her order for a cheeseburger and fries. The food arrived and she ate, consuming the entire meal in short order. It was a treat after her brief experience with airline cuisine and she was even hungrier than she realized.

Sipping her soda, she felt a tap on the shoulder. She turned and was suddenly face to face with Billy Fuller, who had just arrived for his shift, just as Miller had told her he would. Her eyes went wide in recognition as she remembered the fit young man she had met back during the Pearly Whites days and a particularly stimulating scene of a raging erection from one of the many side effects the man endured with the early versions of the genetic teeth. Billy was not quite as lean now but probably the same otherwise which sent a shiver of pleasure through her body.

He said, "Hi Sally. Remember me?"

Sally said, "Ah, yes. Billy, isn't it?"

Billy nodded and said, "Yep, bottom of the food chain Billy."

Sally felt two emotions at that comment. The first—she remembered how Billy had gotten screwed over during the Pearly Whites debacle and felt a tiny bit sorry for him. The second was she found being near Billy led to a serious endorphin release just as it had in the past. She said, "Well, I see you got your teeth fixed."

Billy smiled, reach up and took out his temporary bridge then said, "Oh shure, ish jush perfect!"

Sally closed her eyes and shook her head. She then looked up and said, "Billy, I had no idea they never fixed your teeth."

Billy put the bridge back in and said, "Left me high and dry. No severance, no teeth, nothing. Finally got the job here."

Sally paused to consider his last comment, then pulled a napkin out of the counter dispenser and wrote her phone number on it. She said, "Call me in a couple of days. I might have a better opportunity for you."

Billy looked more than a bit surprised as he said, "Really? What would I do?"

Sally said, "Well, the company is starting back up under a new name, PhoenixGen. I am sure there will be plenty of jobs and I would like to see what we could find for you. I am the CEO now. I think I might have some pull."

Billy broke into a big smile, which demonstrated his prosthetic was not particularly great, but he said, "CEO? Wow! Thanks Sally!"

Sally smiled, nodded, wondering what he might do for her in return. She flagged the waitress, handed her thirty dollars and said, "Keep the change." She then said to Billy, "Don't forget to call." She stood, gently rubbed him on the shoulder, then headed for her Mercedes.

*

Billy was elated. As Sally walked out of the diner, he placed a call to Liz. When she answered, he said, "Everybody needs to get together tonight. I got some news!"

Liz replied, "Well, I can't wait. We all gonna' meeting up at the usual watering hole?"

Billy said, "Yep. See you there." He turned around and headed into the kitchen and for a while he had no problem doing his dishwashing job. Until he stuck a fork in his hand. He soldiered on and showed up that evening, hand wrapped in bandages, at the

Watering Hole Bar and Grill, a dumpy, poorly lit, decrepit joint near his apartment which primary feature was low prices. Frieda and Helga were already imbibing at their recently designated "regular table" located in the far corner of the establishment. A few moments later, Bob wandered in, then finally Liz.

This was not a high dollar liqueur sort of place with fancy entrees. Mostly they drank the cheaper variety of low brow booze paired with a decent guacamole and chips. The inexpensive whiskey did the job each time, making them loud and obnoxious to the other patrons, which was no easy task as most the Watering Hole patrons were pretty noisy and obnoxious themselves.

Liz started with, "So Billy, two questions. What is the good news? And what did you do to your hand?" Billy tried to decide which was more important to answer first—he concluded nobody gave a shit about his hand, so he launched into, "Sally Dinklestern showed up in the restaurant today."

Silence ensued. Finally, Helga asked, "Did you kill or just maim her?"

Ignoring the question, Billy got excited like he hadn't in some time, even though his hand throbbed from the fork wound. He said, "I am supposed to call her!" Again, silence.

Finally, Bob said, "So, what happened to your hand?"

Liz said, "Hold that thought Bob, if you can. Billy, about what Sally wants you to do—why does this matter that you are supposed to call?"

Billy said, "She's working at PhoenixGen as CEO now!"

Frieda said, "Fucking figures. The woman that brought down everything with her squealing is the goddamn CEO now!"

Billy shrugged and quipped, "I may get a job! Well, I mean, no guarantees."

Liz, in a neutral tone, said, "Well, yes, good news indeed. So, who's up for another round?"

The others all raised their hand. After they were served, Liz asked, "So what happened to your hand?"

Billy launched into one of his legendary fifteen minute explanations, including the quirks of working as a dishwasher, care in handling pointed objects and plain old bad luck. Bob dozed off in minute two of said explanation while holding his untouched drink. Spying the man's lack of consciousness, Liz removed his drink just short of him dumping it in his lap, then redistributed the contents to the others.

10

Sally sat at the expensive desk located in the corner fourth floor office that was PhoenixGen CEO central, pondering the vagaries of her life that had led her back here. While Martin had given Sally the position as CEO, she had not yet gotten the benefit of an administrative assistant, so she had to take her own phone calls and actually communicate more directly with the various parts of the organization, such as it was. What it was at the moment was tiny, so at this point, she could manage the minor workload.

A few former employees had reapplied for their old jobs and Sally just pushed them through, as she was not interested in interviewing and wanted to get things on track as quickly as possible, per her employment agreement and what Special Agent Miller expected. For once, working for two masters was not a problem.

Which led to the man Sally knew as "Sonny" being rehired as a security guard, though the criminally inclined gentleman was now required to sit at the front gate for twelve hour shifts as there was only two other security personnel at the moment. Claiming seniority, Sonny took the day shift. Along with that were some lab folks, then the cafeteria crew. The food was less edible than ever, and hours of cafeteria operation were truncated which was actually a positive.

Earlier, she had briefly toured her new environment. Things looked about the same except for a layer of dust on everything from when the place had been closed up. On the desk was a new to her, but otherwise well used laptop that a re-hired and sullen IT person had dropped off an hour earlier. At the moment, she was looking at resumes for the VP of Production and Grounds Keeping slot that was to report directly to her. That person would then be her left and right hand person, as she was not getting more help. It was then that she realized she could help the company, the FBI and her insatiable self. She pulled out her phone and dialed. A moment later, with a cacophony of kitchen noise in the background, Billy answered, "Hey Sally! How ya' doing? I was going to call you later today."

Sally said, "Well, great minds think alike. Listen, I need to fill a position here at PhoenixGen. It would be a job on the production side. High level. You interested?"

Billy said, "When do I start?" Sally giggled and said, "You will have to come in for a… one on one interview, so bring your resume. It's more a formality than anything. Can you be here this afternoon around three?"

Billy said, "Absolutely! Maybe even earlier if you need. It's not like I am in love with washing dishes!"

"Oh, I think three o'clock will be just fine. See you then young man." The call ended and she sat back in her chair feeling stimulated at the thought of the interview.

*

At the same time Sally was talking with Billy, Martin was on a conference call with Mabel Belkin.

An aggressive Mabel queried, "Martin, what is going on with some of the people that are getting hired? Specifically, why is Sally Dinklestern back?"

Though offended by Mabel questioning him, he forced a chuckle and said, "I ran an extensive background on her. She won her freedom from the FBI after she handed over her old boss, she is clean. And we need to get the FDA approval back on track in the U.S which I already have rolling. Finally, we can keep Sally and company busy with that while we use the capital she provided to get production up and running. Now where you come in is the same as before."

Mabel sat back in her chair with an empty expression over what Martin had just said. She finally replied, "What exactly did you have in mind? The foundation has many responsibilities and I'm a busy woman."

Martin answered, "Mabel. Please stop with the act. I know how you bulldozed over Elizabeth Cleaver. We need the support of the foundation to market the teeth, just as before. I know you are aware of that and there is no upfront cost to your organization." Mabel guffawed, "Oh, okay. Just messing with you. We're still in from the clinic side."

Martin said, "Brilliant. I know this goes without saying, but we need you to be very upfront on promotion, maybe open a few more clinics, that sort of thing." Martin wondered if he might have said a bit too much with the last comment as Mabel now looked annoyed. He said, "One other idea, and I think you might enjoy this. Why not have Elizabeth Cleaver work at PhoenixGen? She could be put into some menial role. I understand you have her in a position like that as well, but this could be even more humiliating. The reason I bring her up is that we will need to do some…abbreviated trials of the new teeth to get our final FDA sign off. I think she would make a great test subject."

Mabel raised an eyebrow, then said, "Liz Cleaver being experimented on. I like it!"

Martin nodded, thinking he had perhaps won some goodwill from Mabel. He certainly wanted the money she had, and it was quite obvious what Sally Dinklestern had told him was accurate, that the woman detested Elizabeth Cleaver. He concluded with, "Well, that's sorted. I need to run. I hope you have a great morning. To wealth!" Mabel sighed and said, "Right. To wealth. Bye now!" The big screen on his study wall abruptly went blank. Martin sniffed and went in search of an exotic brandy to shore up his irritated attitude.

*

Recently appointed FDA regional director Art Goldenberry was looking across his desk at Reuben Corpenny. Reuben had a cynical smile on his face as he asked, "So, are you enjoying your new job?"

Art shrugged and said, "I like the paycheck better than before if that's what you mean. And for what it's worth, I know you got railroaded on the last go around."

Reuben nodded in agreement and said, "Listen, I appreciate you taking my call earlier and letting me come in."

Art said, "Well, I know we can use you, if you would like to work on a contract basis. You, more than anyone, realize how we are eternally short staffed. I would like you to run the team that will rework the PhoenixGen tooth certification."

Reuben almost laughed, raised an eyebrow and said, "So they want to bring back the teeth? What kind of world are we living in?"

Art shrugged and said, "Cash driven I believe by the very wealthy. In fact, I have a person you need to talk to, if that is okay. They will call you to explain a… generous opportunity."

"I like generous opportunities. In fact, I could use one."

"So, are you in?"

Reuben said, "I think yes! Who's on my team?"

Art replied, "A couple folks from the last go around since they know the product in question."

Reuben said, "Excellent. I guess I need to get ready to go visit PhoenixGen."

Art stood, extended his hand to Reuben, and said, "Welcome back to the team!" A vigorous handshake later, Reuben was out the door. Art sat back down, sighed, and said to himself, "Just one more year to go baby and I am out of here!" He then made a quick call, gave the person on the other end Reuben's phone number and name. Shifting gears, he started flipping through a brochure for a retirement community in Scottsdale Arizona where he could play golf until he crapped out in old age.

*

Billy's ancient Chevy Vega was smoking its way up the drive to the front entry of PhoenixGen. When he stopped at the guard house, he recognized Sonny, the former/current head of security, manning the entrance. Sonny leaned out from his stool, looked at Billy, gave a contemptuous smile, and said, "You lost?"

Billy smiled back and said, "Nope, here for an interview!"

Sonny looked amused as he challenged, "An Interview? With who? For what? The head janitor?"

"Sally Dinklestern."

Sonny's amusement turned to surprise as he asked, "The new CEO? Why would she want to interview *you*?"

Billy, now irritated at the delay and questions, fired back with, "Why did she hire you? And why don't you call her and ask?"

Sonny said, "I don't have to. I think you are full of shit. Everybody knows what happened with you and your teeth and how you destroyed a perfectly good company after you rammed that bus!"

Billy said, "Hell, it was not my fault! Okay fuckstick. I am calling Sally now!" He pulled out his phone and dialed, while putting the phone on speaker. Sally answered, "Hey Billy, you here?"

Billy said while glaring at Sonny, "Yep, but the so-called *guard* here doesn't want to let me in."

Sally replied, "What? Put him on the phone."

Billy said, "You're on my speaker. I think Sonny can hear you."

Nervously, Sonny responded, "Sorry Ms. Dinklestern. I was confused. You want me to let Billy Fuller in?"

Sally said, "Well, yes, that would be very nice of you Sonny. Oh, and Billy, I'm in the CEO's office."

Billy said, "Got it! And, hey, Sally, Sonny started all this. Insulted me bad! Said I caused the company to go under!"

Sonny, suddenly concerned for his job, said, "Bullshit! I never said that!"

"Did too!"

"Did not!"

Sally, sounding amused, said, "Boys, boys. Calm down. Billy, get your fanny on up here."

Billy said, "Thanks Sally." He ended the call and said, "I need to go asshole!"

Sonny, miffed, pushed the button that raised the guard rail. Billy floored it going through, leaving a cloud of smoke for Sonny to choke on. Still chuckling to himself, he parked and strolled on into the lobby and up to the receptionist, the same woman that had worked the desk back in Pearly Whites days—another rehire.

She handed him a badge and began to give him directions. He said, "That's okay dear, I used to work here and know exactly where Ms. Dinklestern is at."

The receptionist nodded and said, "I'm sure you do, after the way you brought us down last time! And I am not your "dear!""

Billy said, "What? That was not my fault! And I'm sorry about the dear!"

The receptionist said, "Right." She then turned her back on him.

Feeling frustrated at two accusations of having caused the failure of the old company in less than five minutes, Billy huffed off for his interview. Once in Sally's office, she had him sit, accepted his resume and they began to chat while she flipped through it.

Sally asked, "How many pages is this document?"

Billy said, "Eighteen."

Sally grinned in amusement and said, "Eighteen page resume. I hope you didn't leave anything out."

Billy shrugged, and said, "Well, I mean I had to trim it back somehow."

Keeping a straight face, Sally nodded, noting his time in the boy scouts, his weightlifting awards and so forth. Shaking her head to clear her thoughts of Billy flexing in a tight little pair of form fitting trunks, she laid the resume on her desk and said, "So, you think you can run the production line business unit for the company? You will be responsible for hiring the staff, getting the line going, plus you own the groundskeeping of this place."

Billy's eyes went wide. He had been hoping for something like Sally's secretary. This was a whole new area he had not remotely considered. He answered, "Well, sure, I mean I would be willing to give it a go. I gotta say, this is a bit of a surprise."

Sally nodded and said, "Yeah, I thought it might be. But I feel bad about the way you were treated before and think you deserve to be given a second chance and with good opportunities."

Billy nodded thoughtfully and said, "And I get to be a boss?"

Sally said, "For sure. And you and I will… be working very closely." She smiled inwardly at the thought. She then added, "How much notice do you need to give your employer before you can start?"

"Oh, how about tomorrow morning?"

Sally laughed and said, "Sounds grand. You're not curious about pay?"

Billy said, "Better than a dishwasher salary I am guessing."

Sally said, "Oh, a wee bit. Actually, you will get a few stock options as well once we go public. Job pays a hundred thousand, for what it's worth."

Billy sat back, looking stunned thinking that was well over four times his current pay. He said, "That sounds fantastic!"

Sally smiled. She then added the "Special Agent Miller" part of her plan and said, "Um, on staffing. I have a request from one of our investors regarding a person that you need to bring on board. Her name is Elizabeth Cleaver."

Billy tilted his head and asked, "The Elizabeth Cleaver?"

Sally nodded, "Yes, to be hired into the lowest of the low end jobs is what I was told. She'll be coming over from a dental clinic she has been working at in San Francisco."

Billy nodded, wondering what was up, and said, "No problem. I work for you!"

Sally smiled, stood and said, "Well, let me escort you to the lobby." They walked out the door where she nonchalantly brushed her breasts against his muscular arm. He smiled at her as they walked down to the elevator. Billy hit the button and a moment later, the door opened. Both Sally and Billy stepped in, the door closed, and she moved close to him, took his hand and said, "This is going to be so much fun Billy! Sally knew Billy was well aware she was resting a boob against his arm once again. He grinned and said,

"Sure *feels* like it to me!" Thus encouraged, Sally tucked in a little closer.

The elevator chimed as the door slid open to reveal the lobby. Sally and Billy exited, and she offered, "How about a cup of cafeteria coffee before you go?" She could not bring herself to let Billy leave just yet.

Billy said, "Ah, yes! The murky hot brown water beverage that haunts the cafeteria. Lead the way!"

Once there, two of the now rehired cafeteria personnel were wiping down some tables on the path to the coffee pot. As Sally and Billy passed, the elderly woman, not bothering to keep her voice down, said to her coworker, "There goes the man that destroyed this company last time! What is he doing here now?"

Billy and Sally both heard the comment. Billy spun around and said, "It was not my fault! Where in the world is this stuff coming from?"

The woman sniffed and said, "It's all over the Internet you know. You, your gayness, your taking money to be quiet and then ramming that bus to make more money. The terrible way you treated the project manager, Bob Oppenheimer."

Billy said, "Lady, I ask you, what does my being a gay person have to do with anything? Well? And just where might I find this misinformation on the Internet?"

The woman sniffed again and said, "Just type in Bob's blog. Mr. Oppenheimer documented everything right after the company went down the crapper."

Sally, seeing an opportunity, moved protectively in front of Billy, where she rubbed her backside against his frontside, then took a deep breath while thinking delicious thoughts. She then realized the two cafeteria workers were giving her the eye, so she said, "Hi, I'm Sally, CEO as you know. I think you two need to find something else to do." The older woman sniffed again then nodded to her coworker. Both headed back towards the kitchen. Billy did not move away from Sally, so she figured he must be enjoying the experience as much as she was. She took him by the arm and led him away as she tucked Billy in close to her, but reluctantly eased off then sat him down at the table next to the coffee pot.

She got two cups of coffee and sat one in front of him. She then sat next to him and stirred in some cream and sugar while watching Billy closely. She finally said, "You okay?"

Billy said, "Yeah, and thanks for the chance to get to know you better, I have been…on my own for a while. He smiled and Sally blushed as she smiled back and said, "I kinda… hoped you'd like that."

Staring in her eyes, he continued, "However, I just realized why I probably had such bad luck looking for jobs with companies around here. Bob's blog?"

Sally shrugged and said, "Well, that's all over now. It's you and me partner, leading the way to the future."

Billy smiled and said, "I'm bisexual you know. If you get my drift."

Sally giggled as she patted his hand. But then Billy's thoughts returned to the "Bob's blog" comment. He sipped his coffee, made a face at the taste, then picked up his phone and did a quick search. A website with an earlier picture of Bob Oppenheimer came up.

Softly, Sally said, "Billy, whatever it is, it can wait. We need to talk about right now." She gently ran her fingers from his hand to a bicep and smiled.

Billy sighed, set his phone down and said, "Understood."

From there, they talked about the plant build, the personnel requirements and Billy smiled increasingly more. Sally said she wanted him over for dinner tomorrow night so they could discuss details. She felt his pulse quicken where she was resting her hand on his arm—she hoped he wanted to explore her details in depth.

She gave him a long body pressing hug at the conclusion of their discussion, then he was off to his car.

*

The evening of Billy's return to PhoenixGen, another gathering was held at the Watering Hole Bar and Grill. Billy arrived first, then Liz, Frieda and Helga. The three women seemed to be getting on well again. Bob arrived as the others finished their first round of whiskey. He sat down next to Helga at the far end of their corner booth where he was directly facing Billy across the table. Helga frowned, then scooted away from Bob and closer to Frieda.

Billy said, "Well, I have some really good news." Liz said, "Please feel free to elaborate."

Which Billy began to do, then said, "Oh, never mind. You guys would not be interested anyway."

Helga said, "Oh come on Billy. I want to know." She gave him an encouraging smile. Billy shrugged and said, "Um, I am now employed at PhoenixGen!"

Everybody, now leaned in as Liz said, "And?"

"I was wondering if any of you would like a job. I am hiring." Everybody paused to look at each other.

Bob finally said, "Hiring? I thought you went to work at the company we are trying to get information on."

Billy smiled and said, "I did. I am now a VP. VP of plant operations and landscaping in fact!"

Frieda said, "How the heck did that happen? And don't get me wrong. I am thrilled for you!"

Billy gave Frieda a sideways glance as he dove into the phone call with Sally, her CEO position, what she hired him to do and by the end, the mood in their far corner of the Watering Hole was euphoric. Billy then said, "And, on a sidenote, I found out today that I am *the reason* that Pearly Whites went down the crapper." Everybody stopped talking.

Bob said, "What? You, bring the company down? You were a nobody."

Billy scowled at the "nobody" comment, nodded and retorted, "Thanks Bob! But yes, I am the scamp. This is according to… Bob's Blog. Do you remember Bob's Blog, Bob?"

All eyes swiveled to Bob, who looked suddenly hesitant as well as a bit contrite. He said, "Uh, well, I do… sort of. I think it was when I was coming down off all the drugs and alcohol and needed something to do. So, I started to blog."

Billy nodded and said, "Well, let me read to all of you a passage from Bob's fucking blog," as he pulled his phone out and opened the web page. Clearing his throat he began, "The main reason this great company, the greatest work of my life, my sweat, my tears, etcetera, went down in flames was one Billy Fuller. This Fuller man, if you want to call him a man, because he is gay, brought down the company by ramming a bus, taking money from the till by holding the CEO hostage and insisting on money and stock options, and then ratting everybody out to the cops, the fed, the FDA, and so on and so forth." Billy paused, then added, "There are a lot of typos so, perhaps I got something wrong here."

Everyone at the table turned to look at Bob, who was avoiding eye contact and sipping his drink. Frieda broke the silence with, "Bob, if anybody was primo in bringing down Pearly Whites, it was your drunk, drugged up ass that was a big help!"

Bob then sobbed. He said, "I am so sorry Billy. I was fucked up when I wrote that. All drugs, booze, and going broke, my woman had ditched my ass, and I was barely functional." He sobbed again for effect.

Helga looked disgusted and said, "Your woman? Ditched your ass? You dipshit!" Frieda pulled her in close to comfort her, while mouthing obscenities in Bob's general direction.

Liz rolled her eyes, sighed, and said, "You know, somehow nothing this group does surprises me. Now, Bob, no matter how fucked up you were, why would you write such drivel?"

Bob shrugged and said, "Fuck if I know. I am past that. Billy, please, please forgive me. I will post updates about it being all wrong." Billy nodded and said, "Well, that should help eliminate all the conspiracy theories I heard today at PhoenixGen about how I nearly destroyed Wall Street and capitalism with a Ford Pinto!" Everybody looked at Billy, then burst out laughing. The longer they laughed, the more contagious it became until everybody was finally about to run out of air.

Billy then reached down into a sack he had brought with him and pulled out a bottle. He looked at everybody and said, "Let's have some good shit for a change. I bought a bottle of Macallan today! Last time I drank a bunch of this, I got into a fight at a liquor store!"

Everybody gazed appreciatively at first the Macallan, then Billy, and all held out their now empty glasses they had just poured out into the water pitcher. He filled each glass and the group's relief from not having to imbibe crap whiskey was palpable around the table. As the Macallan disappeared, Liz said, "How are you going to hire us? Everybody knows who the fuck we are. Especially me."

Billy shrugged and said, "Fake IDs, I guess. Not sure where to find them, but we should look into it. Frieda, I need a programmer, and I heard you can program. You could work offsite." Frieda shrugged and said, "Yeah, I can do a bit of that. I don't make no claims to being Alan Turing."

Everybody looked at her and Bob said, "Who?"

She continued, "The code breaker from WWII? Billy, I am surprised you have not heard of him. He was gay!"

Billy said, "What about being gay has anything to do with whether I heard of him or not? And how about we make your fake identity name Alan Turing?" Everybody chuckled except Frieda, who was now frowning.

Billy said, "Now we just need somebody to make some fake ID's. Idea's people, ideas!"

Liz smirked and remarked, "Looks like you are getting in the spirit of this VP position."

Billy said, "Thanks Liz. I aspire to be more."

Bob looked confused then said, "Be more what? Gay?"

Billy said, "No, I want to be just like you! Living out of my crappy old plastic sports car."

Bob sagged, so Helga pushed a bowl of potato chips his way.

Liz suggested, "Uh, let's change the subject before somebody has to go into therapy."

Billy said, "Fine. Also, for those of you that have to come in to work in the plant, let's get the hair dyed, the beards going, and the accents working."

Helga said, "Don't know about the beard thing, but I could use my German accent!"

Liz said, "Uh, when did you stop using it?"

With that, the official part of the meeting adjourned with no clear path to getting fake IDs, what accents should be practiced and if the women actually needed a beard. However, Billy had another bottle of Macallan in his bag that they did manage to polish off.

As they prepared to leave, Billy pulled Liz to the side and said, "Liz, I got a request from Sally. Looks like you are going to work for me now instead of the dental clinic. Seems you are being… reassigned."

Liz nodded slowly and said, "So, I don't need a fake ID then?" Billy said, "Nope. I was told to give you a crappy job. I have a plan in that regard. You won't have to do much at all." Liz nodded and said, "That's a relief. Besides, that clinic is more toxic the longer I am there."

Billy nodded, then headed out. Liz pulled out her phone and called Miller to provide her with an update. Miller said, "Liz, this is great! You will be right where the action is." Liz agreed, "I'll keep you posted."

11

As Billy walked into the boardroom and sat down, Sally arrived, taking a seat next to him. A few moments later, Albert Schoonover strolled in.

Albert was purported to be a scientist with real credentials that would do the work of upgrading the buggy tooth growing software to one without side effect that could then be used for production level teeth that could be sold. He had come their way via Martin Crosswaithe who had stated that the man had worked for him previously and was an excellent choice for lead scientist.

Albert seemed a good fit, from his resume in engineering, genetics and frankly, Billy was already underwater on this whole situation in front of him, having never interviewed anyone before, so he had been quick to make an offer. He figured he was covered anyway due to the way Martin had brought this candidate to their attention. Sally had concurred, so today was new hire orientation day for Albert.

Sally talked briefly about how Albert would report to Billy and how he needed to keep Billy in the loop at all times and not bother her. She then smiled, stood and said she was off to get her nails done and gave Billy one last knowing grin before she left.

Albert watched the exchange with apparent interest, but simply nodded. Then he and Billy toured the facility. Albert took notes on a pad he carried with him about the lab, the DNA splicer, (which Billy had no idea how to even power on though he remembered the device from his previous time at the company), and how to get to the cafeteria. Billy then escorted Albert to his office down near the labs on the second floor and gave him a tour of the area—he had more than a passing familiarity with the place.

An IT employee showed up with Albert's laptop, which Billy used as his excuse to leave.

After the meeting, Billy headed to his car. He was trying to get Jerome back from Mississippi and had been texting and sending pictures to his estranged partner about a new upscale apartment he was leasing to entice the man back. Sally had grudgingly cleared him to go if he could get back in an hour or so. Climbing in the Vega that he was also planning on replacing, his phone buzzed with Sally requesting that he return as soon as possible, she had something very important to talk about.

*

Sally, back from her nail appointment, was sitting in her office when Billy knocked. While waiting for his arrival, she had mostly focused on watching a video sent to her by her landscaper of improvements he had been making to her Spanish Villa. It made her homesick—she sighed as she paused it but perked up as she waved Billy on into her office—he quickly strolled in and sat down in the chair across the desk from her. She watched him sit, noticing he appeared a bit more svelte. She teased, "Been exercising?"

Billy nodded and launched into his routines of stretches, bends, crunches, and all the talk of working out had Sally imagining him exercising in the nude. She shook her head. Something about the man always turned her on and she was happy about his switch hitter comment the day of his interview when he broke her train of thought, "So I am working on getting a few essential people in here as quickly as possible."

Sally locked eyes on him, smiled and said, "Sounds good. What do you need?"

He slid some resumes Frieda had invented over to Sally. She glanced briefly at the documents and shrugged then said, "Looks fine. When do you want them to start?"

"Soon as possible if that works. I hope to get them into the plant and one of them out on the grounds quickly to work with Liz."

Sally took another quick glance at the resumes, shrugged and said, "You know your budget. What does this paragraph about programming background mean?" She did not show him what she was looking at, so Billy stood and walked around the desk to peer over her shoulder.

Sally spun around her chair to find her head at crotch level to Billy. It made her want to grab him by his rear. Taking a deep breath, she stood and was face to face with Billy. She said, "Are these people real Billy?"

Billy gulped nervously. He said, "Oh yeah, yep, they sure are real." Sally moved in a little closer and said, "Billy, you know…" Half smiling, Billy said, "Know what?"

Sally said, "Listen, I know you have a partner. I just… find myself…feeling…"

Billy said, "Yes?"

Sally decided actions would be stronger than words. She pulled him to her and settled her right hand on his rear. She said, "I think you get the idea." She smiled expectantly.

Billy's eyes went wide. He did not try to withdraw from Sally's grip on him. He said, "Listen, Sally. Uh, this is certainly tempting. Yes, I am partners still, sorta, with Jerome. And I do enjoy both sides of the coin if you know what I mean. It's just…"

"Just what?"

"We work together."

"We could really work together, if you get my drift."

Sally determined from the hard on that Billy had pressing against her as he now slid his hand down to her rear that he had gotten her drift. She was about to kiss him when a knock at the door ended the moment.

As quick as he could, Billy got back around to the other side of the desk and stood by his chair. Sally, pulse racing, remained standing and said, "Ah, come on in."

The door swung open, and Albert entered. He said, "Afternoon. Would like to talk if you have a few minutes." Sally, still distracted, said, "Uh, right now?"

Albert nodded, looked at Billy and said, "Sorry for the interruption." He then winked. Billy blushed as Sally moved away from her desk towards the window. Albert's gaze followed her.

Billy said, "Well, I should sit down!" He slipped into the chair, trying to keep his back to Albert to conceal his poked out pants. Sally sighed then said, "So what is it that could not wait?"

Albert said, "The lab. I am so busy getting this thing up and running, making things come back to life."

Sally sighed, and said, "Good. Because with all this stuff that I am working on with the production plant and getting Billy going and getting staff hired and…" She trailed off as she was trying to get her mind off the recent close encounter with the buff young man. Her hand movements bumped and partially swung her laptop around.

Albert glanced at her computer screen showing some newly planted Cypress trees at her villa, smiled and said, "Busy for sure. Well, I should go then."

"Have a great day."

As Albert left, Sally signaled Billy to close the door and lock it so they could resume their earlier activities. They agreed to have dinner at her place that night as they kissed and began to explore each other's bodies.

Then her phone rang. Sighing, she realized fun time was over—it was Miller wanting an immediate meeting.

*

Miller was sitting at a fold down table in an old Winnebago that the local FBI office used for surveillance, waiting for the arrival of Sally. Borders sat on the other side. They had parked earlier and were winding up their lunch of fast food hotdogs from the truck stop a mile down the state highway. The desiccated franks tucked into the buns appeared to have been lying in the sun. The old man working there advised that was about as good as their cuisine got as he handed them over.

Borders said, "Well, I thought with enough mustard, sauerkraut and potato chips, this little meal would work. Fuck all, I was wrong."

Miller made a face, nodded, while wadding the last couple bites of what she now called her crunch dog into its wrapping paper and launching it basketball style towards the trash can located on the other side of the vehicle. It bounced off the wall leaving a mustard stain and onto the floor. She sighed as she got up, tossed it in the can and then sat back down as she said, "Another cleanup job for agent Benowitz!"

Border's guffawed and asked, "What is it about that guy you don't like? Besides his personality."

Miller shrugged, "He's a jerk."

A car arrived, skidding to a stop, which had her craning around and looking out the Winnebago's window. It was Sally. She emerged from the Mercedes and Miller waved her on in while commenting, "This is a pain in the ass way to operate. God, I hope she has something useful to say."

Borders agreed, even though she was giggling. Miller looked at her in amusement and said, "I think you're getting a kick out of all this." She then took a deep breath and held the door open for her snitch. It was then she found that Sally had stopped and was staring at her phone and texting. Miller, already irritated, stuck a thumb and forefinger in her mouth and made an earth shattering whistle that got everybody's attention, including a little boy down the way that rolled over sideways with his tricycle and started crying.

She then barked, "Get your ass in the Winnebago Dinkleberg!" Sally proceeded with due haste as Miller looked over her shoulder at the child whose mother came running out from her RV, picked the child up while glaring at her miscreant neighbors. Miller shrugged and resumed her seat across from Borders. Since there was no other seating, Sally sat on the floor, avoiding eye contact.

Miller said, "So, my spy, what's new?

Sally shrugged and said, "Well, as you know, we got the deal rolling with Martin."

Miller said, "Yeah, that's what we sent you to England for. Detail would be helpful." At the same time, Borders scribbled a note and passed it over to Miller who just nodded and passed it back.

Sally said, "What the fuck was that all about?" Borders giggled, then with a deadpan expression, said, "Just… taking notes for future reference."

Sally sighed.

Miller continued, "So, what else? Come on, what the hell is going on in that place?"

Sally said, "We're staffing up and we are making progress." Miller shrugged and said, "We need to get Martin's ass over here in the states. Got any ideas on that?

Sally shrugged again, then said, "I guess we could invite him in for the plant opening when we get to that point. That's when the possibility of actual money coming in would happen."

Miller queried, "And how far out is that?"

Sally shrugged again and said, "Well, a couple months? Maybe more?"

Miller sagged, looked at Borders who was shaking her head.

Sally said, "What? I mean, it's been only about two weeks since this operation even got going. I am doing my part!" Borders scribbled in her notebook and nodded to Miller.

Sally, now agitated, took a deep breath, but before she could say anything, Miller cut her off. "Listen Dinklestern. This is not about best effort, it's about results. You got a sweetheart deal with the FBI and the AG that kept you out of jail, so, use that brain of yours and come up with a plan."

Sally took a deep breath and swallowed. Then she said, "Fine. I will. And why the hell do we have to meet out here in the boondocks instead of in town?"

Miller got a cynical expression on her face and said, "Well, for one, I suspect Martin may have someone watching what is going on. So, coming over to the local FBI office might arouse, oh, I don't know, wait, yes, suspicion!"

Sally was expressionless, then her eyes went wide in a moment of revelation. She said, "I think we might have gotten somebody in the company that is there to do just what you said—keep tabs on us."

Miller queried, "Who?"

"Albert Schoonover. His resume was forwarded to me by Martin himself. And the man is well qualified to get the lab up and get us ready to go. He just reported in for his new job." Miller nodded and said, "Is he American or British?"

"American."

"Well, be careful what you say around the guy. Get me some info on him today and we'll run a background check. Also, if anybody else comes up like that from Crosswaithe, I want to know as soon as you do, even if you don't hire the person. Got it Dinklestern?" Sally nodded. Miller said, "Ok, let's get the hell out of here, Borders and I need to go find some actual sustenance."

12

Bob parked his vette in the usual spot where he used to sleep near Perky Petite's café. Earlier, Billy had instructed him to meet a document forger that went by the Internet persona of Righteous-n-Randy, or RnR for short. Billy had found out about RnR from Liz who had provided him the name. RnR had stated that he/she/they, (Billy could never figure out anything about the person's identity from the secretive communications that were demanded), would provide the fake IDs needed for the Watering Hole gang's employee identifications at a reasonable cash price.

Climbing out of the car, he began walking to a designated meet point at a bus stop bench about two blocks away. When he arrived, no one was there. He looked around, feeling a bit nervous, as he sat down. Five minutes later, a precocious female child walked up and sat on the far end of the bench and slid a sack over to Bob. Bob opened it and browsed through the contents, seeing that it contained his new identity along with the others for Frieda and Helga.

Bob knew nothing about creating false identities but decided they looked fine. He then slid a small sack of his own over to the child that contained the cash needed to conclude the transaction. The little girl pulled a phone from her pocket, took a picture of the cash contents and texted the image. A moment later she got a reply.

She stood, and said, "RnR says nice doing business." She then walked away. Bob felt a rush of relief, but his curiosity was unabated. He watched the child go around the corner, then leapt to his feet and ran towards her last known position. When he arrived at the corner, he peeked around it as if he were on a secret mission. All he saw was the young girl climbing into a nondescript old Toyota sedan that then sped off.

Borders was sitting in her car with a telephoto lens on the camera that Miller had provided her. She began clicking images of Bob as he sat down, then when the little girl arrived, the transaction and when the little courier left. She thought she was done, but then she saw Bob jump up and go running after the child.

She took a few more pictures of him peeking around the corner, giggling to herself, thinking *what a moron*. She placed the camera in the passenger seat of her car and drove around the block, parked on the street outside Perky Petite's then went in, grabbing a booth on the far end of the place. Miller showed up a few minutes later with the little girl who had done the exchange with Bob.

Their waitress arrived with menus, and they waited patiently while the little girl perused the options and ordered some pancakes. Then Miller and Borders submitted their breakfast orders and leaned back as the server brought their coffee and a hot chocolate for their small companion.

Miller said, "Amy, you did good today. Tell your mom we appreciate her letting you come with us."

Amy gave a sunny smile then began sipping her hot chocolate. She sat her cup down and asked, "Was there something wrong with that man I gave the sack? He seemed kinda goofy."

Miller grinned as Border's eyes went wide with amusement. Miller said, "Oh, you know how it is with some of the people we meet. But you're right, he's goofy…but harmless." Amy nodded and continued sipping her drink.

Their server arrived, setting down their orders. As they went through their meal, Borders said, "So, now that we know that some of the original gang is back at PhoenixGen, do you foresee any problems?"

Miller said, "I am counting on them. I expect we will see the level of shenanigans pick up. Everybody seems too relaxed, and we need information now to get closer to Martin and the foundation."

Borders nodded, then said, "So, I love those pictures on the fake IDs, who did them?"

Miller nodded towards Amy as she patted the little girl's arm and said, "Her mom. An ace forger the FBI caught a few years ago but did not prosecute. She has owed me a few favors since then. I hope all our miscreants are able to do the makeup needed to fit the images." Amy looked at the two women and said, "You all are fun to be with, but I miss my mom. Can I go home now?"

*

As usual, Bob was the last to show up at their assigned booth at the Watering Hole. He slid the sack he had picked up earlier from Amy across the table to Billy. Billy laughed at the pictures and then started doling out the IDs to Frieda, Helga and Bob as Liz commented, "I am glad to not be part of this silliness."

Frieda stared at her picture and said, "I have blue hair. Blue hair? What the fuck?"

Liz glanced at Frieda's id, smirked, then asked, "So, what is my job?"

"Grounds keeper. Spend most of your time outside, out of sight," Billy said.

Helga said, "Um, this is my actual picture with my hair streaked in light green. Is that gonna work?"

Billy nodded and said, "Remember, nobody at Pearly Whites ever saw you since you didn't work there back in the day. So, you'll do light janitorial work in the building, which lets you get near the lab where Albert is located."

Helga nodded in understanding.

Frieda asked, "How often do I come into the office to work?"

Billy said, "For now, you work from home after you get your computer. While the plant gets built, I have an office for you. You won't have to go through the lobby, you just come in the rear plant entrance once it is finished." Frieda nodded.

Liz inquired, "So, I get to be the mule moving potted plants and lawnmowers around?"

Billy said, "Nah. You don't have to mow or plant more than you feel like it, nobody is actually paying attention. You actually have a special assignment."

Liz asked, "So what would the special assignment be?"

Billy looked her directly in the eyes and said, "If you are willing, you would participate in the new trials program."

Liz blinked and said, "What? Get one of those teeth implanted in me? My ass!" She then finished off her drink as she took a big swig of cheap whiskey and made a face.

Billy grinned at her and said, "More like your mouth. Besides, you had your bottom wisdom teeth removed years ago. So, you got a slot or two available."

Liz nodded, though she was not smiling.

Bob was still staring at his ID and finally chimed in, "So, I get long red hair. Brown eyes. Freckles?"

Billy smiled, "You're too well known around the premises, Bob. Gotta' keep you disguised."

Bob sighed and said, "Okay, okay, I'm doing it for the band then."

Billy said, "That's the spirit."

Bob asked, "So what's my position? I wouldn't mind my old project manager job at all."

"You actually will perform the grounds work for Liz, so she can focus on the trials."

Bob's expression blanched as he said, "Physical labor? I feel ill."

Billy slapped Bob on the back and said, "Now, that's the Bob I know. And you can blog about it when this is all over!"

Frieda, Liz, and Helga were all grinning as Bob frowned and said, "So this is revenge."

Billy shook his head and said, "Oh, absolutely not Bob. Not at all."

Bob said, "Uh…right."

Billy looked around the table, pulled a bottle of Macallan from his backpack and said, "So, anybody up for some decent whiskey?"

13

Liz and Bob were on their third day of their new occupation, theoretically examining a pallet of potted plants that had been dropped off earlier from a nursery. It was then that Liz spotted Albert and decided now was as good as any for her to make contact. She looked at Bob and said, "Okay mister. I am going in. Keep your ass out of sight because your wig and those paint on freckles look ridiculous."

Bob nodded then began limping off, having strained a calf muscle the first day while lifting some decorative rocks into his wheelbarrow.

Liz noticed Albert was observing both Bob and her. She stopped a few feet short of him and said, "Hi, I'm Liz Cleaver. I was told that I am to be part of the trial program for a genetic tooth."

Albert said, "Liz, so nice to meet you. Yes, I was notified as well that you would be involved."

Liz forced a smile and said, "Great. When are we looking at doing this?"

He replied, "Oh, soon. Don't worry, I'll be in touch."

*

A short time later, Reuben Corpenny was following Albert down the hall to a second floor meeting room. He was musing to himself about his twenty five years with the government and how he had just made more money in the last week than in the previous decade.

His agreement with Martin Crosswaithe was generous and he really never thought he would have his very own Swiss bank account. Albert held the door for Reuben as he entered the room. Once seated, Reuben said, "We are moving this endeavor right

74

along. Just need to get my team in for FDA signoff, get the documentation written up and PhoenixGen to begin a few live trials going with some volunteers. The rest is just procedure."

Albert frowned and said, "Do we really need trials? Again? That seems risky. Does Martin Crosswaithe know?"

Reuben smiled reassuringly, and said, "I had not mentioned it, but they will do nothing to stop the product from being released to the public. We just need the paper trail in case of an audit. Like I said, it's just procedure. Nobody reads the trial reports unless we find problems, which we will not, right?"

Albert shrugged and said, "Uh, right. So, are we finished here?"

Reuben stood and said, "Yep. I will be in touch." He then turned and walked out into the hall, nearly running into a green haired Helga and her mop. He brusquely said, "Watch where you're going young woman!" Helga kept her head down and acted contritely until he was walking away, then flipped off his receding back.

*

The next day, Albert pulled up in his car next to Liz and the hippy looking male he had seen earlier, who abruptly left, limping off with a wheelbarrow in the opposite direction. Albert shook his head, watching the man go, wondering how he got into these situations since going on Martin's payroll over a decade ago where he began working in various well compensated assignments.

His reverie ended as Liz tilted her head sideways and said, "Morning Albert, you buying lunch?"

Albert shrugged and said, "Sure. Climb on in." He went and opened the passenger door to his gigantic SUV, indicating Liz should climb in.

Liz rose to her feet and walked to the vehicle. After she was seated, he helped her snap her seatbelt in place, which made Liz want to slap him for even touching her. She took a deep breath and smiled instead. He then went around, hopped to the driver's side and they were off to pick up pizza.

At the drive by window, Liz asked for a New York sub, which Albert bought out of his own pocket along with the pizza. On the way back, Liz could tell that Albert was watching his passenger out of the corner of his eye as she ate her sandwich. She did her best to ignore him unless he asked a question. A few minutes later, they were back on campus.

He said, "So, you have no objection in transplanting one of the new genetic teeth?

Liz said, "No. It's part of my gig with the foundation and PhoenixGen. Looking forward to it."

Albert said, "Good. We can get you done tomorrow if that works for you."

Liz replied, "My schedule is based on what the foundation wants. So, I'll see you then." She then climbed out of the SUV as Albert waved goodbye. Once he was out of sight, she pulled out her phone and called Miller to provide an update.

Liz then headed over to where Bob was resting against the trunk of a tree taking a nap, legs sprawled out in front of him. She kicked his foot to wake him, taking care to make sure it was the leg that was currently suffering from the muscle pull. Bob's eyes fluttered open as he said, "Fucking ouch! Did you have to do that?" Liz shrugged and said, "Sorry about that."

Bob briefly grinned, then said, "Could you help me up?"

Liz stepped forward, extended her hand, reconsidered at the last moment and said, "Nah, might strain my back. Come on, let's go."

She headed off to find Billy. Bob got to his feet just as Sonny came by on a security golfcart used to get around the company grounds. Sonny said, "Don't you have some rocks to move over by the front gate? They've been there like a week."

Bob had been affecting a southern accent lately with his disguise and said, "Could I get a ride on yer' fancy go-cart mister?

Sonny appeared to consider the request then said, "Nope," and drove back towards the front gate. Bob grimaced as he retrieved his wheelbarrow and limped off to the rockpile.

14

Liz arrived at Billy's office and heard what sounded like a struggle going on. In alarm, she almost knocked on the door but then she heard low voices and a woman saying, "Ok, ugh, that's the way big boy." She waited, not patiently, for the conclusion of whatever was happening. There was a lot of groaning and sighs and finally the expected climax. She then knocked.

Billy said, "Who is it? Can you come back in a minute? We are in a meeting."

At this point, Liz shook her head as she said, "Liz here, Billy. I was wondering if we could talk for a few, got some questions." She could hear them both cursing quietly and apparently struggling to get back into their clothing. Liz then heard Sally say, "Who the hell is that?" Billy replied, "Liz Cleaver."

"You're not doing her too are you?"

"Sally, she works for me, you know that."

Sally pointed out, "And you work for me."

"You have a point, but nothing is going on with me and Liz other than work stuff."

Liz was trying not to laugh as the door finally opened. Sally came through, lipstick smeared, her hair mussed up, and her blouse half tucked into her skirt. Billy looked a little better, though he had forgotten to zip his fly and was obviously wearing no underwear.

Liz again suppressed a grin as Sally gave her the once over and then headed off down the hall. Liz shrugged her shoulders as she walked in Billy's office, and as she closed the door, she said, "Your fly's open dude."

Billy said, "Shit," and zipped up as he walked back around behind his desk and picked up his underwear that he shoved in a desk drawer. Liz headed over to the sofa where she was about to sit down. Billy shook his head.

Liz looked down, saw this was obviously where "big boy" had done the deed and said, "Well, look at that…puddle." She then pulled out a chair from along the wall, drug it over to in front of Billy's desk and sat down.

Billy sighed and said, "So what's up that you had to start banging on the door?"

Liz said, "I was not the one doing the banging my friend. And aren't you gay? And, as you already know, I prefer women. We could trade."

Billy rolled his eyes, "Jeez Liz! I'm bisexual if that helps your imagination. Now why are you here?"

Liz said, "Let's do a quick review. Why did you hire me? Answer. To get inside dirt. Well, tomorrow morning, I get a tooth implant."

Billy sat up as he said, "That was fast. Well, I have been through that implant crap Liz. Pay attention to how you feel afterwards."

Liz shrugged and said, "It's just one and I think we will be fine."

Billy leaned back in his chair and said, "Who else knows at this point?"

"Nobody."

Billy's phone rang. As he gazed cynically at Liz, he said, "Thanks for calling Helga and especially giving advance notice you are coming." She smiled back.

Billy continued with his phone conversation, "See you in a few. No, don't listen to Liz. I will tell you later. Bye." He sighed and said, "Helga has some dirt too. Hang on, let's hear it together."

A couple minutes later, there was a knock. Liz went and opened the door and said, "Hey young lady!" Helga gave a polite nod as she headed over to sit on the sofa. Both Billy and Liz said, "No!"

Helga gave them both a quizzical look, then surveyed the sofa. She raised her eyebrows at her findings and went over to the chair where Liz had been sitting, slipping into it before Liz could. Liz sighed, drug over another chair, and sat down next to her.

Billy said, "So what's up?"

Helga said, "I found out that Albert is spying on us for Martin Crosswaithe. I overheard a discussion between him and the FDA dude, Reuben Corpenny. They are going to do a sham trial and certification with just a few patients."

Liz said, "Yeah, and I am one of them. Good to know though about Albert. Have to say, after the short time I spent with him, I am not surprised."

Billy said, "I need to brief Sally."

Liz said, "With your pants on I hope!"

Billy sighed as he escorted both women out of his office.

*

Liz called Miller once back at her apartment. "This dude, Albert Schoonover. He works for Martin Crosswaithe and apparently is feeding him information about PhoenixGen activities." She added, "Crosswaithe apparently sent the guy's resume to Sally and Billy hired Albert to take the teeth to production level quantities and do some abbreviated FDA trials. Also, there is another person involved in this part. Reuben Corpenny with the FDA. Sounds like he is in on what is going on as well."

Miller said, "I knew about Albert, but this is useful. I am impressed Cleaver. Keep tabs on what is going on, have a good evening." The call then ended. Liz went to her refrigerator, found a package of premade tuna salad and some wheat bread, of which she made a quick sandwich, then sat at her computer, nibbled as she surfed the Internet looking for any information she could find on Martin Crosswaithe and his investment group.

15

The next morning, Liz arrived at work early, wanting to get her tooth insertion over with. She was currently sitting in the conference room across from the second floor lab where she had been situated following the dental procedure, ostensibly to make sure she was doing okay post op.

Albert and a new hire technician were off and on, observing her. A contract oral surgeon named Vinny had done the actual work. Several times Albert reminded Vinny that he was under an NDA that would ruin him if he ran his mouth about what he was doing. The fellow didn't seem to care, commenting that, "I'm here for the cash. No warranty expressed or implied."

She was frankly surprised at how little Albert paid attention to her. She guessed it was because he saw her as the "hired help" around PhoenixGen and unimportant. That suited her, as he talked freely about this abbreviated trial with his technician and the accelerated plans to get the teeth certified in Europe.

Her new wisdom tooth lived up to the earlier appearance of genetic teeth, being pristine and white as could be. The procedure itself was relatively painless with Novocain having been injected around the gums. Even now, two hours after the procedure as it wore off, she felt only a little discomfort.

Compared to patients she had seen at the free clinic after various dental procedures along with her own previous history, this seemed a better way to get teeth repaired or replaced. It made her think about her original plans with the foundation before had gone off the rails. Inwardly she sighed at that memory.

After a quick check of her new tooth, the technician nodded to Albert, who then handed Vinny a plain envelope stuffed with the cash. Vinny smiled, nodded and headed out.

Albert then said, "Liz, open your mouth and let me take a look." She opened wide. Albert peered in, nodded and stepped back. Albert was impressed. "I'm no dentist, but that looks perfect," he said.

Albert sat down at his laptop and started typing. The output of his screen was on a wall monitor. As he typed, he said, to the technician, "This is the last bit of code for the upgrade you and I talked about. Just getting it documented."

Liz suddenly had a very weird experience. She looked at the code and for the first time in her life, thought she understood its functionality. It was odd because she was definitely not a programmer other than some very basic stuff she learned as a teenager, and she had not stayed current or interested. The recognition lasted but a moment then faded.

Albert shut his laptop lid, nodded and said, "Well, looks like we are done here. You can go Liz."

Liz said, "Great!" She wasted no time getting to the door and to the elevators then headed up out to the parking lot to meet up with Bob, who was forlornly raking pea gravel in some islands between parking spots. She walked up behind him and slapped him on the back as she said, "What the fuck up Bob?"

Bob, taken completely by surprise, spun around, lost his footing, and landed in the pea gravel, ass first. Liz laughed and then sat down next to him. With a disappointed expression, he said, "Was that necessary?"

Liz said, "Perhaps not. But it was funny. Anyway, I got my tooth."

Bob perked up and said, "Feeling weird yet? Need to beat up anybody in a parking lot? Oh yeah, you just did!" Liz said, "Pshaw, I just tapped you."

Bob sniffed, "It hurt."

"Poor little baby." She rubbed her eyes like she was crying then added, "Well, gotta go. I got some work to do."

Bob stood, picked up his rake and offered it to her. Liz said, "Not that sort of work. I need to do some research."

Bob nodded, "Great. Keep me posted."

"I just did." Bob looked confused as Liz strolled off, climbed in her car and phoned Billy. Billy answered after nearly six rings with "Uh, shoot, wait a sec. Ok. So how did it go?"

"Fine. Apparently, Albert and his team are still fiddling with the software that runs the Acme gene splicer that creates the teeth, so I am wondering if the teeth are actually fixed."

Billy said, "Really keep tabs on how you are feeling. I mean it."

"I feel fine."

"So did I at first. I'm serious about keeping track of how you are progressing."

"Okay Dad. Gotta' go now." Liz hung up without waiting for Billy's goodbye.

*

Billy looked at his phone then up at Sally who was gazing down at him expectantly as she sat straddled on his stomach. This time, he was in her office with the doors locked and the electric shades drawn in an attempt to keep prying eyes away. She said, "So, what's up since we are taking a break."

Billy said, "Liz got her tooth in, seems okay. And you're wearing me out."

Sally said, "For a guy that exercises a lot, you don't seem to have much endurance."

They both giggled and continued with their prior activity. When they were done, Billy briefed Sally on what Liz had said about the tooth insertion. Sally nodded slowly, thinking to herself, *I need to make a call of my own here in a few.*

16

Helga and Frieda proceeded hand in hand to the front door of the Watering Hole, where Frieda held it open for her partner. Helga said, "How gentlemanly!" They both laughed and proceeded to their usual table. Liz was sitting at the end of the booth with a laptop computer, typing away, oblivious to their presence.

Helga said, "Hey Liz. How'd did it go today with the tooth insertion?"

Without pausing her high speed typing, Liz said, "It was most satisfactory. I believe it was the logical choice as my empty socket was serving no purpose."

Frieda's eyes went wide at the last part about being logical, then walked around behind Liz to peer over her shoulder as Helga slid in the booth from the other end of the table and watched. Helga saw a perplexed expression on Frieda's face and asked, "Something wrong?"

Frieda shrugged, still watching Liz zoom around her keyboard, "Not wrong, just weird. Liz, when in the hell did you learn how to program?"

Liz blinked and said, "What with everything PhoenixGen is doing these days with applied software and genetics, it seemed a good idea to read up on C++, python, JAVA. The languages are all pretty straightforward as it turns out."

Frieda said, "Ah, right. And today, you are writing code like you have done this for years."

Liz nodded and said, "This code is what I remember Albert working on after my procedure." She then stopped typing, reached over and took a sip of her beer, looked first at Helga, then Frieda who had also moved around to where she could look Liz in the eyes. One eyebrow popped up as Liz shrugged and said, "I just remember this code sequence from Albert's screen. Wanted to get it documented."

Helga, in a slow cadenced monotone, said, "You…remembered…it? By just looking at his computer screen?"

Liz sat her beer down and said, "Yes. Not the best error handling in the man's spaghetti code. Poor subroutine layouts, but it is serviceable if nothing disrupts execution."

Helga and Frieda looked at each other with a "what the hell" expression on their faces. Frieda said, "Serviceable? So, does it work, or what?"

Liz took another sip on her beer, pondering the question, then said, "It depends on a lot of variables that I am afraid Albert is not capable of accounting for, but I can. I can fix this, but then again, we aren't here to assist the evil empire."

It was then that Bob came wandering in and slid in on the far end of the table. He looked at Liz, then Helga, then Frieda. He sighed and when the owner, Becky, arrived for his order, he said, "Eh, what is the very best whiskey you have?"

She appeared to ponder for a moment, then replied, "How about something cheap, you know, like within your stingy ass budget."

Bob leaned back, shrugged, then said, "Sold."

Billy arrived and instead of trying to slide in, he grabbed a chair and sat on the outside of the booth, centered where he could scan the entire group. He briefly fixated on Liz with her computer, then said, "Liz. You and a computer? Does not compute. What's up?"

Liz looked intently at Billy, like she was examining an insect from Mars. She said, "You would not understand." Billy, now with an amused expression, said, "Really? Heck, try me, Liz."

Liz paused, now in deep thought. Finally, she nodded slowly and said, "Why is PI the most complex thought humanity has ever had? Why does this infinite number emerge as part of the formulae of the cosmological constant, the Heisenberg uncertainty principle or Einstein's field equation of general relativity? Or just determining the mathematics of circles?"

Eyes wide, Billy took a deep breath, shrugged and said, "You have a point, Liz. Sorry I bothered to ask."

Liz quipped, "Exactly."

Frieda jumped in with, "Listen, we should all be happy. Right?"

Bob said, "About what?"

Helga, imitating Liz, intoned, "You would not understand unless you applied logic!" She gave Bob a big smile.

Billy leaned back in his chair, took a deep breath, then dug out the Macallan in his bag and said, "This group is… getting weird."

Liz paused, looked at the group and stated, "Well, everything is… about to get weirder."

17

Billy was at his desk, viewing cost estimates for the construction of the new production line in the new production plant and not understanding much of what was in the spreadsheet in front of him.

Admittedly, he had avoided mathematics and the sciences in high school, having found body building a more obtainable skillset. However, here he was, in charge of getting the plant built and online, or something to that effect. He briefly wondered if Liz would help him decipher what he was looking at, but then he remembered the other evening and decided she would confuse him even more with her newfound technobabble. Sighing, he kept studying the well-ordered columns of the document, mostly to no avail.

*

At the same time that Billy was in spreadsheet hell, Martin and Mabel were beginning their own conference call to discuss progress, problems, or whatever else was going on at PhoenixGen.

Martin was in New York City. He had arrived several days earlier to meet with various Wall street firms as his investment group was preparing to take PhoenixGen public on the Nasdaq stock exchange. He also had been going out to high end restaurants every night as he wined and dined with old financial partners. Therefore, this morning, he was a bit hung over from his previous evening's excesses.

The video call commenced, and Mabel came on the screen with the two other elderly yet attractive women that attended the calls but never said anything. The video stream coming in was of low quality and her voice broke up at first.

Mabel cursed, "The Internet these days is a piece of shit! Of course, this encrypted tunnel we use to ensure our privacy does not help as it consumes additional bandwidth!"

Suddenly, the connection improved, and both the voice and video quality returned to normal. Martin said, "Well, it appears you corrected the issue?"

Mabel frowned and said, "Um, no, it seemed to straighten up on its own. I tell you, the telecom companies these days are so far behind the times with shit infrastructure. It's amazing this crap works at all!"

Martin, not particular tech savvy at all about video streaming, encryption and how it figured into his wealth obtainment goals, said, "It seems sorted, let's get on with the agenda if you are ready."

Mabel sighed and said, "Sure, sure. So, you are continuing with getting our stock IPO in order?"

Martin nodded then said, "Yes, my exact purpose for being here in New York as you already know. Along with that, Sally is keeping me well briefed on progress at PhoenixGen."

Mabel nodded and said, "She seems to be most useful. Makes good sense since she went in big with bankrolling the revitalization of the company."

"She does appear to have the requisite intelligence. And the funds she provided, well, they have definitely helped. We just have to see how things go with her over time."

Mabel stared back at Martin and said, "I see. Women need a man to keep an eye on them?"

Martin, sensing he had perturbed Mabel with what he considered an innocent comment, decided to change topics, "At any rate! It looks like our own internal trials are proceeding. The first tooth went in without a hitch with your Liz Cleaver. Interesting how you got her in as a trial subject. It seems there are no problems or side effects to worry about, not that the woman is all that smart."

That elicited a grim chuckle from Mabel who said, "So, another insult to women. You need to work on this Martin.

However, we probably do need more idiots on the payroll to experiment on, we'll just make sure they are male."

With no reply handy, Martin simply focused on what he would have to drink once the call was over. Conversations with this woman were like walking in a minefield—he was not used to being thrown constantly off-balance.

In another attempt to deflect Mabel, he said, "By the way, I must ask—what are the names of the two lovely women with you in these meetings? They never speak. I would love to hear any input they may have." He then smiled at the two women, having taken a fancy to the one on the right, hoping she might engage.

Mabel belly laughed and said, "Martin, they are not women, they are AI constructs that our computer systems generate, though I can have them do things for you. Perhaps a strip show?"

Martin, embarrassed by her mocking amusement towards him, said, without much enthusiasm, "Ah, technology. Amazing. Well, I must be off to another dinner with one of the CEOs of a major investment bank this evening that is very interested in our project. Then back to London."

Mabel said, "Sounds boring and…well, I have a foundation to run so, have a wonderful time."

Now it was Martin's turn to be snarky with, "Ah, yes, how is the milking of those billions going?"

Mabel, in mock seriousness, said, "We run a tighter ship these days under my command, and are far better at making sure the money goes where we want rather than to those silly clinics."

Martin nodded and said, "Mansions and swimming pools! Enjoy." The screen went dead as the meeting terminated from Mabel's side.

Martin sighed and stood, feeling stiff and tired. Traveling did not agree with his age so much anymore. He stepped to the bar in his room, poured himself a cognac, and sipped it while he took a moment to reflect on his life, wondering if the pursuit of all thing's money had been worth the effort versus his long ago youthful desire to write action and adventure novels. He shrugged and said,

"Woulda, coulda, shoulda." He straightened his tie, slugged down the cognac, and headed out for his dinner.

18

When Miller arrived at FBI headquarters, a plain manila envelope was waiting for her at the reception desk. It had no return address and read, Attention: Special Agent Miller.

She glanced at it, shrugged, then instructed the receptionist, "Have this opened by our forensic team. I don't want to find out it's full of ricin." The receptionist nodded and Miller continued on to her office. From there, she called Borders who was on her way in, now keeping banker hours with her consulting gig with the FBI when she wasn't seeing patients at the hospital.

Miller really didn't care, if she needed the woman to do anything, Borders made herself immediately available. They agreed on meeting for lunch at Perky Petite's diner. Miller insisted that the place had the best damn burgers in town. With the call over, she stood to leave, as a text came in from Jean-André, her now ex-stud boyfriend.

The man had worn out his welcome, having put too many miles on her personal car, a fancy Volvo SUV that she herself rarely had time to drive and that he could not explain away all the usage. A quick investigation on her part found that he had been milking her generosity while supposedly out looking for a part time job to help with expenses, but instead was making new girlfriend acquaintances.

So, today was his move out day and he was none too happy. He had texted, "Jade, you will miss me, I will see to that!" Miller texted back, "Boohoo, I am crying in my fucking cereal. Best of luck asshole!" She then departed for her lunch date.

When she arrived at Perky Petites, Borders already had them a booth and had ordered the usual. Miller sat down and with a grin, she joked, "That's the least you could do with what you bill."

Borders said, "Hey, you gotta do the right thing for a friend now and then." She gave Miller a concerned look and said, "Boyfriend gone?"

Miller said, "Yep, he texted me that I would be sorry."

"Are you?"

"Hell no. Man was screwing around on me. And piling miles up on my car!"

"Ah, yep, and never gassin' it up if I remember right!"

Miller nodded ruefully and said, "Hard to spend your own money when you are work averse and broke."

A few minutes later, their burgers arrived and as Miller squirted ketchup on her fries, she said, "Well, I guess it's back to the Winnebago trailer park for another pathetic Sally briefing. She's less useful all the time of late." The two nodded at each other as they dug into their lunch.

*

Bob had been walking around with a measuring tape, clipboard and pencil for the last few days, all part of his personally conceived work reduction plan. Whenever somebody saw him, he would stop, pull out the measuring tape near some landscaped area of the campus and take measurements, then start writing on his clipboard.

If anybody had been interested to see what was being written down, they would be surprised to find no numbers, no comments, only some rather poorly drawn figures of dogs, cats, people, horses and whatever else he could sort of sketch—his creative side had recently reawakened, however, his technique needed an upgrade.

He spotted Liz under the same tree where he had fallen down the other day when she had startled him. He walked over and saw her busy typing away on her laptop.

"Mind if I sit with you? I need a break."

Liz looked up, shrugged and said, "Sure." Bob sat, clutching his clipboard and pencil and after a moment, he started sketching. Liz looked over at what he was doing and said, "You could be the next Rembrandt."

Bob, surprised at the complement, said, "Really?"

"Sure. Just keep doing that for the next three or four decades, you are bound to get… better."

Bob nodded, thinking practice made perfect. He flipped to a fresh piece of paper and started trying to sketch Liz. After a moment, between keystrokes, she said "Would you quit staring at me."

"How am I supposed to get your likeness down?"

"Take a damn picture."

"Picture?"

"Yep, then, when I am not here in a minute, you can look at it to refresh your… brainpan."

Bob realized this was a revelation, for him anyway, so he reached for his phone, but Liz had already stood up and said, "I'm headed out. Got some more research and coding to do."

Bob said, "Hey, I did not get the picture I need of you for your portrait!

Over her shoulder as she walked towards her car, Liz said, "Are you surprised?"

Bob took a picture, out of spite, of her walking away. The woman was eternally sharp-tongued with him, like the last cutting comment she had just made, but she was also now so focused on programming, her deep analysis of data and seem to be constantly doing multiple things at once it was scary.

It was part of what had inspired him to try to start drawing instead of raking pea gravel, thinking he also needed a passion and could do more than one thing at a time—if he kept his expectations low on the quality. He stood up and wandered off, clipboard in hand, determined to sketch…something!

*

After their lunch and nonproductive update from Sally, Borders and Miller were back in the office reading a copy of Borders's latest analysis of Martin Crosswaithe and his organization. Miller sighed and said, "What the hell are we supposed to do with this? We already knew the man is a greedy asshole. Everything here just confirms it to the nth degree!"

Borders shrugged and said, "Maybe...money is the bait we need to lure Crosswaithe to his destruction?"

Miller, sounding a bit frustrated, replied, "We gave the asshole two hundred million dollars of Brandt's loot."

Borders perked up and said, "Yes, but that was to fund making more money. So maybe that is the key!"

"To what?"

Borders shrugged. They both sat quietly, contemplating the ceiling, glancing at their watches. A timid knock at Miller's closed office door ended their contemplation. Miller walked over and opened it.

There stood an intern, a hopeful look in her eyes, offering the manila envelope that Miller had asked to have checked by the forensic lab. Miller said, "Thanks," took the envelope and closed the door in the intern's face.

Borders giggled and said, "Try to be nicer Miller. Poor kid was looking at you like you were a god."

Miller shrugged, chunked the envelope on her desk and said, "Yep, it's good to have a role model."

19

Sally and Billy were standing on the production floor of the new plant, gandering at all the construction work that was finally winding down. Moments later Albert Schoonover arrived, appearing impatient and bored at the same time.

Billy's recently completed project was built for capacity with all sorts of automation to stack and move boxes of product around. Robots were the primary labor force. A few demo units whizzed by that Billy was controlling with a game pad as he prepared to explain how the flow of production was supposed to happen.

Billy began with, "So, this guy, robot one, once we get it all programmed, will just pick up a box of teeth, run it over to this bigger box and place it inside. Then robot two will move the just inserted box to just the right spot so when robot one gets back with a new box, or robot X, because you know, there could be more than one or two... oh shit!" The robot acting as "robot one" had gone rogue, running into a wall—at this point it went offline.

Billy ran to robot and kneeled down as Albert looked around the large facility and said, "So, Billy, you figure this out all by yourself? Looks like a big ass waste of money."

Distracted, Billy said, "No, I had help." Which was true. Billy had definitely found help. The problem: the source of Billy's "help" on the plant design was a YouTube site called, "Build your own production line," by Production Line Productions, whose side business was robots and shelving, which they ran numerous well-produced ads for during their video.

Sally, having been lax in her own attention to the details of the facility build, asked, "Um…why is the plant three stories high?"

Billy said, "So we can get lots of shelves in to stack product on." He stopped ministering to the now offline robot and stood,

95

turning to his audience. He gestured as he walked to one of the walls and said, "See the outlines on the floor? This is where the shelving will start."

Albert said, "So we are going to have three stories of shelves? How do we get to the shit in this place we need to ship?"

Billy answered with "Albert. Please. Drone robots. Should be obvious." Sally chuckled and said, "Drones. Robots. Computers. This reminds me of that Vonnegut novel, Player Piano, where nobody has a job."

Dovetailing on her supportive commentary of the unemployed proletariat, Albert asked, "where is the actual part of the plant that grows the teeth? Remember, right now, we got one machine that can kick out about three of your "product" a week. One person would not even need to show up but once a month to fill one box."

Billy paused in contemplation then said, "That's your job Albert. How would I know how to build the box that makes the teeth?"

Albert said, "Well hell. When were you going to say something Billy?"

Sally, sounding a bit pissed off, said, "Have you two even met to discuss this topic? Even once?"

An embarrassed silence was all that came from both Billy and Albert. Sally nodded to herself. She took a deep breath, seemed about to say something, then took her phone out of her purse and started viewing the screen. Billy went over to his robot, and in frustration, kicked it. It came back to life, lying on its side, flipping its mechanical arms around.

Sally said, "Billy, Albert, please get together, get some specs, and get the most critical part of this, this… giant tooth stewpot going."

Billy and Albert nodded they understood, all while avoiding eye contact with each other. Then, Sally nodded to Billy, who walked over. She grabbed his arm and started whispering in his ear as they walked off. Albert watched them, then headed off in the opposite direction shaking his head.

*

Martin was sitting in his study where he had been reviewing a progress report about the plant buildout that Sally had forwarded him. It had been written by Billy, then heavily edited by Sally to make sense. Basically, it told him little about production other than it had four walls and a ceiling. There were building layouts, pictures of shelves, robots, computers, and cardboard shipping boxes along with numerous bills for expenses such as construction work and the like. None of these details provided enough information for Martin to even be able to guess if they would be capable of going into production soon.

His computer beeped. It was an incoming call from Mabel. Martin gave an annoyed look at his screen, sighed, then clicked on the link, opening the session. He said, "This was unexpected. What is going on?"

Mabel shrugged and said, "Just checking in. What's all that paper on your desk?"

Martin said, "Um, well, it is the information about the plant build."

Mabel nodded and said, "And?"

"Ah, there is a lot of stuff to look at, but nothing like what I would call a progress report."

Mabel nodded and said, "So, what are we going to do? How much has been spent? When will they be done? Can we make the money we are thinking we should make? Will your Wall Street associates be pleased? Will you—"

"Um...I understand this is not looking good. What I can't understand is what these people are doing. It is as if they know nothing about what they are making!"

"Perhaps your attention is needed on location, Sir Martin."

Martin said, "You're one heck of a lot closer. Why don't you go Mabel?"

Mabel shrugged and said, "What do I know about making teeth. Certainly not my area of expertise."

Martin sighed, realizing it was not his either, but somebody had to find out what was going on with his money. He said, "I hate California, they tax the rich excessively, compared to the poor and middle class that owe us so much. But I will go."

Mabel nodded, then said, "Outstanding. Will see you next week."

"So, you are going to meet me there? "

"It's a figure of speech. I'll ring you for an update. Now, bye!"

The call ended. Martin scowled, wondering how he had just gotten railroaded into making another trip to America. He also pondered where the two assistants had been that normally were on calls with Mabel. After a moment of reflection, he lost interest, knowing they were just AI generated imagery anyway.

The woman was difficult to work with, obviously disliked answering questions, so nothing much surprised him from this last call. He wandered over to the bar in his study, poured himself a glass of expensive Bordeaux that Nigel had decanted earlier, then sat back down to finish his review of the paper trail mess on his desk. A half hour later, after getting no further, he poured another glass of wine.

His computer beeped an alert. It was from his bank in Cyprus. He brought up an encrypted tunnel that Nigel's IT staff had arranged for Martin to be able to log into his accounts, rather than clicking on email and text links. The security people for SHI had emphasized not clicking on such things, so he followed protocol. Once in his account, he saw where transfers of money from other operations had taken place, but nothing special, as it was only a few million pounds, and they all looked legit. He logged out, finished his drink then rang Nigel to ask him to get his Gulfstream jet ready for a trip to PhoenixGen. Sighing, he strolled away, leaving the plethora of plant build paperwork littering his desk.

20

Sally sat at the head of the boardroom table with Albert to her left, Billy to her right. The topic was the much needed machines to generate production volumes of teeth in the new plant.

Sally had made attendance mandatory for the meeting after a few unsuccessful attempts to get more information out of Albert, specifically the source code the man had brought with him that was currently running in the lab DNA splicer.

Sally took a deep breath, then said, "So, Billy. What do you need that Albert has not provided?"

Billy said, "Albert's source code. We have to have it for the machine that we are having built so that software can be modified to work at production scale."

Sally nodded and said, "Ok. So, Albert. What's the holdup?"

Albert crossed his arms and grimaced at Billy who looked unimpressed. Albert smirked as he said, "Billy is not a programmer. What would he do with it?"

Sally said, "Billy?"

Billy said, "I have programmers that we have hired. They will make the changes for production level requirements."

Albert replied, "I have not met them. So there."

Billy said, "They work remote Albert. How is this a big deal?"

As Albert was about to reply, Sally cut him off with, "How about a conference call. You know, video stuff. We can talk with a production programmer. Would that work for you Albert?" Albert shrugged.

It was Billy that had suggested this to Sally, and she decided to force Albert's hand. Billy had also provided background investigations to Sally, the ones that Miller from the FBI had concocted along with the fake IDs. Those documents indicated all was fine.

Sally said, "So bring up the big screen, let's get this circus underway."

Frieda appeared in her fake identity outfit, (including her blue hair). Billy said, "Hello Thelma."

Thelma/Frieda nodded in response.

Albert said, "So what are your credentials?"

Sally cut him off again, and said, "Albert, this person is not your employee. She is mine. We hired her based on her resume and interviews. We have had her thoroughly vetted. So don't go down this path."

Albert slumped in his chair like a petulant child and said, "That's not fair. I'm a programmer too!"

Frieda said, "That may be, but we suspect the code has problems that preexist your employment."

Her comment got Albert's angry attention as he sputtered, "Oh yeah? And what the hell is wrong with my code?"

Frieda smiled and said "It's more about the old code that you patched. We had a copy of that, and it needs work." Liz had provided her with a bullet list of problems which she now shared on the screen. She read off, line by line, all the deficiencies in the lab software version. After a bit, he slumped even lower in his chair. Frieda concluded with, "We will provide proper structure to the code, effective error handling and the ability for it to be extensible and scaleable for production needs and much easier to work with as the company goes forward with this and other projects." She was reading, again, from remarks that Liz had provided. It was a calculated bluff.

Albert sighed and said, "Fine. Here." He slid a USB stick across the table to Billy who quickly grabbed it and placed it in his pocket.

Satisfied, Sally said, "Very well then. That's settled. Thanks Thelma!" She then ended the teleconference and added, "Billy, get your folks busy. Albert, be prepared to explain any further weirdness in the software and be prompt with replies. Meeting adjourned."

*

Billy felt relieved as he and Sally left the boardroom. He had what his team needed, the team that Sally had no real clue about. The reality was the team was entirely Liz, the new wonder brain. He marveled to himself that ever since Liz had gone off on her tech adventure that was clearly tied, if not understood, to her tooth implant, she had come back and laid out a strategy that appeared professionally and methodically thought out.

Besides the tech aspect, her intricate plan was about getting even, along with making loads of money. She emphasized that, above all, time was of the essence.

Billy knew a big part of his job now was to keep Sally entertained and up to date and block any attempts by Albert to get his sticky little hands on the revised software. He thought, *Nothing like having a few things to do!*

He begged off going to Sally's office, saying he was off to meet the rest of the team to hand over the flash drive.

Arriving at Perky Petite's, he saw his friend Miranda. She waved at Billy with a big smile when he came in. The two former coworkers had a short reunion of grins and hugs by the cash register. She gave Billy a quick scan, patted his stomach and said, "Your looking studly young man, that tummy is back down to size."

Billy grinned. Miranda was just fun to be around and had often made him feel better when he had been sad and depressed during his dishwasher period of employment. She then asked, "The usual?"

Billy nodded, then went to the booth on the far end of the diner and slid in. It was the only one big enough to accommodate the group, and as a side benefit, it also gave them an effective view of whoever came in and out of the restaurant.

Liz, Frieda and Helga arrived together. Liz had her new full time accessory, a laptop, in a bag slung over her shoulder. Bob, unsurprisingly, had not been invited.

101

With everyone seated and having placed their orders, the meeting began. Running down a list of things that Frieda and Helga needed to do to keep Albert happy, Liz was animated, and her enthusiasm was contagious. She then nodded to Billy, who handed over the flash drive. The group was going strong when their meal arrived. It was near dusk, and they sidelined their discussion to eat, just as two other Perky's regulars arrived, Miller and Borders. The two new arrivals were busy talking about their day as a server took their order and appeared not to have noticed Billy's group.

Liz, however, had noticed them. Billy was taking a big scoop out of his banana split when the expression on Liz's face caught his attention. Her eyes were closed, and she appeared to be far away, but then he realized she apparently was listening into a conversation. After a moment, she opened her laptop and started typing. She looked up to see Billy watching her.

He said, "What's up?"

Liz leaned towards him and quietly asked, "What made you pick this restaurant today?"

Billy shrugged and said, "I used to work here, Miranda is a friend, and the food is good. Something wrong with your meal?"

Liz smiled, then said, "No, in fact, I believe it was a grand idea."

Billy shrugged and resumed eating his dessert. As the group finished, Billy told each of them to tip generously or else. He went up front to pay the bill. Heading towards the front of the restaurant, the group passed Miller and Borders. Liz slowed as she went by and gave the two women a cryptic smile, then picked up her pace. Miller's eyes went wide at seeing Liz though she otherwise made no move to acknowledge her snitch.

Billy observed that scene from his position at the cash register. Again, he had to wonder what Liz was up to. He turned back to Miranda, said, "Thanks for taking care of us."

Miranda beamed, placed her hand on his, and said, "Any time!"

In the parking lot, Liz caught up to Billy and said, "Now there is who you ought to be going after if you like women." She grinned.

Billy said, "Oh, Miranda just a friend. Not sure she is interested in that."

Liz said, "You're not very good at reading women, are you?"

Billy shrugged, thinking he had not ever paid that much attention to women until lately, what with Jerome missing in action, though he knew now he could enjoy a relationship with either gender. He changed the subject with, "So, what was going on with the two women in the booth?"

Cryptically, Liz said, "Nothing, I thought I knew one of them, but I was wrong.

*

Back in Perky Petites, Miller and Borders were still talking about Liz. Miller said, "Man, am I ever slipping! I didn't even notice that bunch in the back booth."

Borders shrugged and said, "No problem. The others don't even know who we are."

Miller agreed and added, "Yeah and Liz handled it like a pro," though she felt unconvinced as she munched on an onion ring and wondered. She said, "That smile she gave me. It was so... something." Shaking her head at her lack of articulation, she added, "Boy, was that ever a worthless description. I could just see me on a witness stand. Judge, it was just so... something."

21

It had been about a week since the source code had been turned over to Liz. She had promptly provided an update to Miller that things were moving forward. They talked for a short time with Miller complimenting her for handling the situation in the restaurant like a pro.

Liz thanked Miller while thinking she could help the FBI and herself without conflict if she could keep things moving along in her detailed and extremely logical plan.

For instance, Frieda. The woman did actually have IT skills and demonstrated them when she had configured two racks of servers at the plant after contractors completed the hardware install. Therefore, Liz started sharing more of what she was working on with Frieda, who was not only impressed, but felt like she was being schooled in technology.

It was amazing how well Liz could write software, especially considering she had just started a month ago. When Frieda had once again questioned Liz about this newfound skill, Liz simply responded, "There are lots of online courses and resources to teach yourself. Try it. It really works." Frieda was well aware of online software courses already, but the speed that Liz had absorbed the knowledge was mind boggling.

This morning, Frieda was on a video call with Billy, Liz and their contract electrical engineer, Roger Brown. Roger was designing the circuit boards that would go in the production DNA splicers so was now integral to their efforts. They were about four hours in, and the detail was becoming mind numbing. However, it appeared to be winding down as Roger said, "I've got enough to build the prototype. Should have it ready in about week at the outside. If that goes well, we will get the actual production electronics made for the machines."

Liz said, "Terrific. So, Billy, is the actual production splicer machinery about ready?"

Billy said, "That is my understanding from the company in San Francisco that is building them to Albert Schoonover's specs."

Roger nodded and said, "I have those specifications as well, for integrating the electronic design into the splicers."

Liz nodded and said, "Terrific! Roger, look forward to hearing from you. Let us know if any problems crop up." Roger nodded and dropped from the call as Frieda was scrolling through the source code that Liz had provided. It was organized, efficient and quite readable, for software that is. Nothing like the mess they had gotten from Albert.

She said, "I am glad we are not sharing this with Albert. I don't think that asshole can be trusted."

Liz nodded in agreement and said, "Our... production version of the software is... quite different. There is really no point in sharing it with Albert as it could not be integrated into the lab splicer, the hardware is obsolete and out of date."

*

Miller was sitting at her desk perusing a backlog of emails. While reading one on how everybody in the agency needed to watch their discretionary spending on lunches with other agencies like the CIA, NSA, and that the agency's budget was getting strained this year due to various investigations of corrupt politicians and their various cohorts, a new message popped into her inbox with the subject line, "Santa Clause is here Miller!"

Miller with a quick glance, saw the sender was Borders and grinned as she shook her head thinking what a character the woman was. So, she clicked on the email. When it opened, it did not take but a nanosecond for Miller to realize this was definitely *not* from Borders. Instead, it contained a picture of Martin Crosswaithe in his own study. The note read, *Have you gotten around to looking at that manila folder you sent off to your forensics lab? Oh, and you might want to watch the video I forwarded. Your spy, Liz Cleaver.*

Miller sat back in her chair and stared at the message then suddenly remembered the intern she had run off the other day who had returned the manila envelope Miller had earlier directed her to take to the lab. It was back now, buried under some other paperwork on her desk. Miller began digging through the pile, finally pulling out the envelope. She opened it and peered inside. It contained the three sheets of paper that the lab had scanned and fingerprinted along with a thumbdrive.

The documents listed Martin Crosswaithe's SHI investment accounts offshored out of a bank in Cypress along with the account numbers, current dollar amounts and names of the various entities that were tied to the accounts. Next to each entities name was a single phrase—*fictitious bullshit.*

Miller leaned back in her chair as she read down the list and the amounts of stashed, unaccounted-for cash. She got to the bottom and read the eleven figure total of just under eighty three billion dollars. She immediately called Borders and said, "Get your rear over here to my office. We got some cool shit to talk about!"

She stared for a moment longer at the pages after she hung up and turned to her computer screen as Borders came in and sat down. Miller handed Borders the documents. She smiled as Borders eyes got big. Borders said, "I'm no accountant, but this seems like a hell of a lot of hidden money!"

Miller nodded and said, "Yeah. And this paperwork came from Liz Cleaver! Plus, I got an email telling us to look at the thumbdrive that was in the envelope as well."

Borders walked around the desk and peered over Miller's shoulder, reading the Santa message and looking at the picture of Martin. She said, "I say play it."

Miller grinned as she plugged the drive in, and saw an MP3 file, which she started playing.

It was a voice recording of a meeting between Mabel Belkin of the Cleaver foundation and Martin Crosswaithe. There were some references to illicit spending without detail. Then a short discussion of the FDA certification issues and finally that Martin was on his way to the U.S. to visit the PhoenixGen facility to allegedly sort things out there.

Borders went back and sat down on the other side of her desk. Miller said, "Crosswaithe is coming to Santa Del Lola!"

Borders asked, "How did Liz Cleaver get this information? And that recording?"

Miller shrugged, then said, "How the hell did they send me an email under your name?"

Borders shrugged. She said, "This is like super hacker sort of stuff you hear about in news stories. I mean, just that bank account information alone seems like everything you have been looking for."

Miller nodded, then said, "Here's the issue. Yes, this is all good information, but it is not enough to get us a conviction, or even something to get a search warrant. I will have to talk to our prosecutors, but at this point, we need more detail around these offshore accounts and what they are really used for. Maybe we could investigate the spending of Mabel Belkin and the Cleaver foundation's funds? Or maybe get the IRS involved there? And I'm not complaining, believe me, there is useful information here for sure. Just trying to think of a way forward."

Borders replied, "Crosswaithe is headed here! This might be the opportunity you are looking for." Miller nodded, "Good point. Now we need his travel schedule."

22

Billy fidgeted while awaiting the arrival of Sally and Albert for their final inspection. The plant was ready to go into full production. He had put all the demo robots away and was going to focus on what Sally had talked about earlier, which was a flawless production DNA splicer, and the teeth produced from it.

When the two arrived, Billy led them to the production line. All of them donned protective goggles to avoid the severe snow blindness light effect that emanated from the machine while it made teeth. They then stepped over to the nutrient boxes and watched the teeth form in front of them in record time.

Sally asked, "How the hell is this machine growing the teeth so fast?"

Billy replied, "It's production quality. Not the old and rather primitive lab device."

Sally said, "This is impressive. Can we look at a sample?"

Billy nodded and replied, "Sure," and handed Sally and Albert each a tooth that was in its nutrient container.

Sally smiled, and said, "This is fantastic Billy!" She looked at Albert for his response.

Albert nodded then grumbled, "I guess. Are we done here?"

Sally frowned at Albert's response and said, "Well, you are. You can definitely go." The man scowled and once out of earshot, Sally said, "What an asshole." Billy chuckled as Sally waved goodbye and left.

It was then that the computer station located by the splicer beeped. Billy strolled over and saw a video session already started, so he clicked into the meeting.

It was Liz, who started in with, "Billy, do you like these new teeth?"

Billy said, "Sure. They look great!"

Liz said, "These will have none of the side effects that you experienced last time. If you want, let's get them transplanted so you can get rid of your denture."

Billy said, "Uh, I don't know about that. I really remember last time."

Liz nodded and said, "I know. However, this is my code for making the teeth. You will be okay just like I am with mine. Come on now."

Billy sighed, "Oh, okay. I'm sick of this denture anyway."

Liz said, "Believe me, you won't regret it. The next four off the line are specifically for you. I can get you scheduled in for tomorrow morning with an oral surgeon that ask no questions."

Billy asked, "How would you do that?"

Liz lied, "Um, an old acquaintance has agreed to do the work. No worries."

In reality, she reflected on how she had earlier stolen cash from Martin Crosswaithe in the earlier trial hack on one of his Cypress bank accounts that he had assumed to be a minor shifting of funds to cover normal expenses.

Billy said, "Great, then drinks are on me tonight over at the Watering Hole. Let's get the gang together."

Liz said, "Sounds great. See you there!"

As promised, the next four teeth were perfect matches for Billy's missing ones. He felt relief as he scooped up their nutrient containers and placed them in his backpack then headed out.

*

As promised, Billy's day had gone spectacularly. Liz had picked him up at his apartment and drove him to his appointment. There, a well-compensated oral surgeon did his job without question and the four teeth were inserted. They were on the road back to Billy's place when he got a call from Sally as they were turning into his apartment complex.

She wanted to come over. Billy begged off with, "Sally, please, not tonight. I'm bushed. Been a long day and after all the surgery, I need to let my mouth rest."

Sally suggestively replied, "I'm not interested in your mouth. For now, anyway."

Billy laughed and said, "Yeah, but still, I need to rest."

Sally sighed, "Your loss my friend. Ok, see you tomorrow morning in my office. Bright and early."

Billy looked at Liz and said, "I messed up getting involved with Sally.

Liz said, "You did fine. We might not be here today if you had not—she was instrumental in getting the group inside all of this and she got you back on your feet financially. At least for now, keep her… entertained."

Billy nodded at the wisdom of Liz's words as he climbed out of her car. With a quick goodbye, she drove off.

23

Martin's Gulfstream jet made an uneventful touchdown at Santa De Lola International. Nigel prepared the way for Martin's exit from the aircraft, with footmen assigned to various tasks. With all the proper preliminaries established, Martin, with a certain excess grandeur and sporting a fancy cane with a lion's head, climbed down the aircraft stairs to the red carpet runner that extended from the jet to a waiting limousine that would transport him to PhoenixGen.

Peering at the facilities, he wondered at the conceit of common Americans calling this hickified airport "international." He thought, *Heathrow, this is not!* Climbing into the limo, he commented, "All I can hope for are that these peasants can properly refuel Gulfy." Nigel nodded in agreement about the wretched airfield conditions.

Once all the servants were properly distributed in the caravan attending Martin's limousine, Nigel signaled the moveout to the driver, who was a contract chauffer by the name of Xenophon, a recent immigrant from Greece to the U.S.

The chauffer floored it on the way out of the airport, driving much the way he had learned from years of operating a taxi around Athens, leaving the rest of the caravan in catchup mode and Martin cursing while bracing himself with his expensive cane as he was slewed sideways in the back seat during their turn onto the freeway.

Martin tried dialing Mabel to let her know he had arrived, but his phone would not connect and showed a lack of signal. He snarled to himself, *inferior American infrastructure! How did this country ever become so dominant?*

*

Miller sat in her idling car on a side street situated next to the exit ramp that Martin Crosswaithe would be taking on his last mile to the facility. She had received another Liz email, this time allegedly from the President of the United States, which had made her laugh when she saw it.

In the email, it outlined the arrival of Martin Crosswaithe into the U.S. and his visit to PhoenixGen. Miller realized that Liz had become far more useful than any intel coming out of Sally.

Miller spotted Martin Crosswaithe's caravan exiting the Interstate, on course for PhoenixGen. She nodded to herself and headed toward a rendezvous point with other FBI agents assigned to help. A few moments later, Miller pulled up in an empty parking lot of an abandoned strip mall where the other agents were waiting.

Her phone rang. It was Sally. She answered, "What?"

Sally said, "Well hell, I thought you'd like to know Martin Crosswaithe just arrived."

Miller cynically said, "Thanks for the advance notice. Listen, would you do me a favor in that regard?"

"Uh, sure, what do you need?"

"When Martin gets ready to depart, give me a quick ring. Then wait inside the lobby as he goes to his limo. I'm guessing you will get a kick out of what happens next."

"You got it."

Miller smiled to herself as she climbed out of her vehicle to brief the waiting agents.

*

Back at Santa De Lola International airport, Bob arrived just as Martin's caravan exited. Liz had briefed him three times on his assignment. The briefings had been just with her, and she assured him it was very important and for security reasons, this was their little secret.

The way she had described his special mission, it appeared she had great confidence in his ability to execute the plan and that he was the only person in the group capable of carrying out such a delicate operation. While Bob did not know how she came to those conclusions, he had come to recognize that she was really smart, good looking and had been acting very friendly for the last few days. Her briefings had been stimulating and included Liz outlining each step on a blackboard with basic stick figures and objects, the plan he was to execute. It was all he needed to build a secret agent persona into his plethora of personal delusions about himself.

The focus of his mission was "Gulfy," Martin's aircraft that was currently unattended. He felt a bit deflated as he was expecting various people and security checkpoints that he would have to slip by going in and upon his departure. As there was, nothing was happening near the aircraft.

With a shrug, he parked, walked up to the front of the plane and attached a small black box with a sticky adhesive in an obscure location inside the front landing gear compartment. Then, he scanned the horizon, nearby terminal building, far off aircraft hangars, and all other points of interest he could imagine. Again, nothing presented itself, so he sighed and wandered back to his vette, climbed in, and drove off.

*

Billy had just completed another tour of the plant production facilities that included a robot demo that went off without a hitch. Martin Crosswaithe appeared adequately impressed and was bubbling details about piles of cash to be accumulated.

Martin's entourage then proceeded to the lobby. Sally stayed close, wondering what Miller was going to be able to do after the short notice Sally had provided as this was to be the exciting part of the visit. So exciting, in fact, that she was unable to restrain herself and followed the group out towards the waiting limos.

It was then she remembered she had failed to call Miller. Stepping back and dialing the agent's number, Sally noted a lone limo that parked in the opposite direction of Martin's. On the vehicle's driver door, painted in a fancy script, read, "Walter Weegar Law services."

As Martin exited the lobby area, his entourage suddenly surrounded him as the sole backseat occupant emerged. It was an older looking man, dressed in a three piece black pinstripe suit and sporting a cane of his own. When Martin saw the new arrival, he signaled Nigel who had his people pull back.

Sally inched closer while straining to overhear the two old men's conversation. With Nigel at his side, Martin strode forward from his underlings, flicking his wrist to provide his cane with a bit of flare. He waved at the man emerging from the limo.

The man approached and said, "Martin Crosswaithe. Such a pleasure! I'm Walter Weegar of the Walter Weegar law firm, LLC!"

Martin nodded and said, "So nice of you, Mr. Weegar, to make it here on such short notice. Nigel advised that you come highly recommended. We have much to … talk about."

Their pleasurable introduction was short lived. The FBI had shown up in force as sedans full of agents blockaded the lobby drive, preventing any possible escape route via land. Overhead, a helicopter hovered, with agents repelling down to the ground, further surrounding the two old men and their overmatched attaché of security personnel. Agents then emerged from their well-worn sedans with their weapons drawn. Miller approached with a smile.

Martin sighed, looked at Walter and said, "Got any brilliant ideas?"

Walter shrugged, and said, "I'm a lawyer. Brilliant? Who knows? Win cases in court, absolutely. Obtain large judgements? Always."

Martin considered his options, then said, "Hell of a sales job. You're hired."

Miller approached, badge in the air, declaring, "FBI. Martin Crosswaithe, you're under arrest." She then surveyed the other subjects around her, spotted Walter Weegar, and said, "Walter! Are you slumming about today more than usual?"

Walter smiled cynically and said, "Ah, Special Agent Miller. A problematic pleasure, as usual. Careful how you handle my client."

Miller grinned as she spun Martin around who had tried to hand off his cane to Nigel, which failed, and it clattered to the ground. The butler scrambled for it as she clamped on the cuffs and read Martin his rights.

Martin turned to Miller, shrugged and said, "Let's get on with this charade of an arrest, shall we officer?"

Miller sneered, "It's special agent to you Crosswaithe."

Martin nodded as he replied, "Ah, how very… American." Martin then looked at Walter and said, "Mr. Weegar, please follow us so we can get this annoyance taken care of." Walter nodded and headed back to his limo as Nigel scurried back to his ineffectual footmen and had them regroup into their vehicles in preparation for following their boss.

Martin was then placed in the back seat of an FBI sedan. Two agents climbed in, one next to Martin, the other driving. Miller signaled the rest of her team that they were leaving. She climbed in her car and departed. Several of the FBI detailed to the arrest headed in the opposite direction.

That left Miller leading the way to the FBI office and Martin with his FBI escort, Nigel now riding shotgun with Xenophon in the limo, Martin's caravan of footmen, and lastly, Walter Weegar's limo.

A she proceeded up the Interstate ramp, Miller glanced in her rear view mirror as everyone else followed, then shifted her attention to merging into traffic, which at the moment, consisted of semi after semi in their ingress lane, forcing Miller and the vehicles behind her to a full stop.

A gap finally opened up in the long line of trucks and Miller floored it, followed by the other vehicles, each maneuvering in place behind her. It looked like they were all going to make it but a semi that was passing other trucks in the outside lane made a hard right to get over into their lane—Walter Weegar's limo ran directly into the rear end of the truck. Miller thought, *Failure to yield Walter. Looks like you might get sued!*

At the FBI office, Miller parked and headed in with Martin by her side. The other agents intercepted Nigel's contingent. Martin, unaware of what had happened, to Walter, dove in with, "Where is my lawyer? I demand to seem him!"

Miller grinned, shrugged and replied, "Well, if Walter shows up, which probably won't happen for a while after that accident he had on the way over here, I'll be sure to let you know."

Confused, Martin said, "Accident? What accident?"

"The one where Walter Weegar ran into the ass end of a semi while merging into oncoming traffic on the interstate."

"How is that even possible?"

"Bad driving?"

Martin's shoulders slumped as he went silent. Miller escorted him to the second floor conference room where Borders was waiting.

Miller removed the handcuffs and indicated for Martin to take a seat on the window side of the conference table. She then walked around to her side of the table and sat several feet away from Borders. This left Martin positioned in the middle between them. Miller liked this configuration for peppering a suspect from two angles. However, Martin appeared unphased as he said, "Oh dear, good cop, bad cop? Get on with it please! For what am I under arrest?"

Miller shrugged and said, "A variety of federal crimes. The list is long. Want me to start reading?" She pulled out a piece of paper with a lot of text on it, none of it related to charges.

Martin gulped and said, "Agent Miller…I—"

Borders chimed in, "That's Special Agent to you Martin Crosswaithe."

Martin had to shift his attention to Borders who was smiling cynically back at him as he said, "Ah, yes, decorum. Very well. Special Agent Miller —"

Miller said, "Hold that thought. So here is the deal. We know about your offshore accounts. Eighty three billion dollars, last count."

Martin looked surprised at her knowledge. Trying to maintain his composure, he said, "That's an interesting tidbit of information for you to have. Is this from your informants?"

Borders said, "Believe me, you have got bigger problems than informants Crosswaithe."

Miller nodded as Martin's head swiveled first to Borders and then back to her. She said, "Where does all that money flow and go?"

Martin sneered, "Why, whatever to you mean, Special Agent?"

Miller smiled back just as the buzz of a vibrating phone caught her attention. Martin began to reach for his inside coat pocket, then stopped and set his hand back on the table. Miller shook her head, silently wondering if the agents had bothered to search him at the time of his arrest.

At the same time, Borders computer buzzed with a new email. Borders looked down at the subject line and said, "Make sure Miller looks at this."

A knock at the door. An agent stood with a somewhat worse for wear Walter Weegar, fresh from his limo tango with a semi-truck. Miller waved them in as she peered over Border's shoulder.

Walter looked at his client and warned, "Martin, not another word."

Shifting his attention, he said, "Special Agent Miller, what are the charges?"

Miller held up a hand as she read the email. She then stood, smiled and said, "How about money laundering via offshore accounts for starters."

Walter sniffed and said, "Well, I see we need the bail amount so I can get my client out of here."

Miller said, "Going to take a judge to do that Walter, as you know. And we need to write this up, submit it to the prosecuting federal attorneys. Probably looking at seventy two hours of hanging out with the FBI. Plus, with your client having his own jet and not being a citizen… not sure about bail at all."

While Walter and Miller went back and forth, Martin took a peek at his phone. Borders was watching as he began thumbing through whatever he had just received a few moments earlier. Seeing the man's reaction, she said, "Miller, check out Crosswaithe!"

Miller shifted her attention to Martin, who was now breathing rapidly and uncontrollably, grasping his chest while staring at his phone. He gasped, "Four billion… gah, gone? Just like that?"

He dropped his phone, slumped forward, banging his head onto the conference room table in the process. Borders exclaimed, "The fucker just passed out!"

Walter Weegar glared at her and declared, "That is no way to talk about my fucking client!"

Miller shrugged, "If you still have the fucker for a client." Then Miller said to the agent by the door, "Call 911!"

Twenty minutes later, paramedics arrived. Martin was loaded up on a gurney for a trip to the emergency room. Walter had been on his phone, getting a replacement limo lined up for himself so he could get back to his office to prepare his first billing. Nigel was summoned from the conference room and asked whether he was aware if Martin had any medical condition that the paramedics needed to know about.

He was fluttering about, now totally outside of his element of butlership. Miller said, "Nigel, go ahead and ride with the paramedics to the hospital." A few minutes later, Martin was wheeled away, Nigel at his side holding his master's hand. Walter as he prepared to catch his new ride back to his office, gave an ominous look to Miller and said, "You'll be hearing from us."

Miller said, "Walter, this time, believe me, you are way the hell out of your element. This is no common criminal. Oh, and love the Walter Weegar weather cam stuff you have been doing on the local nightly news. Great view of the coastline!"

Walter sneered and said, "That's quite nice of you Special Agent. And as far as my client goes, I'll be the judge of his criminality! Uh, I mean, innocence!"

Miller smiled and thought, *No, actually, a jury of twelve will.*

24

Albert Schoonover strode into his office, closing the door behind him after peering up and then down the hallway. Talking aloud to himself, he grinned. "So, Mabel Belkin wants to talk to me? Interesting." He had received an email earlier to his personal account with an invitation to a conference call to discuss the future. Sitting at his computer, he clicked on the video link she had provided.

Mabel appeared on the screen. She nodded and said, "Good morning. Well, let's get to it. You are done at PhoenixGen."

Albert said, "Wha, wha, what did I do?"

Mabel gave Albert a stern, scary stare, then laughed and said, "Oh, you're not fired. You have a new assignment! Just messin' with you."

Albert, mouth still hanging open, nodded and said, "Uhhuh. New assignment. And, uh, what would that be?"

Mabel said, "You think you might like Italy?" Albert said, "Well, I would imagine so. But why me?"

"We have a facility there to bring online for making the product."

"So, like is this temporary?"

"Let's see how this goes. I have already arranged a villa for you to stay in overlooking the Mediterranean. Oh, also, I should mention for your earlier efforts, you will be receiving a… large bonus. You have a new Swiss bank account as well."

Albert said, "So, this sounds wonderful. How big is this bonus?"

Mabel said, "I won't spoil your surprise. Info on account access is in another email that I sent. Also, time to get your ticket rolling, first class all the way."

Albert immediately logged into his new Swiss bank account from a link in his earlier email. He turned his attention back to Mabel and said, "You are my hero!"

Mabel chuckled, then added, "Now, Albert, this conversation stays between us. Understood? And definitely, don't say anything to Sally. Understood?"

Albert nodded, thinking he didn't much like the CEO anyway.

*

From out in the hallway, Borders was peering into the hospital room where Martin Crosswaithe had been taken after his emergency room visit for his multi-billion dollar induced collapse.

She had just finished getting a briefing on his condition which appeared to have been a stress induced anxiety event. However, since he was an old codger and had passed out, to be on the safe side, he would spend the night in the hospital. Except, at the moment, he was being dressed by his butler preparing to depart.

Miller came strolling up with a couple of cups of coffee in a small tray. She handed one to Borders who nodded while taking a sip. Also in the room was Walter Weegar. He had gotten a court order for Martin's release that specified Martin was to be taken to a luxury suite at a nearby hotel where he could recover in extreme comfort while the FBI finished filing charges. Walter noticed Miller's arrival and scowled at her, then began whispering to Martin as Nigel tucked in his master's shirt tail.

Miller scowled back, then turned to Borders and said, "Let's talk." The two women went down to a waiting area near the elevator where Martin would have to pass on his way out.

Miller started in with, "So, was Crosswaithe faking it?"

Borders shook her head and said, "Nope, it looks like the old fart had a genuine panic attack."

Thoughtfully, Miller said, "Martin said "four billion just taken". Who could have pulled off a heist like that?"

Borders shrugged and said, "Outside my area of expertise."

Miller then said, "One thing we know for sure. What matters to Martin is…" She paused for effect.

Borders grinned and said, "Money." She looked down the hall and added, "And here comes dah man."

Both women stood to face Martin's entourage as it escorted him to the elevators. Looks were exchanged by Martin, Nigel, and Walter as they passed Miller and Borders. Borders wanted to stick out her tongue but resisted on the professional grounds of being a well-paid contract shrink.

Miller called after them, "See you all very, very soon!" Once the elevator closed, the pair sat back down and continued their discussion about how they might use the four billion dollar disappearance as leverage to get Martin Crosswaithe to talk.

*

Elevator doors closed, Martin said, "Get our pilot on the phone. I want to get the hell out of this country."

Walter looked alarmed and said, "Mr. Crosswaithe, the FBI will never allow that."

Nigel gave Walter a cynical look as Martin said, "Thank you for your profound advice, you small time ambulance chaser. Now, you have been compensated generously for your trouble in this matter, have a wonderful life." The elevator door opened and Martin with his entourage, sans Walter, headed for the lobby.

Nigel was already on the phone with their pilot, advising them of the immediate departure. Martin was shaking his head in disgust, again looking on his phone at the very thing that had made him faint—the theft of billions made by *someone* from several of his offshore accounts. Who could that possibly be? He concluded he had no idea.

His entourage scrambled as Martin entered the limo. All was stowed, underlings moved to their assigned vehicles, and they were on the road to Santa De Lola International.

Nigel said, "Our aircraft is fueled up, we will be in the air within the hour."

The caravan of vehicles arrived as a ground crew pulled chocks from the wheels of the Gulfstream. The flight crew could be seen through the cockpit windows going through their checklist. Martin climbed the stairs and headed to his seat. As he got situated, a cognac was served to steady his nerves. Everyone was in place, and the aircraft sealed up for departure.

He listened as "Gulfy's" turbines came online. Moments later, they were taxiing along as the flight crew obtained clearance for takeoff. Turning off the taxiway and onto the runway, one of the engines shut down. Then the other. Finally, lights went off in the cabin, followed by total silence.

After a moment, Martin said, "What in the devil is going on here? We should be hearing something or other making noise."

Nigel nodded and as he unclipped his seatbelt, the cockpit door opened and the pilot, looking quite out of sorts, said, "I am sorry, but there seems to be some major malfunction in the aircraft's primary systems. It's like everything is kaput."

Nigel, remembering his RAF days when he was a humble airman guarding a flight line, queried, "Kaput? Is that some sort of technical term?"

The pilot shrugged and said, "We need somebody to come out and take a look but first we need to be towed off the runway."

Martin looked distressed and said, "So, Gulfy is a multimillion dollar paperweight going *nowhere?*" The pilot hung his head and nodded in shame.

Martin shook his head and said, "Perhaps I should have kept the ambulance chaser on the payroll a bit longer." A supportive Nigel said, "A judgement call my lord. We will yet prevail."

Martin raised an eyebrow, shrugged, then slugged down his cognac. While it was being refilled, he pulled up Mabel Belkin's phone number and called her. He got a message that the system was unable to complete his call and to please try again later. He flipped his phone to the side then picked up his drink, shaking his head as he sipped.

The flight crew opened the cabin door and slid out an emergency egress ladder to the ground. The pilot climbed down and in short order was on his cell phone, calling into the tower to get a tow arranged. Along with the fresh air that now flowed into the cabin came outdoor noises—a breeze whistling around the aircraft, sounds of vehicles on the distant interstate. It was surprisingly quiet on the runway when nothing was actually taking off and landing. So, after a few moments it was not hard to hear some distant sirens. The wailing sound was obviously getting closer and closer, but their view was blocked by the terminal building and nearby hangars. The sirens abruptly stopped, so everybody went back to waiting.

The pilot signaled the copilot who was standing by the door. A towing tractor was on its way from the terminal building. A moment later behind it came a stream of muted color sedans moving at much higher speed. The vehicles streamed past the startled tractor driver. The alarmed pilot hollered at the copilot, "We've got visitors!" The copilot relayed the information to the flight attendants who relayed the information to Nigel. Of course, since Martin was sitting across from Nigel, he was fully aware as well, and he tensely waved off Nigel's briefing.

The butler surged to his feet in old man fashion, which is to say, slowly, and said, "Batten down the hatches!"

Martin said, "Oh my gawd. Shall we man the poop deck as well? Belay that silly order. It's the bloody FBI, they will cut into us with blowtorches if we try to keep them out."

He then stood and walked to the cabin door. As he watched, one FBI vehicle in the pack went rogue and left the taxiway, making a beeline for them. Martin watched and then to his amusement, the rogue vehicle dipped out of sight, apparently encountering a dip in the terrain between the taxiway and the runway. Emerging from the dip, the vehicle was airborne for a few feet then it tucked down and on impact, slammed forward on its front bumper, where it came to an abrupt halt in front of their plane on the runway with two blown out front tires.

The other sedans stopped uneventfully between the rogue sedan and Martin's Gulfstream. Miller climbed out, along with Borders. She sent two agents over to the damaged sedan as she, Borders and the rest of her crew headed for the aircraft.

Martin, in grim humor said, "Well, so we meet again Special Agent Miller. And, I must say, a more entertaining keystone cops sort of entry I have not seen in ages."

Miller said, "Glad you enjoyed the show. As you might imagine, you're under arrest again and this time, you are going to stay in jail until trial. I think it's pretty clear you are a flight risk. Or more like, a flightless flight risk!" She, Borders and the rest of the FBI contingent burst into laughter.

As their amusement subsided, the agents began the process of getting Martin and his company of co-conspirators out of the aircraft, all under arrest on various charges for aiding and abetting Martin's escape, then came scraping up the remains of the rogue FBI sedan and having it towed off.

It was then that Miller found out that it had been driven by the forever fucking up Agent Benowitz. Apparently, the man thought he would make an impression on senior FBI management by arriving first at the scene. However, he had smacked his face into his steering wheel instead. Miller was smirking at his bloody nose when the other two agents escorted him to her. She said, "Benowitz, how the hell did you ever become an FBI agent?" She nodded to the other two and said, "Get his dumb ass to the ER to get that schnoz looked at."

An FAA contingent arrived to complain about the time being taken to get the Gulfstream off the runway. Miller replied, "Stop being so pissy."

As the senior manager of the facility steamed off, Miller said, "Nothing personal, okay? It's a goddamn crime scene." She then exercised the privilege of cuffing Martin for the second time in a week. He was loaded in the back seat of Miller's car, the rest of his crew in other FBI vehicles. On the way to the office, Miller said, "You still got that five and dime lawyer? You're gonna need somebody better than that."

Martin slumped uncomfortably in his seat, saying nothing. Once inside, he called Walter Weegar whose secretary said he was remarkably busy and that they would not be able to handle his case any further. Miller laughed and Martin was taken off to have an orange suit fitted, all the while with him objecting, "I want a lawyer! I believe I have that right even in this country!"

Miller said, "You sure do. And the court will appoint one if you can't afford it yourself. But for today, we don't want to talk to you. So, enjoy the accommodations."

25

Sally, curious at how quiet things had become lately, strolled down to Billy's office. No sign of any recent activity. Puzzled, she decided to go down to the lab. When she got there, Albert was nowhere to be found. That was damn peculiar as well. Shrugging, she headed to the cafeteria. There, she found the cafeteria crew and some of the janitorial staff having a hearty breakfast at company expense and time. She pulled out her phone and called Miller. Sally said, "Something strange going on around here. Nobody is at work."

Miller said, "What, *nobody*?"

"Well, nobody that matters."

"So, what sort of ship are you running there Dinklestern?"

Sally thought to herself, *Hell if I know. And why did I call this woman?* She replied, "Oh, fast and loose." Miffed, she hung up.

She decided to snoop around the lab. There were some teeth in boxes though the DNA splicer was powered off. She found that curious, as she could not recall it being off since Albert had been hired. She kept snooping around, having previously inspected the facility not long after Albert had gotten it up and running again. The place had the feeling of being abandoned. In his office, she noticed all the junk that Albert normally had splayed around the room was gone. So was his company laptop, which typically he never took home with him.

Frustrated, Sally sent out a text to Billy instructing him to be in the boardroom within the hour, then sent a separate one to Albert. Reluctantly, she again phoned Miller and asked her if she would come to the meeting—she suspected Schoonover might have gone AWOL.

She then took a walk over to the plant. It was recently finished and was scheduled to go into production as soon as the FDA completed their certification. The only activity was some robots slogging around sucking up dust and all appeared in order, so she headed back to the lobby.

Miller along with Borders were already there waiting for her. Sally escorted them up to the fourth floor. On the way, Miller said, "So, I think you might be right about Albert Schoonover. It appears he caught a flight out of San Francisco early this morning that is headed to Rome." Sally frowned and said, "Rome? You mean like Italy?" Miller nodded. Sally said, "Well, that explains that, but Albert took his laptop."

Miller said, "Well, the laptop is company property, correct?" Sally nodded. She continued, "So file charges on his ass for theft. Since he went cross country, that makes it federal jurisdiction. He's making a stopover in Atlanta. We can nail him there."

Sally said, "I need to sort out what is going on. Plus, he's really not needed here anymore so it is not that big a deal."

Sounding irritated, Miller and said, "Your choice Dinklestern."

Sally simply nodded, thinking she did not particularly like Miller and wondered how much longer the agent was going to keep messing with her life.

26

Reuben Corpenny's FDA team had just completed submitting the certification PhoenixGen genetically grown teeth—in fact, he had personally ensured that everything had turned into smooth sailing.

He was also feeling quite satisfied on the financial side of things this morning. He had bet the farm with his Martin Crosswaithe bribe money, going all in on PhoenixGen stock when it went public. The stock was rocketing up the charts. He had sold some the day before and was standing at the Santa De Lola Mercedes dealer, waiting to drive away in a new high dollar coupe.

His salesperson pulled up and gave him a big smile as she handed him the keys. They chatted for a bit—she was obviously flirting with him. He also noticed she did not have a ring on her finger, and was probably twenty years younger than him, so he asked her out on a date. She modestly accepted. Life seemed to be going his way.

A few days later, he got a call from Art to come into the office for a follow-up discussion. When he arrived for the meeting, an FBI agent that Miller had dispatched arrested him and Art for insider trading. Apparently, the FCC had noticed his large stock buy as well as one that Art had made.

It was easy for Miller to make the connection between the two men and PhoenixGen. That evening a story ran in the New York Inquisitor about the arrest of Martin Crosswaithe and how he was now in the custody of the FBI. It also had a paragraph about Martin's failed attempt to flee the U.S. in his private jet with a photo of the aircraft stalled out on a runway surrounded by FBI sedans. Within the hour, other news outlets picked it up and soon it was all over the news.

The next morning, Mabel was sitting in the kitchen of the Cleaver Foundation estate, sipping herbal tea with organic honey, reading the story in the *Los Angeles Herald.*

The kitchen help, all former commune members from the original group under Liz's late mom, and all of which had been forced to ingratiate themselves with Mabel to maintain their indoor status, scurried about, some slower than others due to age.

All these women had learned through negative experiences with Mabel's temper to be subservient. Other more independent members that disagreed with her were summarily moved outside to work on marijuana crops, mow grass, or dredge the various patio pools around the estate. If the member was particularly egregious in standing up to her, they found themselves booted out to the curb—which for most these women, with no savings, no social security records and no marketable job skills, meant living on the street.

Mabel clucked as she looked up at Ethel, one of the original commune members, and said, "Why did we do business with that idiot man?

Ethel immediately agreed, always striving to maintain her distant second slot to Mabel, but not really caring either. She mostly, as top suck-up, enjoyed a private suite in the mansion and wanted to keep it. Also, as she had not had any involvement with PhoenixGen, she had no clue about what was going on or who Martin Crosswaithe even was. She changed the subject, "I was thinking of getting the women out working the north fields today on that new strain of cannabis you are wanting to get to market. They are goofing off."

Mabel grimaced and said, "They always have and always will. Plus, they think I owe them something. They are all slackers. I built this commune. Made it all happen for that ingrate Olivia Cleaver. Then I alone wrestled it back from that Elizabeth Cleaver after making sure her mother was… well you know the story!"

Ethel nodded, being one of the few that had discovered the real truth about Olivia Cleaver. She replied, "You fixed all that as well."

Mabel nodded in approval at Ethel's ability to suck up. The kitchen help was listening, but it was obvious that neither Mabel nor Ethel cared that this core group overheard them. The two women continued their conversation, talking around certain topics so as to not make any obvious declarations of criminal guilt—it was an acquired skillset for the two.

Mabel's phone chirped. She picked up the phone and made a simple Z pattern to unlock it. It was from Martin. All the message said was, "Let's chat."

Mabel scratched her head, sipped her tea and said, "Well, I guess your royal highness Crosswaithe is still with us. He wants to talk."

Ethel raised an eyebrow, "About what?"

Mabel shrugged and said, "Probably needs a get out of jail free card. Still, if he has his phone, maybe he's out on bail." Ethel chuckled as Mabel stood and said, "I'm headed to Patio three to get this over with."

After she left, the kitchen staff disbursed, most of them dropping the charade of looking subservient. One in particular, however, wandered off from the crowd and prepared another herbal tea with organic honey for Mabel. This particular staffer was very new and quite nervous, in fact, it was Helga. Liz had schemed a plan to have Helga accepted into the commune. She was to perform a mission she had volunteered to do.

As it turned out, getting into the commune had been as easy as Liz had told her it would be. Helga had been carefully prepared to get her past the gate guards. Her pitiful story had worked perfectly with Ethel as well when the guards contacted her, which was that Helga was an undocumented immigrant and sex worker trying to break away from her former life and had nowhere to go.

Ethel figured she could use Helga as a sex toy for Mabel to keep brownie points piling up and have her work in the kitchen as well. Therefore, she had sent the apparent street urchin over to the senior manager of the kitchen. The manager then outfitted Helga in appropriate attire, gave her the "three hots and a cot" story, emphasized that was her only compensation and to never to ask for money, then sent her down to the kitchen to peel potatoes.

Helga's effort at getting on the inside had started barely twenty four hours earlier. She now needed to get closer to Mabel to accomplish the next step of her mission, which was to get into the woman's bedroom, (formerly the uber fancy primary suite that Liz and Frieda had occupied).

She put the tea on a tray and headed out the same door, catching up with Mabel just as the woman sat down at a patio table that was equipped with a large computer monitor.

Helga took a deep breath, swallowed her nervousness and approached Mabel with her head bowed. Mabel looked up and gave the young woman the once over then said, "Well, hello my little pretty."

Helga, not having seen the Wizard of Oz, missed the joke, but got the gist of what a leering Mabel was thinking.

Liz had briefed Helga about Mabel's proclivity for young women down on their luck. It was up to Helga now to fill that role in the woman's mind. She said, "I am so sorry to interrupt, I only wanted to provide this drink for you."

Mabel nodded, smiled and said, "Have a seat young woman. And that's a sexy accent. German?"

Helga nodded. Mabel continued, "At any rate, I have to take a call, but afterwards… we can spend some time getting to know each other."

Helga bowed, gave Mabel a radiant smile and pulled a chair around to where Mabel indicated she should sit. A moment later, the screen came to life and Martin appeared. Mabel said, "Well, it looks like you are not in jail! The story I just read said you were being held as a flight risk."

Martin laughed and said, "Well, don't believe everything you read. Of course, the fact that I am on this call with you ought to make that obvious. And who is that gorgeous young woman next to you?"

Mabel stiffened. Martin was being a smartass—the young woman next to her was none of the old man's business. She took Helga's hand and with a cynical smile changed the subject. She said, "Whatever possessed you to come to California to begin with."

Martin shrugged and said, "Oh, I really needed to see what we were spending our money on. And it is looking good, exceptionally good in fact. Now, I just need to get away from this horrid country."

Mabel said, "How are you going to do that?"

Martin said, "Why, I will pay you. You have resources and can do it."

Mabel replied, "I don't need your money, but I believe you will. Lawyers and such."

Martin's expression became grave as he said, "Oh dear. Well, I suppose I have to reveal my hole card now. Would you like me to say it in front of this young woman you seem so fond of?"

Mabel leaned forward, releasing her grip on Helga. She said, "I don't care for arm twisting, or shakedowns if that is what this is becoming. Just what do you think you know old man?"

Martin smiled and said, "Why, that you murdered Olivia Cleaver when she found out you were embezzling profits from HBC. Plus, you engineered Elizabeth Cleaver's removal under false pretenses from the foundation and took over as yours. Should I go on?"

Mabel's expression froze. Helga could sense the fury and confusion mounting in the old woman who clearly believed she was talking with the real Martin Crosswaithe. She took a deep breath to relax. Liz had briefed her on this part saying that Mabel was a dangerous person and to not do anything to make the old woman suspicious.

Martin continued, "Now, about that help you are going to provide."

Mabel lowered her eyes, then raised them, staring straight at the screen, and said, "If you know so much about me and how I finished off that woman's time on earth, you should know you could be next."

Martin acted taken aback, then chuckled, "A threat? Is that the best you have? So, does this mean you won't help me?"

Mabel cynically said, "Oh, I have just the thing to get you out of here. The country that is. Meet me at the location I am texting to you in eight hours. Come alone."

Martin laughed, "Come alone. Not bloody likely. But I will be there."

The screen then went blank. Mabel let out a long sigh, looked over at Helga and said, "Men can be such dicks. But I understand you are remarkably familiar with that part of the male anatomy from your previous work."

Helga smiled and nodded. Mabel smiled back and said, "Perhaps you and I could spend the afternoon together in my bedroom, it's an interesting place."

Helga gave Mabel a seductive look and nodded. As she stood, she felt a surge of adrenalin. The situation was moving fast. Still, she continued, "I would very much like to…engage with you." Mabel gulped and said, "Wow! And again, I love that sexy accent." She then took Helga by the hand, and they set off.

A few minutes later, they arrived at the master bedroom suite. There was a big screen on the wall directly facing the oversized bed as well as one on the ceiling. Mabel put on some of her favorite porn and asked Helga to remove her work dress, which she did, leaving her standing on display in only her underwear. Mabel looked Helga over admiringly and said, "You are some beauty! I'll be back in a few, need to freshen up. Make yourself comfortable."

As soon as Mabel entered the bathroom and shut the door, Helga heard the shower come on. She immediately went to a corner by a double window and felt around for what Liz said should be there. It took her a moment, but she finally located the button that made a hidden door swing open.

There she found an abused looking satchel full of documents and a single tape cassette. She grabbed the items and ran back to where she could put her clothes back on. Far as she was concerned, it was time to leave.

It was then that Mabel abruptly walked out, stark naked, with a sheen covering her entire body of some kind of sex lubricant. She looked at Helga who had quickly stashed the folder under her clothing on an ottoman and said, "Going somewhere? I need you to join me in the shower." Helga was now not sure what to do. Mabel walked over, turned Helga around and undid her bra, then slid down her panties. She then gave a playful shove against Helgas bottom with her pelvis, leaving a lube blob on her rear, along with sending Helga in the direction of the running shower.

Helga felt a surge of panic. This was not part of the plan at all. She knew one thing for sure. The old woman had touched her body the wrong way for the last time. She turned. Mabel smiled and said, "Not yet my little pretty. I have a whole other bottle of lube we need to apply to you!" She then brushed by Helga again, leaving behind more lube globs.

Helga was now getting more pissed off by the second, a feeling she had not experienced since the end of her time with Bob Oppenheimer, except this was far more intense. Mabel went over to the bathroom counter and picked up a bottle of the weird smelling glop and handed it to Helga. She said, "Get busy spreading that love lube! I'll watch!"

Helga looked at the bottle and decided to oblige. As she popped the cap off, she saw that it was designed much like a mustard bottle. She smiled, aimed and squeezed as hard as she could in Mabel's direction, and said, "Right back at ya!"

The lube hit Mabel squarely in the face, clogging her nose and partially filling her mouth. Helga kept squeezing. Mabel began to pivot around on one leg in an attempt to get away and was gagging, trying to spit the stuff out.

Helga realized she was running low and spotted another of many bottles on the bath counter. She chunked the first one in Mabel's general direction, bouncing it off the woman's head, then picked up the other. Her first squeeze put a big blob on the floor and Mabel walked right into it. The woman's feet slid out, one to the front and one to the back–she was suddenly doing the splits, though obviously was rather unprepared. Halfway to the floor, her backfoot slid out sideways. From there she fell over and hit her head on the fancy venetian tile. Helga looked closely and realized the woman was knocked out, at least for the moment, so she ran to her cloths.

She then decided she could not wear the kitchen outfit; she would be spotted too easily trying to leave the grounds. She did a quick scan of the garments in Mabel's closet, found a pair of jeans and a halter top along with some sneakers. She came back out with the clothes draped over one arm and tried to use the kitchen dress to wipe off some of the mess Mabel had made on her rear end. Mabel was starting to stir, tried to rise, slipped again, once again banging her head on the floor—she groaned and collapsed in a heap. Helga grabbed a loose blouse in the bathroom and tied Mabel's hands and feet together like a steer at a rodeo. She then stuffed a dirty sock in the woman's mouth, securing it with a scarf so the woman could not spit it out.

Now was escape time. She put on the jeans and halter top, grabbed the satchel, hesitated, then seeing Mabel's phone, she grabbed it as well. In the hallway, she reached around and turned the center lock on the door handle, pulled it shut and began her escape.

Liz had previously briefed Helga where a rarely used golf cart was located at the front of the residence, and she got there just as a small ruckus began in the house. Having watched Mabel closely when the woman had unlocked her phone earlier in the kitchen, she made the z swipe. She dialed Liz as she climbed into the golf cart. Liz answered and Helga said, "I need you to meet me at the gate now! I have the stuff, but shit has gone south."

Liz said, "Someone better than me will be there to meet you. I will explain later. Just get going!"

Helga took a huge breath, steadying herself—she was on an adrenalin high now, caught up in the action, feeling exhilarated. She floored the cart for the front gate, then wondered how she would get past the guards.

Another golfcart was flying down the drive from the front gate guard shack and it passed her with two large men giving her a hard once over. She smiled, waved, and kept going, hoping her borrowed outfit would work to make her look like she belonged in a stolen golf cart barreling for the front gate.

The distracted guards kept going towards the mansion and she let out a big gasp, not realizing she had been holding her breath. When she slowed as she got to the gate, another guard stepped out and pointed to the curb, indicating she should pull over. She floored it and headed straight for the man. Not entirely an idiot, the gate guard dove to one side and Helga passed him. It was then that a dark blue sedan pulled up and her hopes sank, thinking her escape was over.

The guard was now hollering threats, as he climbed back on his feet and began running towards her as the vehicle in front of her doors opened.

Out stepped Miller on one side, Borders on the other. Seeing the guard, Miller pulled out her badge and her gun as the man was himself reaching for a sidearm. Miller said, "FBI. Keep that fucking piece of shit out of sight unless you want your balls shot off." The guard stopped dead in his tracks.

He said, "That woman cannot be allowed to leave." The man sounded like he was about to cry—Helga thought, *working for Mabel sure seems to lead to lots of emotional crises.*

Miller nodded in mock understanding and said, "Well, tough shit, though I can get a load of FBI agents out here to do full body cavity searches, starting with you. You see, this brave woman in front of you is working for us. Now we are leaving, so don't get all stupid!"

Borders pointed to the back seat of the sedan, and said, "Over here, dear." Helga went under the lowered guard rail and was in the back seat of Miller's car in record time with the old satchel in her lap.

Miller nodded to the guard and said, "You're smarter than you look," as she climbed back in the sedan. She quickly backed out and they were off down the road from the estate.

After a moment, Borders looked over at Helga and said, "What is that smell?"

Helga grimaced and said, "Some sort of gross love lube Mabel Belkin was trying to use on me."

Borders laughed and said, "Wow, must be fun hangin' out at that place!"

Helga replied, "You have no idea!"

Two miles up the road, Miller slowed and rolled into a convenience store parking lot. Liz and Frieda were there waiting next to their car. Frieda ran to Helga, first hugging her, then saying, "What is that smell?"

Helga shook her head and said, "Later," as way of an explanation and gave her a quick but passionate kiss. She then handed over the satchel she had rescued to Liz along with Mabel's phone and a quick demo of how to unlock it. Liz then repeated that process by handing the items to Miller.

Liz nodded towards the satchel and said, "That ought to help you deal with the other part of your equation. It is everything I have on what Mabel did to my mother, especially the tape of their last… encounter. Now, we have to go before we are seen here with you. Just so you know, the contents of the satchel were in my possession for years, given to me by the one of the old commune women that recovered the items from my mother's body before the police showed up the day of her death. That woman personally handed it to me at that time and I foolishly hid it away. Then, I had to leave it behind when I was abruptly evicted from my estate by Mabel. I was afraid if I had tried to smuggle it out, Mabel would have destroyed it if she caught me. So, for what it's worth, Helga was executing a court order I had obtained a week ago. Here's a copy of that order for you."

Miller accepted the court form, then after a brief scan of the document, hefted the satchel. Duly impressed, she said, "Anything else Liz?"

Liz said, "View the contents and listen to the tape. You'll understand, I am sure. I will be in touch." Miller grinned and waved goodbye as Liz, Frieda and Helga drove off.

*

Miller watched their receding taillights, thinking about what had just happened and shaking her head. Liz, it turned out, had been an excellent deep informant and was making Miller look better and better in her new position as special agent.

She climbed back into her car, handed the satchel and phone to Borders while she did a deeper read of the court order. All appeared to be in order. She handed that to Borders as well and they drove off in the opposite direction which took them past the estate. She and Borders giggled as they rolled past the front gate, which now had numerous guards in place. The place was locked down tight. Borders said, "That was some crazy shit!"

Miller nodded and said, "Yeah, this whole bunch we've been dealing with seem to be outsized bonkers."

27

Sitting in the conference room at the Santa De Lola FBI office, Miller and Borders were reading copies the lab had made of the documents Liz Cleaver had provided them. They then listened to the tape of the last conversation between Mabel Belkin and Olivia Cleaver, which left nothing to their imagination about what happened that day. Earlier the lab techs fingerprinted and catalogued all the items, validated the dates of the documents to be authentic along with photographs and then made copies of the tape recording.

Borders shook her head and exclaimed, "Miller! I ain't believing some of the stuff written in here. For instance, these journal entries by Olivia Cleaver? The woman must have been a genius. Plus, that final document."

Miller said, "Yeah, interesting. Liz didn't do the right thing at the time. Why I don't know all the particulars of, but we've got something now."

Borders said, "So there is a case here?"

Miller leaned back in her chair and said, "Hell yes! I just need one more conversation with our friend Liz."

"When is that happening?"

Miller stood and said, "I am heading out to meet her now. I need to go alone. It was specifically at Liz's request. Since she's been really helpful lately, yeah, I am gonna honor her request this time."

Borders shrugged, "See you later then." Miller nodded and headed for her car.

Twenty minutes later, she was sitting in a booth at Perky Petites, sipping coffee as Liz came in and slid in the booth on the opposite side of the table. Their server arrived and Liz asked for decaf coffee and some honey. The server nodded and headed off.

"Decaf?"

Liz smiled and said, "Caffeine makes me hyper."

"I understand a lot of things used to make you hyper. You don't seem so much that way anymore. Calculating would be a better descriptive."

Liz smiled and said, "I'll take that as a complement."

Miller nodded then said, "So, I have read the documents and listened to the tape you provided. Now, this is not going to be fun to talk about, but I need to understand why now is the moment that you finally decided to reveal the contents to law enforcement."

Liz raised her drink, took a sip, then placed it carefully back on the saucer as she looked into Miller's eyes and replied, "I made lots of mistakes after my mother died. I wound up with the foundation and all that went with it. I was most definitely not prepared. In fact, I was a self-absorbed incompetent brat. Without going down the particulars of that failed path, suffice to say my self-focused agenda led to where I lost control of the foundation to the very person my mother most detested and feared and who ultimately murdered her."

Miller said, "Mabel Belkin."

Liz grimaced, "Yes. I need you to know something else."

"Ok. What?"

Liz nodded and replied, "I have… been developing skills in technology."

Miller said, "I saw the one example of what you sent me. Can you confirm what that was?"

"The offshore account information."

"What is the value of those accounts?"

Liz smiled, shook her head and said, "North of eighty billion before recent losses that caused Martin Crosswaithe to pass out."

Miller's adrenalin spiked at that last reply. The woman was telling her the truth—she had not been sure until this moment. She asked, "Recent losses? What does that mean?"

Liz shrugged and said, "The riskiness of being a criminal investor I suppose. Shit happens."

"So, Liz, what's in this for you?"

"I hope to get the foundation back on track, under me. Then, I will embark on helping people as my mother expected me to do originally."

"The free clinics?"

Liz nodded, adding, "And now, even more. Lots more. We can talk about that as much as you want, to assure you of my sincerity."

Miller said, "Your comments will suffice for now and I have what I require for filing charges on Mabel. Anyway, I need to go."

Liz nodded as Miller slid out of the booth and said, "I'll be in touch."

For the first time in a week since Mabel Belkin had been skillfully deceived, waylaid and left tied up in a pool of sex lube, she had decided to check in on the staff.

Her current bedroom was not the same location where the lube attack had taken place but instead a lowly motel-like suite with a tiny bathtub and toilet located in the opposite wing usually reserved for the lesser commune help. The master suite was still being cleaned up and Mabel had decided it would require a thorough remodel if not total demolition.

She made her way down to the kitchen, thinking either a hot tea or a stiff vodka might improve her mood, which was quite black at the moment. A lot of recent events were contributing to her foul mental state. For starters, she still had no idea who the woman was that had worked her way inside the estate and performed the deed. Secondly, her head and neck still ached from twice banging her head on the venetian tile flooring of her own bathroom. Finally, it had been absolutely humiliating to be found lying nude and lubed on a floor by her inferiors. To make that situation worse, when she first awoke, she heard a few of the staff giggling. She had been so out of it, other than her embarrassment, she had so far been unable to determine the giggling offender's identities.

She arrived to find Ethel reading a supermarket tabloid that had a story splashed across it about Mabel's incident. There was even a color picture that appeared to have come off a cellphone camera. It was of her, wrapped in a blanket, a bandage on her still lube-glistening forehead as she was being toted along by several of the staff. All the faces had been blurred out but hers. Seeing the picture, she added item four to her grievance list—goddamn tabloids and whomever the amateur paparazzo was that apparently leaked the story as well as the picture!

She sat down heavily in a chair across the table from Ethel, who peered over the top of the paper at her, then went back to reading. Mabel found that behavior quite unusual coming from her number two, who usually was crawling up her ass to give it a morning kiss. She snapped her fingers at one of the kitchen staff who came over and stood in front of her. Mabel, irritation growing, griped, "Vodka tonic. Three fingers of vodka! Wait, make it four."

The staff member looked over at Ethel who nodded at her. The woman turned and went off to fetch the drink. For her part, it was not lost on Mabel what had just happened. She sat quietly, but her mind was racing over this very unexpected change in staff behavior. She shrugged, figuring it did not take long for the mice under her to become traitorous. A familiar and very dark rage was beginning to come over her.

The staff member returned with her drink, set it down and walked off, no curtsy, deflected eyes, nothing! She snapped again at the woman, "Who the hell do you think you are?" The woman kept on going. Mabel took a deep swig and looked over at Ethel who was still ignoring her. This was rapidly becoming a group passive aggressive experience for her, and Mabel was going to have no part of it. She said, "Ethel! What the fuck is going on here?"

Ethel paused, lowered the tabloid to the table, spun it around and pointed to the story. She said, "You've made us look like fools."

It was then that Mabel realized there was a power play afoot. She said, "Ethel, let's not forget who is in charge here. I can have your ass out on the street in milliseconds. I run the foundation!"

Ethel smiled and said, "I've been in discussions with the staff. It is time for a change, and it is taking place… well, I guess right this very moment." She then snapped her fingers, and two security guards showed up on each side of Mabel, unceremoniously lifting her to her feet as a kitchen staff member rolled a wheelchair over to the table. Mabel tried to struggle but the large male guards strapped her in with duct tape around her wrists and ankles.

Ethel stood and with a cynical smile, said, "So, yep, you are the figurehead of the foundation. But I will be running things. After talking with the staff and offering them a substantially better deal than any crappy thing you would ever do, we all agreed you would be better off in this new position. And we will be sure to provide all the sex lube you need to keep yourself… entertained."

Mabel sputtered, "I will have your asses! Do you hear me? Your asses!"

That was when the intercom beeped and Ethel stepped over to it as she replied, "Perhaps a shipment of your sex lube has arrived."

*

Miller, along with a half dozen other FBI vehicles, were at the front gate of the Cleaver estate.

The same guard which she had threatened to shoot in the balls the night of Helga's escape was giving her dirty looks as she advised him, "You really need to behave yourself unless you'd like a fully escorted trip to a holding cell where I can keep you sitting for days and then charge your ass with something like interfering with a federal office in the discharge of her fucking duties. Your choice bud."

The dirty looks fell away, especially as several more FBI agents came up alongside Miller. The guard hung his head and asked, "So, what do you want me to do…mam?"

Miller told the man, "It's real basic. Wait until I tell you to call in and advise Mabel Belkin she has visitors. Don't mention it's the fucking FBI. Got it?"

The guard nodded. Miller smiled and nodded to one of the extra-large male agents assisting her. She said, "Please keep an eye on this dufus and make sure he stays on script."

The agent nodded then walked over to the guard, giving him a big grin. With that, the gates swung open, and the FBI headed down to the circle drive in front of the mansion.

A few minutes later the guard did as instructed.

Ethel wound responding to the intercom while she had been instituting her own coup on Mabel. She said, "We're busy here. Who the hell is this?"

The guard at the front gate said, "This is Buford, up at the front gate."

Ethel impatiently replied, "And?"

"Uh, well, you have visitors."

"Tell them to fuck off. We are busy."

"Uh, well…they're at the front door."

"What? You let them in and then called me?"

"Uh…"

The doorbell rang and the chime of it reached the kitchen. Ethel declared, "No one answer that!"

A moment later, the doors burst open from an irresistible force. Ethel and others in the kitchen heard, "FBI, don't move" then "FBI, freeze motherfucker!"

Pandemonium ensued. There was a loud reverberation from a flash grenade then everyone could hear Miller cursing, "Fucking Benowitz! Somebody get that retrograde moron out of here!"

A moment later, Miller, her service pistol drawn, walked into the kitchen with her contingent of agents, minus the retrograde moron.

Mabel, still strapped down, screeched, "Thank god agents! I am being tortured by that woman, Ethel, along with these other miscreants!" While likely she would have liked to point a bony finger at her former second, the best Mabel could do was nod her head in the woman's general direction.

Ethel said, "She's lying, and has been in an out of hysteria ever since her attempt to rape a young woman. Due to her head injury, we've had to keep her restrained! I mean, look at her. Look at this tabloid!" With that, Ethel held up the pictures of Mabel for all to see.

Miller laughed and said, "That's pretty funny, I have to say. No, we're not here about piddly things like you all torturing each other." She then stepped over to Mabel, squatted down and said,

"Hey. Mabel Belkin. You're under arrest for the murder of Olivia Cleaver." She let that soak in for a moment while Mabel's eyes went wide.

Mabel cried out, "It was self-defense! I was standing my ground! I was …"

"Right!" Miller laughed again and said, "That's not quite what is on the tape recording we recovered. You might want to get a lawyer. Now, somebody read this woman her rights."

She then stepped over to Ethel and said, "Listen, you're under arrest too! Accessory after the fact. Somebody Mirandize her! I ain't got time for this shit."

Before that could happen, Ethel panicked and tried to run. One of the agents stuck out an arm and clotheslined her, dropping Ethel to the floor. Miller, annoyed, said, "Was that fucking necessary? Are you related to that idiot Benowitz?" The agent hung his head, mumbling apologies.

Mabel was left duct taped in her wheelchair, and a few moments later, she was rolled out to the FBI van. Miller commenting, "Hell, that's way better than handcuffs. Cheaper too!"

Paramedics were called to check Ethel. After a cursory examination, they loaded her up and headed off to the emergency room with an FBI escort for a more thorough assessment.

The kitchen staff woman that had served Mabel her vodka tonic that morning came over to Miller and curtsied, then with head hung down, said, "Can we stay? We have nowhere to go."

Miller looked the woman over and said, "What's your name?"

The woman paused, not used to having to actually have a conversation, but finally said, "Emily. Name is Emily."

"Okay Emily. You are in charge for now. You and the others can stay. FBI agents will be going through the house, executing search warrants. Answer any of their questions, fix yourselves some of that expensive food I saw in the kitchen to munch on out on the patio, and otherwise, just stay out of the way. Got it?"

Emily nodded, a beatific smile on her face. Miller sighed, "Fuck me. This place is nuts." She then headed out to her car, told the agent driving the van with Mabel to follow her, and with that, they departed the Cleaver estate.

*

A brief time later at FBI headquarters, Mabel was rolled into the conference room. Already waiting were Martin Crosswaithe, Borders and two other agents that were sipping on coffee while chomping down some donuts on a tray. Miller sat down next to Borders. Mabel was rolled into position alongside Martin on the other side of the table. Miller told the agents to remove the duct tape from Mabels wrists and ankles. She then began recording the conversation.

Mabel said, "I got nothing to say to you, FBI woman."

Miller shrugged and said, "That's okay. I understand that one of our agents in the van let you call your attorney and that he is on his way."

Mabel replied, "Goddamn right. Walter Weegar will make mincemeat out of you."

Martin looked askance at Mabel, and said, "Walter Weegar? That idiot? I fired him!"

Mabel retorted, "Sounds about right, though he told me he quit on you because you are an imbecile!"

Her smile said more than her words that she had the upper hand. That smile provoked Martin. He said, "You know, I am only here, in this sorry ass set of circumstances, because of you Mabel! You insisting I come to this godforsaken country and this very hovel of a village"

It was Mabel's turn to look askance at Martin. She said, "I never told you to come here. What the hell are you talking about?"

"The meeting in my study. The bloody video call! You were all worried about progress and what we were spending on PhoenixGen."

Mabel looked genuinely lost and replied, "I have no idea what you are talking about! And what about that ridiculous call you made to me, accusing me of murder! Are you the one that turned me in?"

It was now Martin's turn to display a "what the hell are you talking about" expression. He said, "I never called you or accused you of anything, let alone a murder, I've been sitting right here, on my ass, in jail! How dare you! He reached over and slapped the bruised side of Mabel's head.

She screamed, "You asshole!" To her credit, she leapt out of her wheelchair in record time and started slapping down on top of Martin's forehead with both hands, leading with a left, then a right in a rhythmic cadence. It was a stellar performance. Miller was ready to let it go on for a while but then remembered Martin was a bit flakey on the health side, so she signaled the two coffee sipping agents to put a stop to it. One of them got kicked in the shins by Mabel for his efforts, but they managed to get the woman back in her chair and rolled away from Martin.

Then came a knock at the door. It was Walter Weegar. He marched in, went over to stand alongside Mabel, as he gave a dirty look to Martin then said, "Please release this woman. She is not guilty."

Miller rolled her eyes and chunked a file across the table. She said, "You might want to review that evidence before you make more ill-advised pronouncements about guilt or lack thereof."

Walter looked mildly offended but accepted the file, sat down in a chair next to his client and began flipping pages, which included a transcript of the tape recording that was the most damning evidence. Mabel said, "You actually reading or just skimming?"

Further offended, Walter replied, "I was a speed reader all the way back in grade school!" After a few moments, he put the file back on the table, looked at Miller, nodded, then swung his gaze over to Mabel and said, "At the moment, I've got such a huge case load that is taking all the resources of my practice, sorry. Best of luck!" With that, Walter was out the door.

Martin, forehead now beet red from the Mabel slap fest, broke into a huge guffaw and said, "I told you that ambulance chaser was worthless!" Mabel flipped him off.

Miller and Borders both giggled as Miller told the two agents, "Escort these folks to their cells."

29

Before Frieda or Helga agreed to accompany Liz to a court appearance to provide her moral support, they had been clear that their backing was predicated on Liz finally explaining how she had pulled off all the recent events that had fortuitously all swung their way. Liz's explanation was minimalist in nature but hit all the key events and was particularly logical.

Frieda shook her head in amazement and said, "So, your newfound abilities as well as all the events you masterminded happened because of the tooth you had implanted?"

Liz nodded and replied, "I wound up with a lucky hit on the genetic anomaly issues that led to all the problems when Albert created my tooth. The code he had was still defective. Talk about beating the odds in Vegas! At any rate, I found everything becoming quite clear as to how all this technology worked, how to analyze the chaotic nature of the implants and how to use this knowledge to not only fix the teeth for general usage, but how to enhance an individuals' abilities. That was what all the code changes were that you saw me write and why I left Albert with the defective version."

Helga, just as amazed, said, "You knew, for instance, when you sent me into the Cleaver estate that I was likely to have to make a run for it?"

Liz replied, "I apologize for that, but, Yep. I was positive you would manage." She paused, then continued, "I also had captured earlier calls between Mabel and Martin and with that bit of data, I generated deep fake streaming to each of them to get them to incriminate themselves. I also created the device that caused Martin's private jet's systems to have a total shutdown on the end of the runway that kept him here so he could be arrested. I then kept the FBI agent Miller up to date, acting as her snitch, though I obviously did not tell her everything. Took her a while to believe what was going on, but she finally jumped on the bandwagon."

Helga said, "Wow! This is some cool shit Liz! Now what?"

"Other than myself, Billy has the teeth, but his are standard civilian issue. I would really like to enhance you two as well. It would strengthen your natural abilities. Sort of make you a super brain in your specific areas of expertise."

Frieda and Helga looked at each other, nodded, then stepped away for a brief private discussion. When they came back, the women both agreed that they were on board. Liz smiled and said, "Well, let's get on with our next phase. Today is *the* critical day for all of us as well as the foundation's future, especially after all that had come out in the press about the murder of my mom by Mabel Belkin and the subsequent trial. Today is a civil proceeding, and the timing of the filing was another calculation I made." She looked at her watch, then started walking towards the courtroom as Frieda and Helga accompanied her.

She added, "Also, getting this particular judge had been part of the plan." Liz then entered the courtroom and went to her chair. Frieda and Helga seated themselves in a nearby row.

The judge came in, everyone stood, she immediately instructed everyone to be seated, looked at the filing in front of her and said, "This is in the matter of the Cleaver Foundation chairman assignment and the reinstitution of Elizabeth Cleaver into that position. Ok, let's get this show on the road."

The judge nodded to Liz, who stood. She was dressed in a dark blue pencil skirt suit and sounded quite lawyerly as she said, "Your honor, thank you for hearing this case today. I wanted to request permission to approach the bench and present these papers to the court."

The judge nodded, Liz walked up to the judge and held out a sheaf of papers for her to review. Almost begrudgingly, the judge, a cranky older woman with short, dyed red hair, accepted the documents and suddenly looked annoyed at the sheer content handed to her—a lot of her attitude stemmed from the fact that she was sick of hearing cases and desperately wanted to retire. She briefly looked at the documents, then she said, "Please tell the court what you are filing here Ms. Cleaver. I can read this in detail, but we all want to move on with our day. Make your case!"

Liz stepped back to her table, then replied, "Yes, your honor. As you know and as is detailed in my filing, my mother was murdered and the person that did that has been found guilty and is now awaiting sentencing. This same person, Mabel Belkin, stole the Cleaver foundation from me for her personal gain. The foundation was my mother's legacy to me. To be blunt—I simply want it back."

The judge nodded then said, "Judgment for the plaintiff. Next!" She gaveled down, looking even more pissed off as she reviewed her upcoming docket, as this was her first case of the day.

Liz, obviously quite happy, grabbed her paperwork, then she, Frieda and Helga headed out the door. In the hallway, Liz whispered to the other two, "That was way easier than even I had hoped for."

They swung by the court clerk's office directly off the courtroom, and after about an hour, obtained affidavits showing Liz back in charge. She looked at Frieda and Helga and said, "Finally."

Out in the hall were a gaggle of reporters waiting for them because she had earlier leaked this court appearance.

Liz stepped up to one of them. The reporter, as it turned out, was Pulitzer nominee Carson Wells from the Los Angeles Herald who had been quite useful to Liz in the past when she had previously had control of the foundation. She smiled and said, "Well, hello Mr. Wells."

The reporter smiled and got right to the point with, "Call me Carson, please. How did things go today in court?"

Liz smiled, grabbed Carson by the elbow and maneuvered him next to her, so they were both facing the news media cameras. She replied, "It went well Carson. The judge ruled in our favor, I am back in control of the Cleaver foundation, and based on the results of the murder trial, Mabel Belkin is going to finally see justice if not execution. Now, if you will excuse me, it has been a stressful morning."

She nodded to the cameras, then stepped away and with Frieda and Helga now flanking her, they pushed through the crowd of reporters who were all asking questions. Liz smiled, waved and wished them all a lovely day, but kept moving.

They no sooner got out of range of the reporters when they ran into Miller and Borders.

Miller said, "Liz, nice to see you. You're sure gussied up today. What gives?"

Liz, not all that surprised to see the special agent and her cohort, said, "Um, just a civil proceeding today special agent." Miller nodded and said, "So, did it go like you planned?"

Liz said, "It did. All went well." Miller said, "You don't have to be so coy. We just watched your interview with the reporters on Border's phone."

Liz smiled and said, "Ah, right! And, yes, I have gotten my legacy back."

Miller nodded carefully and said, "Well now, that's a big deal. Try to use it well."

Liz nodded back, "Thanks for the advice. So, you all are in the courthouse today?"

Miller nodded and said, "Yeah, you know, FBI stuff. Crime never stops." With that, Miller and Borders headed off.

Once they were out of earshot, Frieda said, "What do you think Miller was implying? It sounded almost like a warning."

Liz pondered for a moment, and as her logical side kicked in, she said, "I will have to think on this as to why she is here. It could be legitimate court stuff, then again, Miller might be messing with me, it is her modus operandi. FBI agents always think everybody is up to something, it's their raison d'être. One thing for sure. Whatever made me useful to her is now in the past. So, she likely is looking for her next project."

The three walked on to the parking lot, where they all climbed into a limousine she had hired for this special occasion. Liz had told the other two women it was time to splurge, but just a little bit. There were no objections, so they were off to the Cleaver estate.

*

Miller and Borders watched from the third story window in the courthouse as Liz's entourage climbed into the idling limousine and departed. Borders said, "So, what are you thinking?"

Miller sighed and replied, "Well, what do we know at this point? We have Mabel Belkin's confession that included how she provided intel to Liz to assist the woman with the coverup of millions of dollars in Foundation funds before Mabel kicked Liz out. Plus, Liz allegedly had an inside informant that she used to damage the former Pearly Whites corporation that led to its bankruptcy while she profited."

Borders asked, "So why not arrest her now?"

Miller said, "Mabel is a problematic source since she is a convicted murderer."

Borders asked, "Even with the documents, stock trades and offshore cash transaction data that Mabel provided?" Miller nodded and said, "Thing is, there is no way to know Liz directed her to do that. And Mabel, shortly after executing these transactions, kicked Cleaver to the curb and took over the entire operation until the murder rap wound her around the axle. Other than Mabel's assertions, Liz looks legit and could easily claim in court that this was all Mabel's doing, and we don't have any proof otherwise. So yep, we need corroboration."

Borders considered for a moment. Then she said, "You remember what Mabel said in her statement about Liz and Frieda running things together?

"Yep, and?"

"Well, I noticed in reviewing the documents that Mabel mentions how at one point, Liz hired Helga Krantz. Helga, at that time, was dating Bob Oppenheimer. Oppenheimer was right in the middle of the genetic tooth project."

Miller perked up and said, "Interesting. I can arrange for Oppenheimer to come in and talk to us, but he is still working for

PhoenixGen. If we talk to him, he might very well tell Sally and company and then it would get back to Liz Cleaver."

Borders sighed and said, "Good point. Well, let's head out for a burger at Perky's and consider our next move." Miller nodded as they headed for the elevator.

*

On her arrival at the estate, Liz's new security contingent was waiting at the front entrance. These were all women that had worked for Liz in the past, mostly former law enforcement at some level or another. She had gotten them in place under a temporary court order after Mabel's arrest to keep an eye on things while the legal process was in motion to place the foundation back under Liz. The old guards that had worked for Mabel, all male, were there as well, wondering about their jobs.

Liz climbed out and approached the women, nodded, thanking them for their work. She then approached the men and said, "Ok, dudes. Got new assignments for all of you if you're interested. Check in with Hellene at the front gate for details." The men perked up, realizing they were not headed for the unemployment line.

Liz and company then proceeded to the large portal entry of the mansion itself. As they exited, Nigel and his crew were there, standing at attention, awaiting orders.

Liz nodded, patted Nigel on the shoulder and said, "I enjoyed our talk on the phone the other day. I must say, it was a wise decision to sign on. Martin is likely… unable to help with your current employment predicament and I can relate to being left in the lurch."

Nigel smiled and said, "Whichever way the wind blows, madam!"

Liz returned the smile, then headed on in to meet the rest of the staff. She had already arranged for Chef Alfonzo and his partner Langley, her former employees, to restart their employment and begin culinary training for the kitchen help. For his part, Nigel was to work with the household staff and for the first time since arriving, every person was going to be paid fairly for their labors to go along with their room and board.

Everybody lined up as Liz, Frieda and Helga headed out to visit the fields of marijuana that had been planted by the dozen women which Mabel had previously held in bondage-like conditions of uncompensated work. They then had the women follow them back to patio number one for an afternoon buffet along with time for them to take their first swim in the pool and enjoy a day off. Liz stood on a small dais that had been set up and as the whole kibitzing staff got seated with their meal, she tapped on a champaign glass and smiled. The crowd fell to silence.

"Thank you all for staying with us. I know it might not have been an easy choice and in some of your cases, you might have felt you really did not have a viable alternative. Well, let me say, that all that abusive work environment is ended. Today, you are all employed, and you will be well compensated. You will also have a pension system and the Cleaver foundation under my watch is going to make sure that it is funded. For those that would like to stretch themselves to another level and work on a college degree, we will help. And finally, health care will be free!"

That led to a round of applause and Liz, like a practiced politician smiled and nodded, then continued, "Listen, more to come on the details. But for now, be assured, you will be cared for. For starters, we begin with free dental checkups and make sure everybody is pleased with their teeth's appearance. We are going to have an onsite dentist. We have, as they say, the product to make sure each of you have brilliant, lovely smiles!" Another roar of approval went up. Once the applause dropped away, she added, "Now, enjoy the day and to all our futures!"

30

As Sally walked through the PhoenixGen lobby, she felt upbeat, especially considering the wild fluctuations of her situation since Special Agent Miller had forced her back into the U.S.

She ran through an abbreviated list—Martin, in jail; Mabel, in jail; company stock, doing well; Liz Clever, her new ally.

She stopped in the cafeteria and got a cup of coffee, had a pleasant exchange with some of the staff, then proceeded to the production plant. On her walk, she ran into Billy, who was headed in the same direction.

Billy smiled and said, "Well, today is the day. First shipments out the door. Hard to believe it's real. Cleaver foundation is taking the first batch for work they want to do over at the estate for their employees. I think we might be seeing Liz and company in just a few minutes."

After Sally smiled noncommittally, Billy took a deep breath, then dropped, "Oh, I also meant to say, Jerome is on his way back. I think we finally have things patched up."

Sally gave Billy a wistful look and shrugged, "Well, it was fun while it lasted."

Billy blushed a bit, then nodded towards the double doors in front of them and said, "Come on." He shoved them open and headed onto the production floor with Sally falling in behind him as he proceeded to a computer console.

Sally watched the robots for a few more minutes, took one last look at Billy, then headed to her office. However, before she got there, the phone rang—it was the receptionist saying that Liz, Frieda, and Helga were in the lobby. She responded, "Cool, on my way!" as she changed course.

157

She greeted the Cleaver foundation trio and after a brief exchange, guided them to the production facility. On arrival, Billy flung open the double doors. The group entered; their path lined with waist height robots at attention on both sides.

Liz giggled at the sight and said, "Nice work Billy!" Billy smiled.

Liz turned to face them all and said, "This is a victory for both PhoenixGen and for the foundation! The teeth will help so many people who will be better off for all your efforts."

Nods went around the group. Billy then pulled out his phone, tapped some commands into it and the robots began scurrying about to get the boxes loaded into a rental truck that had arrived just a few minutes earlier as part of Liz's contingent that had accompanied the women from the estate.

Sally stared at the person overseeing the product getting loaded and said, "Is that Nigel?"

Liz smiled and nodded, "Yes, he is most helpful to us."

Sally asked, "How the hell did that man wind up working for you?"

"Well, to quote directly from the old butler himself, it's *whichever way the wind blows*. He and his people were left stranded by Martin's criminal activities, I made an offer he decided to accept."

Sally nodded, while reflecting on her initial visit to London when this all started, thinking, *people are weird*.

Liz continued, "Also, if you all are interested, I would really hope all of you stay on in your current positions. We need your expertise, the FBI is about done with their investigation, so, I think you all are back to square one with the law."

Billy's ebullient grin spoke louder than words. Sally nodded, looking thoughtful.

Liz, noting Sally's reaction, added, "Let's talk in private before we all head out. I have some ideas for each of you that I think will suit you. Also, I need to pick up those special order of teeth I programmed in, they are to help Frieda and Helga with…

replacements they need. Our private dentist is about to show up at the estate."

Billy nodded and stepped over to a locked shelf he had set up that was dedicated to special orders from Liz. He opened it and retrieved the two teeth in question that were in a special environmentally sealed case, handing them to Liz. Liz then signaled Nigel who walked over to them. She gave him some special handling instructions, to which he nodded, took the sealed case and left.

With that, the ceremony was done. Liz invited Billy and Sally out to the estate for a fancy dinner night, a date to be set in the near future.

*

Back in his office, Billy was gazing at his computer screen, running over some of the latest accounting. Recently, he was finding himself a lot better at seeing the big picture on this sort of thing. So, while reviewing this latest information he came to a peculiar line item in the payroll column. It seemed that somebody was working vast amounts of overtime. It made him wonder who it could be, since the company to date was pretty much an eight to five operation, Monday through Friday.

Liz, Frieda and Helga had been hourly, along with Bob. However, the women had all officially resigned when Liz had reclaimed the foundation, so this could not be any of them. That left only one hourly person in Billy's business unit—Bob Oppenheimer. It then occurred to Billy he had not seen much of Bob lately on the grounds, or even around the plant, especially since after work drinking with the group had ended.

Billy shook his head in sudden aggravation. It would not surprise him to find Bob doing something dumb like falsifying a timecard entry. Also, Billy had been pretty much rubber stamping the time reporting in the past since he had trusted his allies. Plus, he had struggled a lot with his responsibilities as he had grown into the job. So, it pissed him off to find that Bob might have been fucking the company while working under him.

Plus, Billy didn't want this to get in front of Sally and have her question his management abilities just as his job became a full time deal. He sighed, picked up his phone and called Bob.

*

For his part, Bob believed he had adapted well to being the sole hourly employee under Billy, as nobody paid him any attention and that he could do nothing in the form of actual work full time, even if the pay was lower than he desired.

These days, he now focused on his new artistic endeavors such as abstract paintings, (it was easier to just make squiggles on the canvas than rake gravel).

He had been purchasing more and more paint, brushes, canvas and other art goods when it had occurred to him that he could cover his costs by turning in a bit of overtime. Of course, he did not work it, but he quickly discovered it was not hard to turn it in. Which he had, slowly ramping up his "efforts" over time as the money began to recharge his coffers.

Therefore, on this bright and cheery morning, he was at the Santa De Lola Art Depot, a boutique establishment that catered to local creatives, picking up some new colors for his latest work in his burgeoning portfolio that he had entitled, "My Art, in Color!"

It was while mentally juggling the esthetics of chartreuse versus lime green that his phone rang. Miffed at having his concentration interrupted, he pulled the offending device from his back jean pocket, wanting to hurl it across the room. Patricia, the proprietor, having become somewhat familiar with Bob's erratic behavior, shook her head no. He sighed, then noticed who was calling him. He answered, "Bob here, can I help you?"

Billy, on the other end, said, "Bob, where are you right this moment?"

"Um, I am…in the supply shed at the farthest reaches of the grounds. Whatcha need?"

Billy said, "Ah, I see. Well, what I need is you in my office, and now."

Obfuscating, Bob said, "Darn, I was just headed out to lunch! Did I mention that?"

"You did not. Now, turn your car around and come back to my office. We have a serious matter to discuss."

Bob, wondering at the hostile tone of Billy's voice, asked, "Uh, are you pissed off? You sound pissed off."

Billy sighed, "Bob, what I am feeling does not matter. Get to my office and do it now."

Bob stared at his phone. Billy had actually hung up on him without awaiting a reply. He sighed, grabbed a tube of each of the chartreuse and lime green paint, paid Maggie and high tailed it out of the store.

*

Billy, while waiting for Bob to show up in his office, was gazing forlornly at his computer screen, now even more aghast at the numbers. He had at first dragged out an old calculator—the damn thing had failed to power on. He then had resorted to pencil and paper and when that failed due to his lack of math skills, he went online and downloaded a calculator app for his phone which allowed him to enter Bob's hourly wage, overtime and totals hours which generated some impressive six figure earnings. Bob knocked at his door and Billy waved the man on end without looking up from his monitor, indicating he should take a seat in the chair in front of Billy's desk.

Bob slipped into his seat and said, "So what's up?"

Billy sighed, shifted his attention to Bob and said, "Good question. Tell me, how many hours in a week do you think it is humanly possible to work?"

A nervous look passed over Bob's face as he said, "Well, I suppose it depends on what you do. Like… if you sit at a desk, or work in the fields, or…"

"Let's use, for example, your job, Bob. How many hours?"

"Um, ah, okay, well, forty minimum, but then all the maintenance on the shovels, wheelbarrows, tracking inventory like pea gravel, fertilizer…"

Billy cut him off again with, "How does one hundred twelve hours in a single week sound? For each week for the last two months."

Bob gulped, nodded and said, "Well, yes, it has…been brutal, what with Liz, Frieda and Helga all resigning. I have been the lone ranger of late, as you are well aware."

Billy, looking bored, said, "Bob, don't fuck with me."

Bob, feeling cornered, lost it and suddenly flared, "Fuck with you? Don't fuck with me! You are sitting in that chair because of me. I am the one that put the band back together while you were running a dish line."

Billy glared at Bob and responded in kind, "And I got you the paid do-nothing position you are in now. And you are taking way too much advantage of it!"

"Bullshit!"

"No bullshit! Bob, you are making our numbers look bad! Somebody is going to notice besides me and then what?"

"Our numbers? Well, hell, Billy. Liz, Frieda and Helga bailed, went back to the foundation, never gave me a second thought. And who the heck is looking out for my wellbeing? Who? I'll tell you who, it's me!"

Billy sat back in his chair, shook his head at the man defending his thievery as honorable, then looked Bob directly in the eyes and said, "Sorry for your travails Bob. But you're putting both of us at risk with this…bullshit. You're reassigned to indoor janitorial work going forward and will not wander outside of the building during work hours unless under my direct supervision."

Bob stood, gave Billy a hurt, angry look and said, "Janitor? I'm outta here!" He then huffed out of the office.

Billy sighed, walked to his door and hollered at Bob's receding back, "Be sure to drop your wheelbarrow off at the front desk! Asshole!"

31

Liz was chatting with some of the kitchen staff while once again hosting her employees, this time out on patio three. She had arranged for Chef and Langley to fix the crew a special brunch and had invited the women to all indulge themselves and take a swim in the pool. Having pools at every patio had been something she had made sure were installed during her first reign over the foundation and now she wanted to make sure they got plenty of use.

A call came in from the front guardhouse on the intercom. Langley answered then signaled Liz, who stepped over to see what was going on. It was the guard advising that Dr. Kermit Balm, the newly hired Cleaver Estate oral surgeon, had arrived and was reporting for duty.

A moment later, Dr. Balm was driving his elderly Mazda sedan behind a golf cart leading him to the just completed dental facility located on the south side of the mansion. Liz excused herself from the group and headed over to meet the doctor.

When she arrived at the new clinic, Dr. Balm's physical appearance confused her. During the earlier video interview, he appeared to be a much more substantial man, more like a running back than a dentist—she immediately suspected that he had used some AI effects during that session. As it was now with him in person, he stood about five foot four inches and was thin and wiry. He was sporting spiky black hair accompanied by a matching goatee and Salvador Dali sort of mustache. His broad red and blue striped T-shirt, vanilla colored shorts and open toed brown leather sandals completed his ensemble, though what the man was aiming for defied Liz's fashion sense to define.

Dr. Balm stepped forward with a big toothy grin and extended his hand. Liz accepted and up close, noticed that the man's spiky

164

hair had a distinct male pattern baldness configuration towards the back of his skull.

Liz said, "Well, this is a surprise. I thought your arrival was still a few days out."

Dr Balm shrugged and in a deep bass voice the defied his size, boomed, "Well, nothing like getting on with the show!"

Liz gave a dubious nod and added, "Uh, yes, I suppose that is true." The doctor responded with another large toothy grin.

Liz had to admit to herself, the man had a substantial set of glistening white teeth, and she was trying these days to judge people on performance, not appearance. Plus, his supplied credentials were quite impressive.

With introductions now complete, Liz gave the doctor a tour of the new facility. He nodded, making numerous comments about the technology on display that indicated he knew what he was talking about. By the end, Liz felt a lot better about her new hire.

Liz said, "I have two of my people I would like you to work with soon, today if that is possible. They both need a tooth replacement. Over here, are the specific teeth for them." She then picked up one of the acrylic cubes holding a tooth in suspension and handed it to Dr. Balm.

He peered inquisitively at the tooth, shook his head and walloped out, "This is amazing. And it adapts as I understand it, to the patient's gums."

Liz smiled, again somewhat surprised at the volume and deep bass of her new employee. She said, "I see you have been reading up! Yes, it even helps with regeneration of damaged nerves.

"Fascinating. Regenerating the pulp area makes it truly a genuine component of the person."

Liz smiled, then added, "So, these particular teeth for Frieda and Helga, who I am sure you remember from our earlier interview and are specifically constructed for their… special needs. We should get them in as soon as possible. I will put an H on the one for Helga. An F on the one for Frieda." She located a sharpie and marked them up.

Dr. Balm, once again with his toothy smile, replied, "ASAP!"

Liz gave another nod and said, "Okay, well, I am off. Frieda and Helga will be over shortly. After you are done with them, they will show you to your quarters and arrange help with moving your belongings into place."

Another toothy grin appeared in response. Liz shrugged to herself, smiled and headed back to the mansion for a conference call with some journalists to discuss the latest plans for the Cleaver foundation and PhoenixGen alliance.

Before that meeting, she pulled Frieda and Helga into a newly built soundproof study and said, "Dr. Balm has arrived. It's time for your tooth insertions if you are still up for it."

Frieda and Helga nodded as Frieda said, "Liz, we appreciate your efforts and this opportunity."

Liz smiled and said, "Getting one of these teeth will put you both on top of your game like you never have experienced before! You won't regret it, I promise."

Liz stood and jokingly ordered, "Now, off with you!" Then she added, "Actually, sorry to rush you out. But I have this damn call coming up!"

Frieda replied, "We understand Liz. See you at dinner." With that, the two women departed.

Liz smiled to herself, then pivoted to her next task. She proceeded to the new press room that had been recently created by converting one of the numerous dining rooms dotting the first floor. It had state of the art cameras, microphones, along with professionally installed lighting. She walked in and sat at an expansive mahogany desk as her staffers showed up.

These particular women had shown interest in technology and video production and were currently in training by the company the equipment had been purchased from. Today would be their debut of their new skillset.

Their job was to operate the gadgetry in the press room as well as doing any makeup/hair/clothing picks for foundation members that would appear before the media. One young staffer tweaked

Liz's makeup, comber her hair and gave her the nod that she was ready.

Liz reviewed a list of journalists she had invited, including CNB Online, Wall Street Guardian, the New York Herald, Los Angeles Herald, Boston Tribune and Chicago Post, among some of the more prominent news organizations. Liz said, "Ok, let's get this production rolling." She drew a deep breath, let it out, looked at her staffers, then nodded—the interview began.

Twenty heads popped up on the big screens on the far wall. When each journalist was signaled to ask a question, the system would move their stream to a larger screen in the middle of the array to enlarge the person, which would make it easier for Liz to determine positive or negative facial expressions accompanying their question. It was the latest technology and had worked well in earlier demonstrations that Liz had attended when they bought the system.

The interview started with a scripted introduction that Liz quickly rattled off, "Hello to all of you, and thank you for attending today. Today, the Cleaver foundation wants to announce that it is moving forward in every major city in the U.S. to get the long promised free dental clinics up and running now that the teeth are FDA certified. Our staff here at the foundation has expanded, we have contracts that are getting facilities in place and are actively interviewing for local staffing. Also, as we are going into these oft overlooked urban neighborhoods, we are trying to help revitalize the area with some contemporary looking remodels that put local folks to work. With that, I will take questions." Liz then looked down at her notes, knowing the first question would be from Carson Wells, for which she had a prepared answer.

However, a reporter from the Dallas Upright somehow got to the front of the queue and launched from his own prepared script with "So, Miss Cleaver, Henry Coal, Dallas Upright. About the recent conviction of Mabel Belkin, I have a few questions."

Liz raised an eyebrow, but interjected, "You can call me Liz, thought I believe the Los Angeles Herald was ahead of you."

Henry Coal, not one to yield the floor, continued, "So, Liz. What happened? This homicide got so much press and there was such overwhelming evidence. How did this case stay buried for so long?"

Liz smiled and said, "Listen, Mr. Coal…if that is really your name, I mean, you might change it to Diamond? Anyway, it is painful for me to talk about my beloved mother and her murderer Mabel Belkin, who was just sentenced appropriately to the death penalty. So, let's move on. Carson? You had a question—"

"But why Liz did this take so long?" Coal interjected, still not observing decorum and appearing moderately irritated at his name being subjected to ridicule. Liz could see her two new staffers were frantically trying to move the man off the middle screen, but since this was a surprise and they were just learning the system, they were struggling.

The one named Maggie was furiously pressing buttons on a panel and suddenly, every single person merged into the center screen at the same time giving each one of the reporters an indicator on their end that it was their turn at bat to ask a question. A cacophony of voices surged in.

There were follow-ups on asshole Coal's question, then about foundation spending on the new clinics, and about if Liz was going to keep wearing colorful tank tops. For whatever reason, the longer it went, the dumber the questions became. Liz looked at Maggie, who began backing out her earlier settings and the screens returned to normal with Henry Coal still at center screen.

Maggie hit one more button, this time the correct one. Asshole Coal was gone, and Carson was up. With a wide-eyed expression, he began, "Wow. Technology these days. He paused, looked at her encouragingly then continued, "Anyway, Liz, tell us more about your vision you articulated in our interview we had earlier, which can, by the way, be watched on my new podcast, Carson Wells News-a-thon!, immediately following this session."

Smile frozen, Liz wondered what had possessed her to talk with the press in the first place. Bulling her way forward, she launched into her prepared remarks that emphasized positivity in their efforts at the foundation and with PhoenixGen, their trusted partner who was now at full production capacity.

A glazed look returned to most of the journalists' faces, though in the end, Liz had managed to regain the narrative, therefore, the nature of the follow-up questions from the other reporters were more on track, and the session ended on an upbeat note. After the call was closed down, Liz sighed and headed for her room to lay down for a bit.

32

Dr. Balm had sped around getting everything ready by the time Frieda and Helga arrived. After Liz departed earlier, he plunged into preparation, priding himself on his speed, efficiency, and perseverance, though the work had only taken twenty minutes.

He had noted earlier that the facility definitely had a production line set up to its layout and based on stated expectations during his job interview with Liz, he would for the first month have a lot of patients coming through this high volume environment. While not particularly good at juggling multiple elevated pressure situations at once, he was certain, well, fairly sure anyway, that he could handle it if he could maintain his own cadence.

As he thought about it, he decided he would have to sort out that cadence and document it in a flow chart over a beer or two this evening, which he could then put up on the wall behind the patients.

In front of him were four dental chairs, marked, A, B, C, & D, with associated shelves to access dental tools and supplies—all of that seemed straight forward enough. The production line design, however, reinforced the one problem that plagued him his entire life.

He stared at the letters, at first seeing A, E, D, & O. He closed his eyes, then looked again, and with his years of practice, was able to get the right order and letters in his mind. Still, it was always tough work, so he would have to focus. Again, he needed to work at his own cadence and briefly considered grabbing a quick beer from the refrigerator in his new apartment to set the pace.

While concentrating on maintaining cadence, he had also taken the two teeth that Liz had scribed with an F and an H and set them next to where Frieda and Helga would sit during their procedures.

When the women arrived, they went through introductions. He was trying to make a positive impression on his first two patients, so he boomed, "Ah! So nice to meet you. I understand you are Frieda, and you are Helga." He pointed incorrectly to each one as he said their names.

Helga said, "Oops, no, I'm Helga. That's Frieda. You got it backwards, but heck, first day, right? So…can we call you Doc?"

Dr. Balm, not one to stir the waters on his first day, said, "Certainly, call me Doc, Doctor, the Docster, if you like, or just call me Kermit."

Frieda and Helga looked at each other, then back at the doctor. Frieda said, "You know, I kinda like Kermit. I mean, we are not so formal around here."

Helga said, "But I like Doc!" The two women grinned at each other.

Dr. Balm said, "Okay then, how about Doc Kermit?"

Helga shrugged, then went over and sat in her chair. Frieda said, "I just want to get this over with. Ok, Doc Kermit, let's get this moving!"

Dr. Balm, now not sure what they were going to call him, declared, "ASAP!"

With that, he gave them each a dose of Novocain, then laid out his dental tools with great exactitude for each one of his tasks he had to perform during the implants. The women chitchatted about how cool the new clinic was.

Helga then said "Sorry Doc, too much coffee this morning. Gotta use the little girl's room." She got up and headed over to where the bathroom was in the back of the clinic.

Frieda, not really into dental work since a childhood cavity that brought back painful memories, was getting nervous at the delay. She climbed out of her chair and began to pace around. When she finally sat back down, it was in Helga's spot.

Dr Balm, seeing the change, grabbed the two teeth, looked at the letters, which swam in front of his eyes. He focused, then sat the one down for Helga in what he thought was chair F. He then realized that was chair A. Not sure, but thinking he had it right, he reversed them at their respective positions. He figured, no harm, no foul, they were just teeth anyway.

Helga returned. Frieda said, "Doc Kermit, please do mine first. This is scary."

Eyes wide, Dr. Balm said, "Okay, you are first!" He was pointing at Frieda while avoiding saying her name for fear of getting it wrong.

Two hours later, both women had new teeth inserted. The procedures had been uneventful, so he now relaxed and had them rest for a bit while every ten minutes or so, he checked to see how the teeth were performing in their new environs.

He was impressed, they were doing everything he had been told they would do, and they looked natural. He said, "Amazing technology! Well, you ladies are free to go now!'

Frieda and Helga thanked him for his work and offered to help get his possessions moved into his new digs. He declined, having arrived with his entire worldly possessions crammed in a single backpack that was in his car parked out in front of the clinic. They shrugged and said, "Later Doc!" and "Have a nice day, Kermit!"

Finally on his own he took a deep breath of relief. Staying employed had always been difficult for him, but perhaps this situation would be different this time.

He then, with what he considered to be his trademark competence, tossed all the waste into a bio marked trashcan, swept the floors for any errant debris, went out to his car and retrieved his backpack and carried it into his new apartment located at the back of the clinic.

He rummaged around the fully stocked refrigerator that included a stack of frozen pizzas and a twelve pack of some microbrew ale. He decided to have one ale but cautioned himself to use restraint as sometimes he over-imbibed. An hour later, the other eleven were empty as well and Dr Balm was snoozing on his new sofa.

33

Billy's arrival at the Cleaver estate was precipitated by an earlier phone call that morning with Liz where she offered to let him get a few more of his gray/yellow teeth replaced by Dr. Balm. In the call, Liz had said, "Listen my friend. You happy with your new teeth so far?"

Billy replied, "Liz, these are great. No side effects. Nothing but four nice looking front teeth."

Liz responded, "Alright! So, let's do a few more if you want. We can do them at a pace you like, but for starters, how about the lower front four? Give you a more balanced look."

Billy didn't even hesitate, "You read my mind! And thanks Liz!"

Liz giggled and said, "Thanks, you're sweet for saying that. So. You and Jerome? Back together?"

Billy said, "Soon, he's arriving the day after tomorrow. I got Sally to give me some time off, so we are gonna vacation down south in Baja!"

Liz sighed wistfully and said, "Baja. Wow! I need to go with you guys. Need to work on my faded tan. At any rate, not this time around, but maybe some other time soon!"

Billy replied, "Bring your buds, I bet Frieda and Helga would love it too."

Liz said, "It's a date." After a few more pleasantries, the call ended.

Enthused on this clear and sunny morning, Billy had driven over for his appointment as he wanted to impress his old partner. Okay, it was more than that if he was being truthful with himself. His enthusiasm was partly driven by looking better, as well as a subtle passive/aggressive response to earlier inferred insults that

Billy remembered Jerome laying on him after his first debacle with genetic teeth.

Billy was driving his latest acquisition, a fully restored and considerably upgraded, 1972 Ford Pinto. Candy apple red on the exterior and sporting a sea foam green leather interior with matching carpet. He thought the car was a real beauty. Along with the appearance package, a turbocharged V6 and paddle shift six speed had been installed, along with extensive traction control modifications and heavily modded suspension.

The Pinto was now more a sports car than the old economy vehicle of its bygone era. On the drive over to the estate, Billy had taken great pleasure in handily defeating some hotted-up Mustang during a stoplight challenge. The Pinto had performed per the specifications that Wild Child Eddy's Custom Designs had promised, and Billy had left the "Stang" in his dust. Billy's attitude was extremely positive as he drove onto the estate and parked in front of the dental clinic. Climbing out, he patted the Pinto on the hood, then strode in for his appointment.

Dr. Balm was busily working on several of the staff of the estate. He paused when he saw Billy and walked over with a clipboard in his hand, which he extended to him while belting out in his deep bass, "Take a seat, please fill this out, and I mean everything, leave nothing blank, be sure to print clearly and don't use contractions. ASAP!"

For his part, Billy grinned and nodded, as he surveyed the doctor while wondering who the wiry little man used to manage his attire, as he was in desperate need of a dry cleaner and definitely a tailor.

Dr Balm was still wearing the same outfit from when he checked in with Liz five days earlier. Now however, there were some food stains, mixed with patient blood stains, mixed with beer stains, on his broad striped red and blue T-shirt. His vanilla shorts looked the worst for wear as well.

Billy sat down, pulled out the pen fastened to the clipboard and started filling out the form. He realized it was no normal medical form by the time he got to page three of the double sided documents. He lifted that sheet and saw two more pages below it. Figuring he was beyond all that due to his relationship with Liz, he set the clipboard aside.

Two hours went by, more staff members piled in. Each was attended to before Billy. He leaned around from his chair, looked out the door, and saw a short line of staffers awaiting their turn. At hour three, frustrated and a bit pissed off, he stood up to go check on his position in the queue. One of the marijuana field hands quickly grabbed his empty chair.

He walked up and tapped Dr. Balm on his shoulder, as the man had dozed off next to a patient. The doctor snorted to life, with an "ASAP!"

Billy, startled, jumped back, not sure what was next. Dr. Balm shook his head as he returned to planet earth and gave a toothy smile to Billy.

Billy said, "Sorry to bug you, but I need to get my work done. Can we get this mule train runnin?"

The doctor smiled, and said, "Sure, sure. Did you get your form filled out?"

Billy replied, "No, I am a personal friend of Liz Cleaver, and she is the one that set this up for me. Look up Billy Fuller on your list of patients for the day."

Dr Balm, hungover, was having problems just identifying what day it was, but hearing Liz's name invoked, he nodded and said, "You are next! Just let me, uh, finish up here."

He then tapped the woman in the chair on her left knee, which reflexively made her lift her lower leg, and said, "You, out of here! ASAP!" The woman looked at him groggily, still under moderately heavy anesthesia. She shrugged, crawled out of the chair and wandered off. Dr Balm indicated for Billy to have a seat.

In one smooth move, Billy was in the chair, mouth open, and staring at the ceiling. The doctor rumbled, "So what can I do you for?"

Billy, a bit put off, said, "Liz said all four front bottom teeth? You are aware, right?"

Dr. Balm smiled and nodded, and said, "Sure, sure. Just checking!" He then wandered off and returned a few minutes later with four teeth. He said, "Okay, gonna have to put you under for this one!" He then proceeded to anaesthetize Billy, who slowly faded off into the black.

Later, who knows how long, Billy woke up in his chair. The room was empty except for Dr. Balm, who was scraping a bunch of waste into a trash bin. Less than totally awake, Billy mumbled, "Am I dumb? I mean, done?"

Dr. Balm replied, "Sure, sure. Just take it easy, lay there, rest, um, and when you feel okay, uh, you can leave! I, on the other hand, am outa here!" He then headed off to his adjoining apartment and fridge, which had been restocked earlier with more microbrew ale.

Billy faded off but awoke again two hours later. He sighed, saw a big mirror on the dental tray and since the doctor had kindly left the light on above him, Billy inspected his new teeth–they were beautiful! He smiled to himself, staggered to his feet, stumbled out the door, and into the Pinto. From there, he did a backout burnout, then floored it out of the estate, the gate guard hollering at him to slow down as he flew by.

*

Earlier, back at PhoenixGen headquarters, Bob was pushing along a mop bucket on wheels, carelessly slopping water down a hallway as he approached Billy's office shortly before the man had departed for his tooth insertions. He had overheard the brief conversation with Liz, which pissed Bob off—here he was again, being shunned while Billy lived the high life of an overpaid VP.

So, when he heard Billy getting ready to leave, he hid himself and his mop bucket in an alcove. Billy came out of his office a moment later, whistling some happy tune as he headed off to his appointment.

Bob then wandered into Billy office and with no one around, sat down at Billy's computer and logged into his old Bob's Blog, where he wrote up a nice little diatribe that he posted, then logged off. Feeling better, he went back to his new job and checked, (but did not restock), toilet paper capacities in several bathrooms before heading out to lunch.

34

The next morning, Frieda stirred awake, feeling distinctly hypersensitive. She looked over at Helga lying next to her and felt like crying. All she could think was how much she loved the woman.

She wiggled across the bed until she was spooning her girlfriend and had one arm clamped around her for a massive hug. Helga awoke and sat straight up in bed, ending the moment as she claimed, "Dibs!" on the bathroom.

Frieda started weeping, wondering why her best friend and lover was ditching her for a bathroom. She lay there, listening to the shower starting. Helga was humming some tune, then another, then another while she washed.

Frieda curled up and started bawling. It was all so weirdly beautiful. A short time later, Helga emerged, dressed in a jogging outfit. She exclaimed, "Gotta run. Literally. Then, when I get back, I gotta do some reading on some topics related to artificial intelligence and physics and chaos theory. Then, well, I have more reading to do, probably at the library, but don't have time to talk about it." She jogged out the door and down the hall to run laps around the estate.

*

Now on her run, Helga's state of mind had gear shifted into hyperactive. Everything was swirling around, informing, disinforming, as she was making new conclusions and discarding old ones. She needed to study all of this further and it seemed there would be no higher education facility there to help.

Her most profound thoughts were about the way humanity tended to misbehave. While working on her PhD in psychology a couple of years back, she had been primarily focused on emotions but now, everything was about searing logic. She realized as well;

she had seen something similar happen in Liz and it seemed logical to her that the woman had added that functionality to her own profile programmed into her tooth.

The primary question in her mind was how she would properly pursue this path in the time she had left on earth before she reached her expiration date. So much to do and all of this was going to require extensive funding, focus—she needed some deep plans and needed them now. She smiled to herself as she picked up the pace.

*

For her part, Helga's morning jog left Frieda feeling crushed. Did the woman not love her anymore? She was not sure. She moped her way out of bed, into the bathroom and suited up in the same clothes she had been wearing every day since getting her new tooth—fashion seemed so trivial now. It was life itself that mattered, and it had been an emotional rollercoaster since that day. It was as if she could sense everyone else's emotions.

There was a knock on the door. She shuffled over and found Liz standing there giving her a big smile and a hearty "Good Morning!"

Frieda instantly perked up and felt exhilarated. She replied, "Well, good morning to you Liz!' She then gave her boss a big hug.

Perplexed, Liz smiled at Frieda, surprised at the sudden gush of emotion. She shrugged to herself and went back to why she was there. "Breakfast on patio one?"

Frieda was suddenly ravenous. She said, "Feed me woman, feed me!"

Liz, her smile fading, nodded, and said, "Okay… Uh, meet you downstairs in the kitchen."

Frieda nodded vigorously, but instead of meeting on the patio, she tagged along behind Liz, chatting about a romance novel she was reading, global warming, how pretty Liz looked in her current outfit, wondered if the staffers were wearing weird perfume, and a myriad of other rapid fire, nonessential, before breakfast topics.

Liz nodded politely at each comment until they got to the kitchen, at which point, she excused herself and said she had to go to the bathroom. Frieda's emotions crashed back to severely depressed, and she started weeping again.

Chef Alfonzo brought her a hyped up latte and said, "This should buck you up!"

She slurped it down, burning her tongue, and said, "Please, Chef. Some really crispy bacon and a load of scrambled eggs! With British style toast! And Oatmeal I'm starving here, starving!"

A puzzled Chef Alfonso nodded and said, "Uh, certainly. Um, yeah, somebody will be back with your rations in just a few minutes." He then rumbled back to the kitchen, telling Langley he was up next. Langley, wise to this sort of loosely defined assignment, dispatched the newbie, Nigel.

Helga arrived fresh from her jog as Nigel came out and asked what she would like to eat.

Helga appeared in deep thought, then asked, "Have you considered the ramifications of the food coming out of Chef's kitchen? Is it sustainable? Will I get gas? Is it delicious and nutritious? What sort of algorithms does Chef run against the palates of his customers here at the estate? And look at Frieda. Are you going to just let her order any old thing she wants? I mean, check out that waistline!"

Frieda started weeping, exclaiming, "I'm fat!"

Nigel, looking from one woman to the other, nodded at Helga and said, "Of course, the usual then. Be back in a jiffy!" as he high tailed it back to the kitchen.

*

The main reason Liz had made a rapid departure from the Frieda/Helga breakfast fandango was due to a video conference call she had coming up with the team at PhoenixGen. Frieda had been making so much noise, for the first time in a long time, Liz had felt her anger dragon start to rise.

She had rapidly suppressed that emotion as she wondered where all the chitter chatter erupting from Frieda had come from. Before she could consider the matter further, the middle screen came to life with Sally and Billy who were sitting next to each other.

Billy was rambling on about having his lower teeth swapped out and was quite obviously having trouble modulating his voice. He sounded like a pentatonic music scale, with his voice going from low to high, mostly adding volume on dramatic minor notes and a few sharps and flats. He was also speeding up and slowing down his tempo. Sally was staring at the man with a befuddled expression. Finally, Liz said, "Billy, calm down please."

Billy harumphed across two octaves and shut up, though his right leg was jiggling up and down.

Liz cleared her throat as she watched. Sally shifted her attention from Billy to her and said, "Uh, so how much of that did you hear?"

Liz said, "I don't know. Maybe thirty seconds worth?"

Sally nodded and said, "Yeah, he's been doing this since he came in this morning. Kinda weird. Anyway, the morning briefing. Shipments are going out to all twenty clinics the foundation now has in Alabama. Next, Alaska with their two clinics, nothing in Arizona yet, then Arkansas—"

Liz interjected, "Terrific! and this sounds great! Oh, and I wanted to remind you all, dinner is coming up tomorrow night at the estate for the two of you! Chef Alfonso is preparing a massive feast, lots of variety for any tastes. I really look forward to spending time with everyone."

At the last part, Billy made a high pitched squeal, again attracting everybody's attention. Sally said, "Did you have something to add Billy?"

Billy launched back into his recent dental work and talked in detail about how happy at first Jerome was when he saw them, but now, Jerome was asking questions like, did Billy feel okay, normal, or was he having urges to ram city buses.

Sally, still unhappy about having her active sex life with Billy terminated said, "Billy, I really don't give a hoot what Jerome thinks."

Billy squirmed in his seat and chirped, "You need some no fault sex?"

Sally said, "I'm fine, thank you."

Shaking her head while watching all this, Liz said, "Alrighty then. Sounds like… a date. Please show up around seven! Now, I gotta go!"

She terminated the call, again wondering what was going on. She leaned back in her chair and tried to do meditate, which failed, so she then did a finger by finger check of how her last manicure was holding up—she found nothing interesting in that pursuit, so finally, she decided to take a walk around the grounds to clear her head.

She first wandered by Patio five and found one of the pool techs with a running garden hose, spraying water into the pool. Curiosity piqued, she walked over and asked, "What are you doing young lady?"

The woman turned and recognition flooded her features. She said, "Liz, I am on to something. I don't know why I had not thought of it before!"

Liz asked, "And what would that be?"

"Watering. I mean, we want things lush. So, I will water!"

Liz replied in an amused tone, "You're watering a swimming pool?"

The woman gushed, "You are so right! Thanks for the recognition!"

Liz stepped back and gave the woman a questioning once over while realizing the morning that had started out damn peculiar with Frieda was getting more bizarre by the minute and with each encounter she had. She walked off and decided to make the rounds of the estate to see if this weird vibe was happening more widely.

Her first stop was at the dental clinic. As usual, there was a small line out the door of staffers awaiting their customized tooth insertions. She slipped in through the side door, saw Dr. Balm busy with four patients, nodded to herself and left without making a fuss to slow any of the doctor's progress. Besides, based on previous conversations, she found herself thinking, *the guy is half looney*, though he did seem to be cranking out a lot of tooth swaps based on his daily report.

She then strolled down to the forty acres of what everyone jokingly referred to as the marijuanie patch. Several of the field hands were busy irrigating the field, however several others were not working on anything cannabis related.

She stopped and asked each of the unengaged people what they were doing. One was working on chapter three of a novel she was writing, holding up her laptop screen for Liz to peer at. Another was starting and stopping sprints, claiming she was preparing for the Olympics. Two others were doing kung fu moves, or dance moves, or some sort of moves—she could not figure out what the women were actually doing.

Adding this to her list of weirdness while scratching her head, she headed off. She found similar problems with the mansion staff, kitchen staff, and Nigel's footmen. She could not put a finger on the problem. Something in the water? Too much Internet streaming and social media? None of it made any sense as she tried to apply logic to the situation. She would have to do a deep dive of her own to analyze this mass bizarre behavior.

She permutated, cogitated, and ruminated. Finally, it occurred to her there might be a problem with the production teeth that she had missed, but that just did not seem possible. Still, she decided to double check her work.

She went to her private office no one else knew about and logged into the production systems at PhoenixGen. She ran through the code, the calibration routines, the equations. She could find no issues, and all was working as she had designed. Which led her back to considering other variables. After several hours, there was one thing she knew for sure—she didn't know what the problem was, but it definitely seemed to be getting worse.

*

Miller and Borders were lunching again over at Perky Petites as Borders was scrolling through a webpage on her phone. She suddenly looked up at Miller and said, "Guess what! Bob

Oppenheimer just posted on his old blog about what he is referring to as "shenanigans" at PhoenixGen and the Cleaver foundation.

Miller said, "Interesting," then took a big bite out of the burger that had just arrived before continuing, "So what does the man have to say?"

Borders kept peering at her screen while munching on her fries, shaking her head and finally said, "Well, it's kind of incoherent but it seems he suspects some sort of criminal collusion. Now, we do know this about Oppenheimer. He was quite close to what happened during the first go-around of defective teeth at the old company. His title as I recall was lead project manager. Also, he was the person dispatched to pick up the false IDs we had made back when Liz was your primary snitch, though not sure how that fits in. Yet, all this seems indicative that he was plugged into something that was going on."

Miller said, "Hmmm. Project manager. False IDs." She shrugged, "Well, maybe this is a path into the labyrinth of illegal activity that Liz was up to back then because we know that his ex, Helga Krantz, also went to work for Liz at that time. There has to be some connection. How about we get a meeting with this Bob character and see what he actually knows."

Dipping a fry into her ketchup, Borders said, "Gotta start somewhere."

<h1 style="text-align:center">35</h1>

Disgruntled FDA regulator, Simon Gibson, had been dispatched to the Santa De Lola office on temporary duty for one simple reason. After Reuben Corpenny had been arrested and the story hit the news, the FDA brass had hastily arranged this trip as they were wanting to cover their asses.

In a feeble attempt by the local staff to lessen his stress at having to be away from home for an extended period, Simon was given a decent view of downtown with a corner office. The problem with the decent view idea; downtown Santa De Lola was mostly older three and four story office and retail buildings, all rather poorly maintained. Half were closed and boarded up. For a west coast town, it had a rustbelt vibe, what with all the retractions of big business and the associated cashflow out of the community to the bay area over the last two decades.

Sighing to himself, Simon set about getting the office arranged to his liking. He got a wireless printer installed, his computer, had some bookshelves brought in with a plethora of FDA sort of literature, and finally, a small Mr. Coffee which he immediately put to work with some freshly ground beans he had picked up on the way from the airport.

Sipping on a cup of Sumatran, he got an email message from the front lobby advising him of a person of interest that wanted a quick callback. There was a number and the only thing identifying the caller was the person had said their name was, Jerome, Billy Fuller's now permanent ex.

Curiosity peaked, Simon returned the call, especially after a bit of research where he read about the history of Billy Fuller and PhoenixGen.

Jerome, as it turned out, wanted to unload about how angry he was. His explanation was short and to the point—Billy was an idiot to get involved with this genetic tooth company once again, regardless of its name. After the call ended, Simon decided to take a drive over to PhoenixGen.

At the gate, he waved at the new gate guard, (Sonny had been fired after he got caught stealing cash from the cafeteria tip jar), held up his FDA credentials and said, "Hello there. I am here to visit with Sally Dinklestern. FDA official business, very important."

The guard gave a noncommittal nod then made a quick call to Sally. A moment later, he provided Simon with a parking tag and waved him on through the front gates.

On arrival in the lobby while waiting at reception, he checked his watch. It was only half past nine. He nodded, figuring everybody should already be at work, which meant he'd be winding everything up in time for an extended lunch hour. Sally herself showed up and after handshakes, she inquired, "Mr. Gibson. Such a privilege to have you here. Whats up?"

Simon said, "Ms. Dinklestern—"

"Call me Sally, please." as she smiled disarmingly.

"Sally then. Sally, we need to talk in private. How about you and a few of your other senior staff attend?"

Sally' tone turned suddenly cautious, "Um, well, I don't know if we can accommodate a last minute out of the blue meeting. I mean, darn, folks are busy, the plant is humming product out the door, you know how it is... we are trying to get this ball rolling to supply a much needed product."

Simon nodded, then added, "Too busy to keep this place selling your product?"

Sally glanced at the receptionist who was obviously listening in to the conversation. She nodded and replied, "Um, let's go up to the boardroom and let me see who I can round up." With that they were off to the elevator.

Sally's panicked mind was racing as she was the only person at the moment that could talk at all, what with Albert gone and Billy struggling to even be comprehensible. Once situated at the boardroom table, Sally got right to it with, "So, here we are. Now, how about telling me what brought you out our way." She again gave Simon a big smile.

Noncommittally, Simon smiled back and replied, "I'll get to the point. How's Billy Fuller doing Sally?"

Sally said, "Billy? Why, he's on leave at the moment. His boyfriend, Jerome, broke up with him again and even before the latest situation, Jerome had been putting the poor guy through hell for the last year or so. I think it's finally over as best we know."

Simon with an understanding nod, intoned, "That is sad."

Sally replied, "Yep. Sad. We all feel bad for the guy. So much pain lately in that relationship, I mean it has been a rollercoaster for all of us." It took all she had to not roll her eyes at her own comment. She added, "So, are we done here Mr. Gibson?"

She stood but Simon remained seated as he said, "Uh, you all might want to sit back down. You see… I got a call this morning from Jerome. Billy Fuller's ex, as you just pointed out. He was at the airport, getting ready to fly back to Mississippi and he wanted to relate to me the latest reason for the final breakup between him and Billy."

Sally sat back down fidgeting nervously.

Simon grinned and said, "So, is Billy here or not?"

Sally said, "Nope. He really is out on leave trying to pull his life together."

Simon nodded and asked, "But not from the breakup, right?"

Sally said, "Sure he is. Seeing a therapist at right this very moment."

Now impatient, Simon said, "Okay, Ms. Dinklestern, from what Jerome said, Billy Fuller had more teeth implanted. Since then, he has had some serious side effects and is acting very weird. Billy told Jerome the whole story and apparently his symptoms are quite audibly obvious. I even have a recording that Jerome is sending me that he graciously made. When I get it, I can play it for you."

Sally said, "Simon, listen, this is likely some other issue, our teeth were FDA certified, right?"

Simon stood and said, "Maybe, but this is peculiar. Just want to be sure we have a safe product and since I was flown out here for the very purpose to look into the final certification process, I am sure you understand."

Sally said, "Goodness! So, what now? Are you going to shut us down?"

Simon shook his head and replied, "No, no, leastways, not immediately. But I will be back here pretty quick, say, this time tomorrow. And I really need to see Billy as well at this next meeting or things will get seriously worse around here for your company. We need to get this resolved quickly." Simon then stood and departed.

Sally sighed and picked up the phone.

36

Shortly after Simon's visit, Liz received an urgent call from Sally. She now knew that something had to be wrong with the teeth as that was the only common denominator with all the recent events, the perfect example being that after the implants Billy had received at the dental clinic, he had awoken the next morning and embarked on his new yodeling behavior. Then there was all the strangeness going on with various staffers at the estate that had also received new teeth versus the ones that had not that were still acting normally.

The good news—at this moment, Billy was being picked up by Sally. They had shut down production and produced four new teeth to swap out the lower four that Billy had just gotten a short while back, which had delayed Sally as she was also the courier.

Liz had checked and double checked that the new teeth for Billy were correct. She had then reviewed her work and checked the earlier ones for any possible anomalies. Everything appeared in order. To be on the safe side, the new replacements had no enhancements, they were the box stock version intended for the general public.

The clinic had been cleared of other patients when Liz arrived and started talking to Dr. Balm about the situation. Her first question, "Doctor, can I see Billy Fuller's records? I need to confirm the serial numbers on those teeth that are engraved in them line up with what was sent up here." She then sniffed the air, wondering what smelled so bad in the place.

Dr. Balm became agitated after her request for records and said, "Why, certainly, certainly. Now, let me see, let me see, serial numbers. Where did I put that information? Ah, yes! Be right back!"

He headed off and Liz nodded distractedly as her phone buzzed with a message from Sally to advise she and Billy were a minute away. It was then she heard a car door slam and tires burning rubber.

Liz ran to the front door of the clinic only to see Dr. Balm headed out at high speed. She immediately called up to the front gate and hollered through her phone at the guard, "Shut the gates, hold the doctor, do not let him leave! And keep him alive, we need him!"

She was not clear why she felt she needed to add the part about keeping him alive as it was unlikely the guards would murder him, especially as she had required them to turn in their sidearms, what with all the strangeness running rampant through the staff.

Though the guards failed to get the gates shut, she needn't have worried because as Dr. Balm arrived at the front gate, Sally and Billy turned off the roadway into the main entrance directly in front of him. Sally was driving the new custom Pinto because Billy had refused to come without it, citing abandonment issues with Jerome and that he couldn't stand to be without his beloved car. Which led to the total destruction of said Pinto when Dr. Balm whacked into them head on. Thankfully, only minor bruising occurred to the occupants of either vehicle.

Shortly thereafter, two golf carts arrived at the gate. Dr Balm was summarily hogtied to one cart and driven back to the clinic by a footman. The other was loaded with the unmodified teeth and Billy, once Sally could coax him away from his car, the man was in tears. Sally then drove the cart to the dental clinic.

Sliding to a stop, Sally grabbed the teeth as Billy slogged into the clinic. Once she was inside, she was struck by the doctor's appearance and realized he smelled pretty bad. Billy was already in his dental chair and the footman that Nigel had sent was keeping an eye on Dr. Balm as he did pain killing injections around Billy's lower front teeth.

At Liz's insistence, some quick x-rays were taken, and she went over to look at the results on a computer. It was then she realized, these were not the teeth that were supposed to have been installed in Billy.

The serial numbers were for various staff members, one of which was wanting to become an opera singer. Mystery solved on his voice behavior. Another tooth was for a staffer that wanted to be a rapid fire sports announcer. Again, the constant barrage of commentary symptom was now explained. She didn't bother to look up the other two teeth, they were about to get yanked anyway.

Liz now knew that *Dr Balm* was the variable she had not been able to sort out. It also meant all his work would now have to be kept secret and immediately undone by somebody they could trust and was a competent dentist, because based on what Sally had told her, Simon Gibson from the FDA was about to run a microscope up the ass of PhoenixGen. That meant the new trustworthy person was going to be expensive and had to be located quickly.

Liz sent the footman into the attached apartment with the doctor with instructions to get the man cleaned up. The footman asked if they could just hose the doctor off which got a negative response.

Not only was Dr Balm rather smelly, and still in his original outfit from the day of his arrival, he was quite unsanitary yet was needed to do this last swap with Billy. So, when they returned twenty minutes later, the doctor was outfitted in some scrubs that had been provided earlier but which had been hanging untouched in a closet. They were too big for his slight frame, but clean, so the legs were folded up about six inches each, held in place with paper clips.

With the smell factor way down, he was put to work on probably the most important patient of his now short term Cleaver foundation career.

Liz was closely watching the doctor when one of Nigel's footmen commented, "That man drinks a *lot* of beer." Before she could say anything, Sally asked, "What do you mean by a lot?"

"There's like a kajillion bottles laying around in that apartment!"

Sally queried, "Kajillion? And how many is that?"

The footman replied, "Eh, a lot?"

Unsatisfied with the answer and with nothing else to do, Sally did her own bottle check. When she returned, she said, "Wow. There is a shitload of beer bottles lying about that dump."

Liz said, "Shitload? How many in that number compared to a kajillion? And dump? It's brand fucking new!"

Sally said, "*Was* is more like it. Nothing like a bad tenant."

Liz noticed that Dr. Balm was getting more agitated as they talked about his beer bottle collection, and the deteriorated state of the apartment. She said, "Hey, let the Doctor concentrate. We are distracting him."

By now, Dr. Balm was shaking so hard, he could not hold a dental probe, let alone accurately insert some teeth. Liz signaled the footman to grab a chair for the doctor to sit down in. That was just before Dr Balm croaked out, "Oh shit!" and keeled over. Immediately pandemonium broke out.

Liz cried out, "Oh hell, I think he's dead!"

Sally exclaimed, "Really?" She then took a hard look at the man and asked, "So why is he still breathing?"

Liz ran to the sink, poured a cup of cold water and ran back to the doctor, pouring it on the man's face. Dr. Balm sputtered back to life like an old tractor and levered back to a sitting position, exclaiming, "ASAP!"

Sally sighed, "Get that man some beer!"

Liz said, "Uh, is that a good idea?"

Sally shrugged and said, "Heck if I know. But it might steady his nerves. I mean, it's pretty obvious he needs something."

Liz capitulated and the footman was sent back into the apartment then returned with two open microbrews which were handed one at a time to the doctor. For his part, Dr. Balm swigged them down faster than one would have imagined possible. A few minutes later, he was up in his chair. Two more beers were brought out and after they were gone, he was approaching full functionality, so the teeth replacements proceeded.

Billy was sedated so that he would stop rambling, because Dr. Balm said it was hard to remove his teeth while he was talking. The doctor was kept on an ale drip during the process so as to keep him steady. Liz specifically handed Dr. Balm each tooth and pointed to the socket that needed that particular one.

An hour and a half later they were done. Sally had joined in at the end to rub Billy's shoulders as the man regained consciousness. He reached up and gently squeezed her hand as his awareness returned.

Thirty minutes later, Billy, now awake and sounding normal, said he wanted to go to the Watering Hole to forget about the loss of the Pinto. Sally agreed to take him there. She left him at the front entrance to the bar with "Be sure to show up in the morning. We got Simon Gibson to deal with and I need you there."

She drove herself home, ordered a pizza, then plopped down in front of her big screen, wondering about how she got to this point in her life when all she had started out to do a couple of years back was to be an efficient administrative assistant.

Back at the estate, Nigel arranged for Dr. Balm to be loaded onto a bus bound for West Virginia. Liz gave the man a sizeable chunk of money, and warned him, "If you run your mouth, we'll have you gutted with a dull deer antler!"

She needn't have feared. Dr. Balm had so much short term memory brain damage from his decades of drinking, he had a hard time remembering how many ales he had consumed for breakfast let alone what he had been doing at the Cleaver estate for the last month.

Finally, back in the mansion, Liz had Chef Alfonso fix dinner for all the staff and footmen that had helped with the latest toothcapades. After dinner, she gathered Frieda and Helga off to the side for a private moment to explain what had happened to each of them with their own teeth and that it would be rectified.

Frieda started bawling and Helga said she'd sleep on the idea, thinking she might now be better off. Liz silently disagreed but let that last comment slide for the moment—it had been a long day plus she was ready for bed.

She waved at the two women and headed off, wondering and worrying if enough had been done about the Simon Gibson problem. She laid with covers pulled up to her chin most the night staring at the ceiling in contemplation, finally drifting off to sleep around dawn.

37

Bob was climbing into his vette at a local gas station when Miller came up to him and held out her badge. His eyes went wide as he held up his hands while saying, "Please, don't shoot!"

Miller gave him a look that told him she was wondering if he was an idiot, (a response he had seen from many other people in the past). He tried to smile it off with, "I was just joking."

Miller nodded and said, "I'm not. Special Agent Miller here. You and I need to have a conversation." Bob said, "Why sure, sure… uh… about what?"

She said, "Park your car over in one of those spots across the street, we are going to go for a short ride. I'll bring you back when we are done." Not having ever talked to anyone in any federal law enforcement capacity, Bob said, "Uh, okay."

After he parked, Miller, with Borders in the passenger seat, pulled alongside his car. He climbed into the back seat of the FBI sedan, and they were off. They parked a couple of miles away near a city park and went over to sit near a fountain on some benches.

Bob was curious at the precautions the two women were obviously taking and felt kind of jazzed at the thought of his situation. It reminded him of when he had placed the transmitter that disabled Martin Crosswaithe's plane. He even decided to open with that.

"You know, I am the one that placed the transmitter that was used to disable Martin Crosswaithe's jet."

Miller said, "Oh wow. So, sort of a special assignment by Liz Cleaver for you. You must be good at that sort of thing."

Bob puffed up at the compliment and said, "Yes, yes it was special. So, what can I do you for?" He then gave Miller a big smile.

Miller did not respond, she simply looked at Borders. Borders said, "So, Mr. Oppenheimer, we see you are blogging again about PhoenixGen. It sounds like you have discovered there are some problems there. Care to talk to the FBI more about what is going on?"

Bob suddenly was feeling transported to a wonderful new world. Here he was, pissed off at Sally, Billy, as well as Liz and company. He knew something was afoot again with the teeth, just hearing Billy yodeling the other day, again while pushing his mop bucket about. He said, "Please, call me Bob! And, well, yes, it looks like side effects once again."

"You were in on all of the problems last time, weren't you?"

"Uh, yep. I was the project manager. Now, I didn't create any problems myself. No, I just got paid to be the…project manager."

"Did you know Liz Cleaver at that time."

"Uh, yeah. She stole my girlfriend, Helga Krantz, when everything went to shit."

"Stole her?"

"Figuratively speaking. Gave her a cushy job, used her to get information out of me when I was at my low point."

"Ah, so, this low point. Is that like when you were drunk and drugged up most the time?"

Bob leaned back, suddenly wondering just how much these two new. Obviously more than he had expected. He said, "I admit I was overindulging, my job was so, so… stressful. Some evenings, I flat had to medicate myself to sleep."

Miller interjected, "So Bob, if you can remember, let's talk about what you told your old girlfriend back at that time."

Bob, his memories more than a bit foggy about a lot of the events of that time, (and yes, there had been a lot of booze and pills), did his best to elaborate. Miller nodded in encouragement as Borders took copious notes, though a lot of what Bob was piling on was contradicting his own statements and nonsensical. After a bit, Miller told him to stop. They got back in the car and dropped him off a block from his vette.

Sally woke up the next morning with a plan. It had been riffed into existence during the night and she refined it earlier this morning after a call with Liz.

At first, Sally had thought her plan was risky, but then decided she was sick of different FDA officials' constant attempts to undermine the product and the company. She and Liz agreed they should go for it.

Simon Gibson had just parked his car and was walking into the lobby of PhoenixGen. He had come prepared with the suspension order he had printed out and planned to file with the FDA after this confrontation, which he was looking forward to only because he could then head back to his home in Kansas City. He was whisked by reception, handed a badge, and escorted up to the fourth floor. When he arrived, an intern led him into the boardroom and brought him coffee and rolls. He shrugged to himself and decided to indulge, knowing no minor graft, as he saw it, was going to influence his decision making.

While munching on a doughnut, Sally arrived, grabbed the chair across from Simon and sat down. He looked at Sally as he swigged down some coffee, smiled, and said, "Delicious. Thanks for the warm welcome."

Sally smiled back and said, "Sumatran, your favorite from what I was told. Think nothing of it."

Simon replied, "So, cutting to the chase, where is Billy?"

Sally answered with "Should be here in a moment."

"I hope not too long."

Sally gave a polite nod in response.

Ten minutes passed. Simon kept checking the time on his phone, thinking he had a flight out in two hours. In a stern voice, he stated, "You all aren't taking the FDA seriously. Listen. I believe I have all I need to shut this operation down. I have an eyewitness, some recordings, all that sorta stuff. It seems your company is definitely hiding something."

Sally responded with a grave nod at the first part, then a graver shake of her head in disagreement at the last part as she looked up and said, "Billy! Come on in!"

Simon's head swiveled. There in the doorway of the boardroom was a smiling Billy who sat down on the edge of the table, and said, "Sorry to be late Sally, traffic was heavy this morning. And hello Mr. Gibson. Sally said you wanted to meet me in person."

Simon immediately felt confused at this turn of events. Nothing about this man's tone or behavior seemed to match the information he had gotten from Jerome or the recordings to which he had listened.

Sally said, "Mr. Gibson, please feel free to talk with Billy as much as you need, and you can check his implants as well if you wish." Simon, now wondering if Jerome had just been an angry lover acting out due to a breakup, decided it was time to wrap things up. He stood and walked up to Billy, "Please you show me those bottom teeth Mr. Fuller!"

Billy smiled and opened his mouth. Simon saw nothing but perfectly normal teeth, top and bottom. He stepped back and considered. Either way, shutdown or approval, he was done with this last minute situation that had been thrust on him by FDA senior management, though approval meant he would not have to be involved further. Shutdown might have him brought back out here to do further work. It was ultimately an easy decision. He said, "Sorry for any confusion, I was obviously given misinformation earlier. I'll file my report with the FDA that we are all done here."

Sally said, "Wonderful!"

Simon nodded and said, "Well, I have to catch a flight, so I must be on my way. Thanks for your cooperation and best of luck with your new business." Sally and Billy stood and a moment later, Simon Gibson was high tailing it to the airport.

Liz was on patio three with Dr. Thornton Watts. They had just finished a sumptuous dinner, following the doctor's arrival from Teddington England on a Cleaver foundation provided jet, (formerly the property of Martin Crosswaithe—Liz had acquired the aircraft on the used luxury jet market for a fraction of the price of a new one).

For her new dental surgeon hire, Liz had been beyond meticulous with interviewing and had run a comprehensive background on the man in front of her. The doctor's credentials had been confirmed by a very respectable security firm. It was now time to formalize a business relationship.

Liz said, "So Thornton, I appreciate your flying in on such short notice for this discussion."

Thornton smiled and said, "It was no problem, Liz. And by the way, I love your new jet, quite the comfortable flight. I also understand your dilemma and the need for the utmost discretion in our new arrangement. So, I think the only remaining item to discuss is… compensation?"

Liz nodded and slid a contract with a pen on it across the table and said, "If this works, just sign at the bottom." Thornton accepted the document and began reading. His eyes went wide, and an unforced smile crept onto his face. Liz nodded to herself as she waited. Thornton placed the document on the table, signed it then slid it back to Liz. Liz looked briefly at the contract, smiled, and said, "Welcome to the Cleaver foundation. I think you're gonna like it here."

Thornton said, "Terrific. So, first things first. How many patients need a replacement tooth?'

"Thirty eight. Standard teeth for now so the people can renormalize. Once we are caught up there, we will visit the plant, get you introduced to the staff there. We have a lot to do to ramp up activity at our clinics and we can visit some of them as well that are out here on the west coast."

"Do we have time this evening to visit mt office?"

Liz nodded, not mentioning that they had just completed a total sanitizing of Dr. Balm's former abode, (it had been quite a bit worse than they had first estimated), but all was in order now.

Once the inspection was completed, Liz said, "Come on back to the manse for the evening. We have a really nice room for you to stay in. No point in bunking here, least for tonight." Thornton nodded and the two strolled back to the mansion with Liz talking excitedly about what would come next.

*

The next morning, Dr. Watts was waiting for his first patients. He glanced at the list, there were only two names—Frieda Hansen and Helga Krantz.

Liz had installed a fancy espresso coffee maker and Thornton decided to put it to work making what he hoped would be many cups to come. As he sipped, Frieda arrived. He escorted her in and offered a cup of java. She agreed after a moment. He could clearly see she was in a very convoluted emotional state.

He didn't want to pry, but he needn't have worried as Frieda led with, "I am so happy you are here Dr. Watts!" She started giggling in pure happiness.

He nodded and said, "Nice to meet you, Frieda. Please, call me Thornton. I assume from what Liz told me we will be seeing each other often around the estate."

Frieda beamed at him as she sipped her drink, then made a face, started looking angry as she said, "Vile! It is vile!" Thornton said, "You don't like espresso?"

Frieda suddenly looked sad and said, "I guess not. Maybe we should get on with the procedure." She then beamed, "Liz said I will feel much better afterwards!"

Thornton gave a reserved nod and indicated the dental chair he had earlier prepared for the procedure. After the tooth swap, he checked on her every ten minutes until he was convinced Frieda was doing okay. An hour later, he did a final examination of her new tooth and said, "That should be good for now. Let me know immediately if you have any problems."

Frieda nodded as she climbed out of the dental chair and looked around the room. They were still alone. Gingerly feeling around the back of her jaw, she smiled and said, "I wonder where the heck Helga is?"

38

As it turned out, Helga was in Stanford, where a few years earlier she had been forced to abandon her efforts to get her PhD in psychology when she migrated to the United States. Money had been the primary deterrent to her plans. Now, however, she had self-funded her latest excursion by dipping into a significant chunk of the cash that Liz had liberated from Martin Crosswaithe's hidden reserves, (the same cash decline that had made him faint).

She had carefully hidden her more miniscule transaction—she was convinced it would be hard for Liz to find, no matter how smart she was now. Helga had also re-applied for and been accepted into a PhD program. Her master's work was more than enough for the university.

Today, she was looking around for a place to live, visiting various furnished apartments. After three showings, she settled on a modest abode that would not attract much attention to herself.

She was busy unpacking when she received a knock on her door. Thinking it was probably the technician dispatched to hook up her Internet service, she walked over and threw the door open.

Much to her surprise, Liz and Frieda were standing there smiling amicably. Frieda was holding a tray of drinks from the local coffee shop a block away. Helga said, "Uh… hello."

Liz nodded and Frieda said, "Hey there, can we come in and talk?"

Helga, realizing she must have made a miscalculation, began running new permutations of how to proceed. When nothing viable rose to the top of her thinking, she said, "Uh… sure."

She stepped away from the door and the two other women entered. She then ran out into the hallway, but once there, she discovered Nigel and one of his footmen smiling at her by the elevator and another footman that waved who was standing at the other end of the hall by the emergency exit. She sighed and trailed back into her apartment.

Liz was already sitting on the sofa. Frieda had set the tray of java on the kitchen counter. It was obvious neither had tried to pursue her. Helga sat across from Liz as Frieda offered her a coffee, which she accepted.

While she was taking a sip, Liz said, "Listen, Helga, I think it's great you want to go back to school, finish your PhD, and as I recall, that was the original arrangement back when you worked for the foundation before. So, we can move ahead with that if you please."

Helga, surprised, nodded carefully, then said, "But?"

Liz looked at Frieda, smiled and then said, "But, that tooth needs to come out and be swapped back for one that will enhance you properly as we originally intended. It's up to you, but again, that old tooth needs to go, it will mess you up over time more and more."

Helga considered the offer. The generosity was beyond anything she had calculated. It made her realize her tooth was not working as well as she had believed it was. She said, "How did you find me so easily?"

Liz shrugged and said, "Oh, the GPS in the car. We simply tracked you. Plus, I knew you had taken the money earlier and finally, realizing you were in Stanford, I reached out to some contacts at the university and found out you were enrolled. By now, I am thinking you realize that your tooth was only working in a partial and at times, defective way."

Helga nodded and said, "Obviously. So, I can stay here?"

"Absolutely, if you get the tooth removed."

"Deal."

Frieda then asked, "So, does this mean you and I are done?"

Helga said, "Not at all Frieda. But can we work this out once I get my tooth replaced? You could stay here with me as well if you like."

Liz said, "Sounds like a plan. Let's get back to the estate, get that tooth swapped, then get you back here by this evening. The foundation helicopter is getting fueled up now at the Palo Alto airport. By the way, you can keep the money you took, that was actually pretty clever, though detectable. Plus, we can get you in a nicer place."

Liz frowned as she made the last comment while she surveyed the modest apartment. Helga nodded and shortly after that, they were all headed out.

*

In reality, things had not gone as smoothly as Liz had made it sound to Helga. When Frieda reported Helga missing and they discovered she had gone on the lamb, there was a mild panic. It did not take long to realize she had taken off in one of the Mercedes that Mabel Belkin had purchased.

The vehicles were all parked in a six car garage that was situated under the estate, (the empty slot was sort of obvious and the gate guard confirmed the fact when they commented they had noticed the bright red automobile departing the estate). After that discovery, it had taken Liz a few days to notice that there was a major withdrawal from the Crosswaithe Generosity Fund, as she had come to refer to it. She had to dive into the details of that before she concluded that Helga was the culprit.

The rest she easily solved once she thought about it. However, Liz had an epiphany—she was slipping, becoming sloppy in her new methodical approach to life. She recognized she had done some clever work earlier when she was motivated by getting even with Mabel and regaining her legacy and fortune. The issue, she realized, was when that challenge had passed, Liz had started to relax and allowed herself to be distracted with day to day details of the foundation, the estate, and PhoenixGen.

She vowed to herself to stay alert. So, when they flew up to Stanford, she was already getting resources in place to help her track the various people she had been working with since she had departed her time at the free clinic down in San Francisco—some of those people were potential issues. In addition to all of that, she designed a second tooth to enhance her abilities even further.

Once they had come back with Helga and got her sorted out, Liz booked herself in as Thornton's next patient. She was determined to remain on top of any situation.

*

Bob was sitting in the waiting area of Santa De Lola Customs waiting on his beloved Corvette while twiddling through an old copy of Auto and Motorist, now steamed about the insulting article where a Corvette had been paired up against a Mazda Miata on a close course race track full of hard curves and switchbacks.

The vette had lost.

The point of the article: Vettes were not near as good in the handling department on a tight, curvy course as the Miata and the vette's excess power did nothing to help it, in fact turned out to be a detriment that assisted it in losing traction in curves. He tossed the magazine back on the table, wondering if the owner of the shop had put it there on purpose.

As far as his own car was concerned, there was nothing being added back that he had earlier sold off, all that mattered to him now was getting the unsightly holes from the removed accessories patched up so that the car looked proper once again.

The repairs were something he was funding out of the money that he had recently gotten for his paid informant work for the FBI, which after his interview with Miller and Borders, now appeared to be over, (except for a warning he been given to not leave town, he might need to testify). It made him feel a bit better after the Billy episode where he had gotten reassigned to being a building janitor, but he was still only a building janitor which did not pay all that well. He sighed.

At the counter the owner, Fred Bar, was waving him over. Bob sauntered over and Fred led him out to the garage. There in front of them sat Bob's vette in all its glory except it was not what he had thought he was paying for. It was now fully restored with all its former over the top accessories. He frowned, turned to Fred and said, "I can't afford this, what the heck were you thinking dude?"

Fred smiled and said, "Here's the keys. No payment necessary." He then turned and left. A thoroughly puzzled Bob watched Fred head back to his office. He shrugged, climbed in his car, whereupon he saw an envelope in the passenger side seat. He opened it up and found a note—it was from Liz Cleaver and was inviting him out to the estate for dinner that evening and to text her number with a "Yes" if he planned to attend.

He felt a sudden excitement and wondered if his situation had just changed for the better. Then he wondered if Liz knew about his FBI conversations. The woman had used him before to get what she had wanted; he felt he should be cautious. Still, his vette was back to full functionality, which left him giddy.

He decided, after doing his best to analyze the situation, to accept the invitation. He texted the reply to her number and then drove out of Santa De Lola Customs with a plan to put the vette through its paces. It worked great and he was having a grand time speeding around until he got pulled over by the California Highway Patrol and issued a ticket. He cursed silently to himself as the lawman handed him a ticket and commented on how nice his car looked.

For the rest of the day, he kept his foot out of the accelerator pedal and went back to work, where he pushed a mop bucket around for a bit, then left to go home so he could shower and change clothes for his dinner date.

He then headed out to the estate, arriving early, was flagged through the gate by an Amazon-sized brunette gate guard that flashed him a big grin and had him park his vehicle under a well-lit, covered parking area. She then drove him in a golf cart down to the mansion. He smiled back, wondering if he might be able to get a date, (it had been more than a while) and made small talk. The guard was friendly, but professional and demurred at his offer to go out for drinks some time. He sighed, but realized there were a lot more women at the estate he might be able to hook up with.

At the front of the mansion, Bob was greeted by a British footman, who led him out to patio one. Waiting there was Liz and Thornton. Chef Alfonso and Langley were preparing their meal. Langley served them all some wine, with a special vintage Liz had acquired. Bob was thrilled to see that it was a 1982 Lafite. He loved this stuff, but like other aspects of his lost fortune, this liquid gold had been off his menu for some time. He nodded to Liz who smiled back as he swirled his glass and sipped, then asked, "Are Frieda and Helga here?"

Liz shook her head and said, "Nope, Helga is back in school, I think you remember she had ambitions to get a PhD. Frieda is commuting back and forth between Stanford and here."

Bob nodded and said, "So, just us then."

Liz, a contrite expression on her features, said, "Bob, if I may, I am sorry about you're not getting a new position here at the Cleaver Foundation. I assure you; it was a temporary oversight. I am hoping that starting tonight and going forward, to rectify that unfortunate error."

In a cynical tone, Bob said, "Uh, sounds great! What did you have in mind?"

"We need a manager for the grounds. You would have a crew working for you. It pays well." Then just like she had done with Thornton, she slid a contract across the table to him. He nodded, picked it up, saw the generous offer along with a lengthy nondisclosure agreement that was pretty specific in its language about maintaining the trade secrets of the foundation and associated personal and business relationships.

He did not dwell on the NDA language, but instead, returned to staring at the generous offer. He grinned, signed both copies and handed them back.

Liz nodded and said, "After dinner, Langley will show you to your new quarters, if you decide to stay here with us on the estate. Frankly, I would recommend it. Free rent, so to speak, save you even more money."

Bob said, "Wow! Liz, uh, this is way more than I expected!" He could hardly wait now to tell Billy to go take his janitor position and shove it where the sun did not shine.

Shortly after that, dinner was served. While munching on his Caesar salad, he bit into a crouton that fought back. Hearing a cracking sound, he winced in pain, realizing he must have broken a tooth. Thornton came over and gave a cursory look, then said, "Yep, cracked down to the root. It will have to go!" Liz exclaimed, "Oh, darn, Bob, so very sorry! Did I mention we have free dental care here as well?"

Bob shook his head, trying to smile. He said, "I've got more than one tooth giving me a problem, been a while since I could afford a dentist."

Liz said, "Not to worry Mr. Oppenheimer, we have you covered!"

39

Miller and Borders were waiting in a coffee shop down the block from Helga's new apartment address. Earlier, Miller had contacted the woman and asked her to drop by and visit after her class was over that morning.

Helga showed up, grabbed a cup of coffee at the counter and then came over and sat across from Miller and Borders who were situated in a corner booth at the back of the place—she had earlier been advised by Liz not to be surprised if the FBI paid her a visit, so she felt no undue stress.

Since the day she had gone back to the Cleaver estate and had a new tooth swapped in to replace the one that Dr. Balm had mistakenly installed, Helga had felt herself return to her old personality, but better in many ways. She now could practically read other people's minds by following tic's, facial expressions, body language and voice tone. The longer someone talked to her, the more she could divine their purpose and their emotional state. She had already impressed her various professors as she was working through the curriculum. For this sudden visit out of the blue, she was thinking of it as "lawdog day finals".

Borders opened the conversation with, "So, Stanford! That's sort of like going to Harvard. I must say, I do miss my alma matter."

Helga nodded, realizing from the slight squint in Border's eyes that the woman was not thinking Stanford was up to Harvard standards. Lie number one had just been made. Helga also suspected the woman was also trying to use Harvard as a way to throw her off kilter in the interview. Helga decided the best tactic in this conversation was to maintain a therapist sort of position in her responses.

She said, "About? Like? I would say that is a fair approximation Dr. Borders, well done! We can talk more about yourself when you feel ready. Of course, I also went to a top university in Germany for my masters. I am sure you know how it all matters." Borders smiled back, looking somewhat bemused.

Miller said, "So, quite a turn of fortune winding up here. Care to explain who is footing the bill? Just a few months ago, you were working in a convenience store."

Helga nodded and said, "Special Agent Miller. What a pleasure to finally make your acquaintance. I have heard… so much about you."

Miller's expression showed she was hesitating with how to proceed, then Helga saw in the set of the woman's shoulders a shift to being more aggressive. Miller frowned, then said, "Care to answer my question?"

Helga thought about the tone and modulation of Miller's reply, along with her expression. The FBI agent thought she knew something and wanted to lead her down a path. She said, "Oh, the answer is straightforward. Elizabeth Cleaver is why. You see, while I was previously working for her, she had promised me as part of my employment contract to allow me to return to school so I could complete my PhD. And now, she is simply following up on that promise since she got the foundation back on track. You might recall the Mabel Belkin incident where I recovered the evidence you needed for that conviction."

Miller nodded and said, "And this prior employment, this is this from when you provided her inside information on what was going on at Pearly Whites?"

Helga smiled gently at this ham-fisted approach, wondering how the woman had ever managed to become an FBI agent, "I did not provide any sort of information to her about the company, let alone *inside*, because I never worked there."

"But you were living with Bob Oppenheimer who was. You should know we have talked with him as well."

Helga nodded, "If you talk to him, you might find his... recollection is pretty broken. Bob was in really bad shape mentally at that time. Most days, he was, sadly, on drugs and alcohol at the same time. He was mostly rather incoherent."

Borders queried, "What do you mean by "mentally"."

"As I just said, he was drinking a lot, taking illegal drugs that he got from sources he never revealed to me and seemed to be hallucinating a great deal. You might talk to him about the illegal drugs, perhaps that would lead you on a case into the drug underworld. At any rate, it was really quite impossible to hold any sort of meaningful conversation with the man during that interlude."

Borders looked at Miller and Helga could see the two women knew each other well enough that they communicated this way as part of their interrogation technique—it was a kind of bluff that might work on some people. However, this interview was not going the way they had anticipated. Helga maintained her calm demeanor, knowing the two were about to ramp up their efforts.

Miller said, "Listen, Ms. Krantz, we know Bob was telling you things about problems at the old company with their teeth. Are you denying that? And before you answer, this ties back to financial transactions that are quite illegal at the federal level. We have evidence that Liz Cleaver and Frieda were being fed this information."

Helga noted the transition to being more formal in how she was being addressed, then the accusation and threat of federal infractions. She responded, "Wow, you should pursue this evidence! However, I reiterate, the man was never coherent, in fact, as I mentioned earlier, he's not particularly coherent even today. Have you bothered to talk to him? You really should. Not sure that one could ever have derived much in the way of useful information to make any sort of viable conclusion from what Bob Oppenheimer often babbled about...bless his heart."

Borders was now writing furiously on a pad of paper and slid it over to Miller, who nodded and slipped it back. Helga waited them out.

Miller said, "So, we have you on record denying all allegations?"

"What allegations?"

Miller, now becoming impatient, barked, "About the foundation, illegal insider trading information, flakey offshore activity, it's a long list."

People over in the coffee line were now looking in their direction. Borders nudged Miller, who hadn't realized she was getting overly loud. Helga said, "I am afraid, Special Agent Miller… and Dr. Borders… I really can't help you out here at all, your allegations make no sense to me, based on the experiences that I recall from that time. In fact, if necessary, I would wind up contradicting this in a court of law if called to testify. Anyway, I am sorry if you made this trip for nothing. You really have the wrong impression about me."

She then took a large sip of her coffee as she watched the two women try to hide their disappointment which was fascinating to her. She was definitely learning a lot here that she felt she would be able to use in her private practice once she completed her program.

Miller sighed and stood. Borders followed suit, gathering her coffee and notepad. Helga glanced at the pad and noticed there was nothing but actual scribbles instead of detailed notes, further confirming that Border's earlier activity had all been a bluff.

Miller said, "I believe you might consider getting an attorney Ms. Krantz."

Helga remaining seated, shrugged and said, "Well, probably not, they are kinda expensive and I am a college student and an immigrant, just trying to make it in this great country. Again, I am sorry you have gotten the wrong impression about me."

Miller squinted hard, obviously restraining herself and said, "Funny. Have a nice day."

Helga replied, "You too!"

Out in the car on their way back to Santa De Lola, Borders said, "Shit, that was like she was interrogating us! What did you think?"

Miller said, "That woman is calculating, smart and frankly, I felt like I was back at the academy in Quantico. We've got to get some better evidence on this bunch than Bob Oppenheimer. For sure, I don't think we are going to flip Helga Krantz easily if at all."

They continued down the road discussing their meeting, not noticing the nondescript old Toyota pickup several car lengths behind them that was maintaining a discreet distance. Inside the Toyota, was one of the ex-cops, Alice O'Reilly, who was now on Liz Cleaver's payroll.

Alice had been assigned to keep track of these two women's comings and goings. She had, in the past, worked undercover and for years had been tracking down dirtball drug dealers until she had a bad run in with an errant FBI agent that had left her bitter over the fact the agent had destroyed the case she had been building for over a year. She had no love of the agency and Alice was happy with her new job.

Plus, Liz had also provided Alice with a replacement tooth for one that had been lost during the very dust up that led to her undercover roll being exposed, again by the imbecilic FBI agent when during a raid, he had struck her with the butt of his pistol, mistaking her for one of the perps. She would never forget Agent Benowitz, that much was for sure.

Bob was relishing his new assignment as manager of landscaping. First off, Liz had made sure his broken tooth had been promptly replaced along with two others that were in bad shape and that had been a relief—the pain of the one that he had shattered on the hardest crouton ever known to the human race was a distant memory now.

Also, it helped that his two direct reports were extremely attractive females that kept him occupied with meetings. He had so far failed to make headway to possibly dating these two, however, both of them had agreed to pose occasionally for his painting and sketching that he was fully engrossed in even more than before—Liz had given him a bit of time off each day to focus on his hobby. It was now an obsession. He was really getting proficient, drawing what everyone at the estate said were Picasso grade renderings with a Renoir-like color palette.

When not moving a brush around, or making a sketch, he spent his spare time learning French and Greek as well from his two lovely assistants, and over the last few weeks, he was using each language more and more, mixing it into his English effortlessly, or so it seemed to him. It appeared to him that he was inventing the most natural of languages and he used this hybrid form increasingly, to the confusion of whomever he was trying to communicate with.

It didn't seem to matter however as his assistants, Mariam, who spoke Greek, and Danielle, who spoke French, kept things running like a top around the grounds, effectively isolating him from unneeded contact with people. Plus, they both spoke far more fluently than him and tried to enhance his lousy enunciation, which further kept him distracted as they corrected him while he painted their portraits over and over again on what seemed to be an infinite number of blank canvases that arrived daily.

Done for the day, Mariam and Danielle, one on each of his arms, led him to patio fourteen for dinner and then three hours later, after he was stuffed with pizza and thoroughly snockered on Bordeaux, he wandered to his room. As he drifted off to sleep, he wondered if he would ever get beyond pizza with either of the two.

*

Borders was now obsessively preoccupied with combing through all the files that the FBI had looking for any sort of clue that would help Miller nail Liz Cleaver with some sort of financial money laundering scheme.

Her determination was driven by two things. The first was she didn't want to have to return to talking to actual emergency ward patients at the hospital she was on leave from for this FBI gig, which paid better than her old job. The second was, if Miller succeeded, Borders succeeded and perhaps they would get another big case. This went back to reason number one—she preferred the FBI gig.

There was an underlying irritant to her current efforts as well. Helga Krantz. The woman had clearly outmaneuvered both Miller and Borders without breaking a sweat during the ineffectual interrogation in Stanford. Borders did not care for being on the receiving end of that kind of action and wanted to show the woman she was every bit of capable of psychological warfare. Hell, the woman was not even a shrink yet. Sighing to herself, she kept digging.

Miller entered the room and with a nudge, broke her concentration. When she looked up, there was a cup of herbal tea in front of her. She chuckled, accepted the offering and Miller smiled, went around the desk as she set down her own drink, then plopped into the chair across from Borders. The two sipped their beverages for a bit.

Miller said, "Find anything new?"

Borders leaned back and said, "Still hunting. There were so many shenanigans going on with this crowd back at that time."

Miller sighed, "So is there anyone left to talk to? Have we missed something?"

Borders shrugged, "There are some people, former employees for one, a Martin Crosswaithe relative for another, but they have never come up in any of the earlier conversations we have had."

Miller asked, "Like who?"

"Well, Trace Orbaugh, the relative. Then a couple of scientists, though their actual names are not mentioned."

"I doubt Orbaugh would be of any help since he is the grandson of Martin Crosswaithe and is living out of the country these days. What about the other two?"

"I don't have much. Just that they were two scientists in the middle of working on fixes. Then they disappeared when shit went south."

Miller sat up and said, "Now, that's interesting. Maybe nothing. Lots of employees were simply dumped with the collapse of the old company, but still."

"What are you thinking then?"

Miller shrugged, "Perhaps we should locate these two mysterious scientists and have a talk."

*

Liz was chatting with Frieda and Thornton on Patio three. Thornton said, "Dr. Balm is recovering nicely. How'd you talk him into returning?"

"Oh, a wee bribe and a promise to help make his life considerably better, i.e., no more dyslexia or desire to over imbibe."

An hour earlier, Thornton had completed a multi tooth insertion procedure into Dr Balm, which to Liz meant she was feeling more secure than she had earlier that day.

"And he will be reliably reticent to talk about his earlier activities?"

"Yep! For one, he remembers little about his time since he was drunk even while working. And he is looking forward to his new gig in San Francisco running our free clinic without having his earlier conditions interfering with his work. Plus, I had the pleasure of firing Adams, the previous asshole that Mabel had hired."

Thornton guffawed then asked, "Liz, since we are winding down on the local staff activity you brought me on to sort out, I was wondering what you had in mind going forward?"

Liz replied, "Oh, did I not mention this? I am opening a clinic in Grand Cayman. To go along with that there is this lovely beach side condominium, just waiting for the doctor that will lead up that operation." Thornton smiled and said, "Fascinating!"

Liz smiled, "Yes, fascinating and lucrative. Are you interested?"

Thornton said, "Do you really have to ask?" The three all broke out into a chuckle.

Liz then said, "One more item. About Bob Oppenheimer and his teeth. Did you get all four installed?"

Thornton nodded and said, "Yep. He only knows about the three that needed replacing however."

Liz nodded, then stood and said, "Perfect. Sorry, I have to run, have an update call coming up with Sally and Billy. Enjoy your new assignment Thornton."

Moments later she was back in her ultra secure fourth floor office looking at one of the new modified Wi-Fi emitters she had designed. She had then worked with their contract electrical engineer, Roger Brown, to have the emitters installed at key locations around the estate. The man had been quite happy to have another gig after successfully completing the production teeth project.

She opened the wireless control app on her phone she had written and had several test teeth with her as well that responded just as they were designed to do with the new system. She nodded to herself, then opened a conference call with the PhoenixGen team.

Sally came up first, then Billy. She nodded to them and said, "Hello partners! How are things going today?"

Sally replied, "Well, we now have our first orders coming in from dental clinics in Europe. Plus, we have the sales team moving here in the U.S. Some of the more forward looking dental surgeons that see the writing on the wall have reached out to us already. Mostly they are asking about discounts."

Liz shuddered at the last part and said, "We are already offering them dirt cheap."

"Yeah, though one of these dentist blogs on some social media site and wrote that once you put in a genetic tooth, you are unlikely to see the customer again until they need some other work."

"Hmmm, perhaps we should provide some of my complimentary croutons to help drive more business."

Billy and Sally went silent and exchanged mildly confused looks with each other, then Liz remembered they were not in on the joke of Bob's tooth breakage. She decided to drop the matter and said, "So how about those EU orders!"

Billy said, "Got a large shipment going to France, then Italy, then Spain."

"Excellent."

Sally said, "Yep, we have accounts set up and they are billed at shipping. By months end, we should have our first revenue stream."

Liz nodded and said, "Let's make sure Wall Street knows. That should give the stock a boost. Oh, and by the way, would love to have the two of you out this Friday evening, it's time to have another big dinner and Chef Alfonso has some great new recipes to try out on us! Can I count you both in?"

Sally and Billy both nodded. Liz grinned and said, "See you then!"

40

Miller was prepping for a call with an FBI legal attaché in Bridgetown, Barbados. The time difference of four hours along with the attaché they had been assigned, who asserted to be working on their own top priority assignments, had led to a week's delay in getting this meeting off the ground.

During that interlude, Miller had dug up the names of the two scientists that had previously worked on the genetic teeth at Pearly Whites. The first person was Fiona Kendle, the lead scientist with a deep background in genetics. The second was a former college professor, named Samuel Heneky.

Borders came rolling in just minutes before the call and was examining the files Miller had put together. As she read the documents, she said, "So, these two former employees had made money off the failed stock of the previous Pearly Whites though all the transactions looked legal?"

Miller nodded and said, "Yeah, it looks legit, they were selling options they had received that were exercisable. However, I also accessed phone logs for the two and saw where Fiona Kendle had several calls with Liz Cleaver at different times."

Borders nodded thoughtfully and said, "Interesting. Why would the lead scientist, working for the old company, be talking to Liz Cleaver?"

Miller replied, "It's suspicious as shit in my opinion. Plus, there actually was some sort of arrangement with the previous management team of Pearly Whites, that the foundation would fund the plant production build out in a partnership scenario. Mabel Belkin claimed that Kendle and Heneky visited the estate at least twice by themselves after that arrangement was signed. Which matches up with dates in the phone log."

Borders said, "Ah! So, this looks promising then."

Miller nodded, turned to her computer and started the conference call with the Barbados office. A moment later, the attaché came on. His name was Victor Vasquez. He said, "Good afternoon Special Agent Miller. May I ask, who is that with you?"

"This is our FBI psych consultant on this case, Dr. Borders."

Victor nodded and said, "Nice to make your acquaintance Doctor. So, Special Agent Miller, you would like for me to talk with these two people, Fiona Kendle and Samuel Heneky?"

Miller said, "Yep, just like the earlier email stated, which we cc'd your boss on." She noted Victor looked a bit annoyed at her bringing up his boss. She continued, "And, as per that email, if they can corroborate what we believe happened, we need to see if these two can be forced to work with the FBI on the case we are working on."

Victor continued to look annoyed. He said, "Ah, okay, however, they are in Aruba. That means I have to travel there for this. It's all day for me to fly there, then the time I spend running them down, getting statements, and then a full day of flying back. And that's if the damn airlines are on time."

Based on his tone and explanation, Miller no longer needed to wonder if Victor was irritated. What she didn't know was that as an extracurricular enterprise, Victor and his wife were running an exotic destination travel business and had loads of customers flying in from Canada to spend a week traveling around the Caribbean at the same time he was expected to have to take this trip. Not that she would have cared.

She said, "Uh, Victor, jeez, sorry, I must be all confused. You see, your boss told me you do this kind of shit all the time! Was he wrong?" Victor was clearly agitated now, but shook his head and said, "No, no, he is right. Just the timing is not great."

"Boohoo Victor! Do we need to talk to somebody that is interested in the assignment?"

Victor caved at that point—his boss had recently become aware of his side endeavors and had probably picked him for the very reason that he was more interested in touring islands than doing FBI work. Sounding beaten, he intoned, "I will be headed out day after tomorrow."

"Terrific! Well, any questions, just holler! She reached for her mouse to kill the call and said, "Lazy fuck." Her mouth was quicker than her mouse work. A now insulted Victor reared back in his chair just as the screen went blank.

*

Sally and Billy were waiting next to each other in the front lobby of PhoenixGen when Liz's helicopter arrived in front of the building. They grinned at each other as they boarded the aircraft. Moments later the craft was back in the air.

Ten minutes later, they set down at the estate and were escorted by a footman to patio fourteen.

Langley came over, welcomed them and nodded to a wine waiter who took their drink order. Billy asked for a Macallan then said, "You should really try one Sally." She demurred and requested a top end Giesen Pinot Grigio instead.

As they sipped their drinks, Frieda came out, her own drink in hand and settled in next to Billy. Shortly after, Liz arrived and sat down by Sally, effectively sandwiching their guests between them. Billy laughed and said, "Listen, I promise, we have no plans of running away. The others laughed and over the next half hour, as appetizers were served, they talked a little business but mostly pleasure.

As dinner progressed, they were now into their fancy salads, which had Billy exclaiming about how wonderful Chef Alfonso's hand mixed Caesar dressing was. Next, they were considering their entrees when dinner was unintentionally interrupted.

A fleeing Bob Oppenheimer came running out onto the patio, flew by their table and dove into the pool that was a few yards from where the dinner party was seated. Right behind Bob were his two agitated assistants, Mariam and Danielle, who were shouting at him, though what they were saying was only partially understandable.

Mariam was using Greek, Danielle was using French, both were interspersing English into their high volume commentary.

Bob resurfaced. Everybody at the table was now on their feet and Liz said, "What the hell is going on here?"

Bob hollered back at her. He started in English, then Greek, then French. Every sentence was a rolling tumble between the three languages. Liz just stood there nodding to herself.

Billy said to Sally, "That guy really has finally gone totally nuts."

Frieda walked over to Liz. She said, "Uh, you don't seem too surprised."

Liz gave Frieda a look that indicated she should drop her line of inquiry, which she did. Liz then said, "Mariam, Danielle, what is going on here?"

The two women came over and excitedly jumped into an explanation. Mariam said, "Bob is becoming way too touchy feely of late. He grabbed both my boobs a minute ago while supposedly getting me positioned for a portrait."

Danielle nodded in agreement and said, "Earlier, he fondled my butt!"

Liz kept a straight face and said, "So, this is about sexual harassment of the worst kind in the workplace?" Mariam and Danielle nodded in agreement.

Liz turned to Bob and said, "Bob, what do you have to say in your defense? Is all this true?"

Bob, looking frantic, began his multi-lingual babbling defense. Liz was gently shaking her head, and it was apparent to everyone she was struggling now to keep from laughing. She turned to Liz and said, "Have Nigel and his crew come and fish that lunatic out of the pool."

Moments later, Nigel's crew surrounded the edges while Bob continued to babble from the middle of the pool. Liz sighed and directed Nigel to have his crew retrieve Bob so they could get on with their dinner.

The footmen dove in, Bob tried to dive under them, though to no avail. After Bob was captured and escorted away, (he never stopped babbling the whole time), Liz promised Mariam and Danielle they would get a bonus for putting up with Bob and not to worry ever again about the crazy man. Dinner resumed.

Billy asked, "What the hell was that all about? I mean, Bob is definitely weird, but that was off the scale insane."

Sally shrugged and said, "I liked the part where they chased his ass into the pool."

Liz and Frieda giggled, then Liz said, "Well, we have been working very hard with Bob, trying to get him in shape to be a valued team member. Sadly, I think the time for that sort of effort is over. What do you all think?"

Sally said, "Fire his ass."

*

The next morning, Bob was fed, then escorted to Liz's office for his exit interview. Liz ignored his babbling, handed him a severance check of one year's pay along with his severance document that he signed without reading. Liz looked at the signature, nodded, and a copy was given to him. Liz reminded him he was not to talk about the foundation or PhoenixGen to anyone. If he kept his mouth shut, he would get a second year's payout in twelve months.

Bob was then accompanied to his corvette and escorted by a golfcart security detachment back to the main gate where he peeled out, shouting angrily, though incoherently, his voice fading away in the distance.

Liz was still at her desk when Frieda showed up and said, "Could we talk?" Liz nodded so Frieda entered, closing the door behind her. She sat across from Liz and said, "What the hell was going on last night?"

Liz smiled and said, "Well, you know, Bob broke a tooth. We fixed that and along with several more implants that were customized for him so I could resolve a problem."

Frieda said, "And that problem was?"

"Bob. He knows too much about what went on back when you and I were trading stocks to recover foundation funds."

Frieda nodded slowly with understanding, then said, "So, this was a way of shutting him up without cutting his tongue out."

"Essentially. I personally needed the man gone, can't stand him, but if I dumped him out into the world in his normal state, the FBI would likely get him to cooperate. You and I could be arrested for what we did back then. Serious jail time sort of arrested. So, I am eliminating loose ends, which he definitely is."

Frieda nodded and said, "Thanks Liz for being on top of all of this. Listen, I wanted you to know I still care about you, and it is clear you are taking care of all of us with your actions." She paused, smiled and asked, "What do you think about if we gave our old relationship another try? Helga and I talked, she is good with it as well."

Liz smiled and said, "Sounds like something I would like to return to as well." The two stood, embraced with a kiss, then headed out for a late breakfast, holding hands as they talked excitedly to each other.

41

Bob was beyond confused at this turn of events. In his head, he was, the man that had orchestrated getting everyone back together. He felt he had done everything asked of him, he had worked hard for his money, hard for the company and foundation, and here he was, unemployed, incomprehensible, and shoved to the curb. He also knew there was no way for him to squeal about what had happened, as his severance document, which he had finally read, had strict penalties if he were to go back online and resume Bob's blog. Plus, he was scared of Liz these days, the woman was very different in the way she effortlessly controlled events.

His bank account, for the time being, was in good shape as he had deposited the check he had been given and knew he would get even more later. While all of that was fine, it still left him wondering what he would be doing in the future now that he could not talk legibly to anyone. And that was another thing that confused the hell out of him. He was now moderately fluent in three languages but could not make a sentence that that was only in one.

Oddly, he could write in each language just fine. He just could not speak. It was part of his obvious consternation when trying to explain his problems the night of his breast/ass Dunkirk that led to his dismissal, (he had to admit to himself, however, he had misbehaved with the two women).

He sighed, sinking into a deeper funk over his dilemma. He decided it was time to go into a bar, sit in a corner and drink himself under the table.

Once there, he placed his order by pointing to the menu. The place had some decent booze, so before long he was snockered. Once in that state, he began plotting, though the plotting was like it normally was for him when intoxicated, and he was getting nowhere.

Closing time arrived and the burly owner came to his table, shook him awake, as he had dozed off. It was time to close out his tab. Bob tried to explain his situation, the owner said, "What the fuck did you just say?" Bob tried harder and the owner rolled his eyes and replied, "Listen buddy, pay your bill, then leave, I gotta life besides this place." Bob handed over his debit card, then after the transaction was complete, he wandered out to his car where he fell asleep in the front seat.

A few hours later, a Santa De Lola police car was shining its lights into his front windshield and a cop was having Bob exit his vehicle. Still quite inebriated, Bob rattled off indecipherable answers. When that didn't work, he tried using his arms and hands to emphasize what he was saying and that led to a misinterpretation by the officer that Bob was threatening him. Shortly after, he was on the ground getting handcuffed, placed in the back seat of the cruiser where he sobbed as he watched his beloved Corvette being towed off.

Once at the police department, the shift lieutenant was pulled in to listen to Bob meander through multiple languages. The lieutenant suggested they take Bob to the emergency room as this could be a medical issue going beyond just being drunk. Once at the hospital ER, he was checked over by a nurse who then alerted one of the shift doctors. The doctor tried for a bit to sort out what was going on. After a bit, he turned to the cop and said, "I have no clue what is going on here unless the guy has had a stroke, but I do recognize words from three different languages. The only thing we can do is run tests on him."

It was then, next to the bed that Bob was laying on, that he saw a pen and notepad. He grabbed them and started writing out an explanation written entirely in English.

The doctor looked at it, handed it to the cop, who read it. They nodded to each other and then Bob was taken back to the police department where he was left in the drunk tank to sober up overnight.

The next morning, Detective Friday came in and was reading the previous night's arrest reports. When he came across Bob's, he thought something seemed familiar about the man's name. He read the handwritten statement the arresting officer had included from when Bob had tried to write down his situation. After a moment, the detective decided to visit him.

Friday recognized Bob immediately from his prior experiences with the company Pearly Whites some months back. He had Bob escorted into an interrogation room. Bob was shown the police report and his earlier scribbles from the hospital. He pointed to it and with a pleading look, made squiggle marks with his right hand like he was writing.

Friday shrugged, retrieved a notepad and pen which he pushed across the table to Bob, who went to work, essentially writing an essay, again all in English, then slid the notepad back to Friday. The detective read the document, grunting to himself occasionally like he was going to laugh, but finally nodded and said, "So, you had three teeth transplanted into your yap by a dental surgeon at the Cleaver estate and that is why you now speak in three languages at once?"

Bob nodded in the affirmative.

Friday smirked, "Right. Question, however. What is this symbol or picture, or whatever, after the first paragraph?"

Bob looked where Friday was pointing, then wrote a note on another sheet of paper, "I was just riffing. It's just my creative side shining through."

*

Agent Victor Vasquez was boarding his flight back to Barbados at the conclusion of his trip where he had interviewed Special Agent Miller's two subjects. While he had been more than pissed off after the way Miller had treated him, especially ending their earlier call with an insult, he had soldiered on, doing what was required of him.

As it turned out, the trip had been more than worthwhile, but for reasons quite different than what Miller had hoped for. First off, Fiona Kendle and Sam Heneky had been the most gracious hosts when he arrived, displaying no apparent concern at his just showing up out of the blue at their recently purchased seaside home that they were in the process of moving into. He had to admit, the place was a really nice, new construction, and modern in esthetic. They had escorted him out to their beachside veranda where they all sat and talked.

Victor started with, "So, you are both former employees of the firm that was known as Pearly Whites, is that correct." Both Fiona and Sam acknowledged that fact.

"Did you ever leak information to Elizabeth Cleaver of the Cleaver foundation about problems that the company was having with their product?"

Both Sam and Fiona denied any knowledge. It was then that lunch was delivered from a local seafood restaurant— the fresh caught snapper was delicious. At the conclusion of the meal, Victor wrapped up his questions—he had everything he needed to get this investigation out of his hair.

Fiona said, "I have never met an FBI agent. What a cool job." Victor shrugged and said, "Well, after nearly twenty four years, I am ready to retire."

Both Fiona and Sam smiled as Sam said, "I can see how it must be an extremely challenging job. What are you going to do in retirement?"

Victor grinned and said, "Well, my wife has already started a travel business. We've got a large contingent just arriving today back in Barbados. I just love those tourist excursions. We trying to make it fun for our customers so we can build up repeat business."

Fiona chuckled and said, "Wow! You interested in maybe having a partnership? Sam and I have been thinking about this exact sort of thing ourselves!" Which led to a long conversation and since nothing else was on the official business agenda, when Sam offered him some expensive whisky, he accepted.

So now homeward bound on his flight to Barbados, Victor was excited and could not wait to tell his wife, Maria, about the opportunities that the two of them now had in front of them. He planned to turn in his retirement papers as soon as he got his report sent off to Special Agent Miller.

*

After watching Sanchez depart for his flight, Sam Heneky gave Fiona Kendle a hug and said, "Boy, I never figured we'd get this lucky again."

Fiona nodded and said, "I couldn't fathom dealing with all the things that happened to Liz after we headed to Paris. No wonder we never heard from her until now."

Sam smiled and said, "The woman came through on her earlier promises!" They kissed, then headed down to their private beach for a swim.

42

Miller sat down excitedly at her desk and logged onto her computer. The writeup from Victor Vasquez had arrived and she was convinced this was the nail in the coffin of Liz Cleaver. However, as she read down through the report, she became more and more glum.

She shook her head, wondering if she should just fly to Aruba herself and question the two suspects, though she knew her boss, Supervisor Special Agent Salton, would never approve such an expenditure for such a weak case. Silently cursing to herself, Borders came strolling in with a smile on her face as she bit into an apple she was snacking on. Miller grumpily asked, "So what the hell are you all cheery about?"

Borders, rather than answering, said, "It can wait for a moment. What's up?"

Miller sighed and said, "Well, that attaché accomplished exactly jack shit in Aruba. In fact, he has cleared Kendle and Heneky of any wrongdoing. It makes no damn sense!"

She then got up from her seat so Borders could sit down and read the report. Borders, once done, leaned back and said, "That is weird. But hey, let's shift gears for a minute." She took another big bite out of her apple as she exited Miller's seat and went to the chair that she usually sat in on the other side of the desk.

Miller said, "So, my gears are shifted. What's up?"

Borders finished swallowing and then said, "Got a call from a Detective Friday over at the Santa De Lola police department. He and I met back when Billy Fuller had side effects from the early versions of the genetic teeth. He advised that they had arrested Bob Oppenheimer the evening before and the detective was talking to Bob, sort of, this morning. Friday is saying that some teeth that have been implanted into Oppenheimer have done some weirdass shit to him."

"Like what?"

"Well, for starters, he is now speaking in French and Greek, as well as English."

"Bob Oppenheimer? Speaking in three languages? Hell, he was not particularly good at English from what we found the last time we talked to him."

"True. Well, the times, they are a changing."

Miller nodded slowly, shrugged then said, "It's not like we've got something better to do. So, let's tell Friday we are on our way over to the PD and to hang on to Oppenheimer until we get there."

Borders nodded, whipped out her phone and made the call as they headed for their car. Once at the police department, Friday led them to his office. After everyone was seated, he said, "So, take a look at this." He handed over Bob's written statement from the night he was arrested and the one he had written when talking to Friday that morning.

The two women read them. Borders looked up and said, "So, detective, he can write in any one of three languages, but he speaks in all three at once?"

He nodded and added, "Also, he claims the implanted teeth did this. Now, if that is true, we are again looking at side effects like we saw the first time around, though so far, no buses have been rammed."

Borders laughed, remembering that whole earlier rather cataclysmic event which had wound up drawing her into her current gig. She said, "If this is a side effect, it is beyond any psychological phenomena that I have ever heard of. Where is Mr. Oppenheimer now?"

"Well, we dropped the earlier charges against him for drunk and disorderly as well as attempted assault of a police officer and he is at his apartment. He said, or wrote, I should clarify, that he really wants to fill you in on what is going on with nefarious misdeeds, as he wrote it, over at the Cleaver estate."

Miller, feeling suddenly upbeat at this turn of events and said, "We have plenty to talk to this guy about." Moments later they were out the door, headed to Bob's place. Once there, Bob handed them a bunch of hand scribbled documents. While Border's looked at them, Miller decided to treat Bob to lunch while he explained the situation to them.

At Perky's, Borders asked, "So, Bob, please, using your mixed language skills, please elaborate on what is going on." Bob did and Borders looked impressed. She glanced over at Miller and said, "His French words sound great!"

"He made sense?"

"No, but his enunciation is wonderful. I took French one and two back in high school, for what it's worth. Anyway, he is mixing the three languages, just like he wrote in his statement. Part English, French and the rest is Greek to me." Miller rolled her eyes at the pun.

Borders looked back at Bob and continued, "So, we read your assertions about how this happened. We get that this is a problem, but it does not exactly help our case. What's changed in that regard." Bob nodded, now equipped full time with a notepad and pen. He wrote, "When I got the teeth, some of what was foggy about the time at Pearly Whites became more…clear." Interspersed were some symbols similar to what he had drawn when with Detective Friday.

Miller, after a quick read, said, "And? What do you now know?"

Bob wrote that he could detail what they did during various conversations. Miller nodded and said, "We need you to testify to all of this in court. You interested?" He wrote, "I am willing, ready and want to screw Liz Cleaver royally!" Again, the symbols were interspersed.

Miller giggled as she handed the last comment to Borders. She said, "So how do we get you back to plain old English?" Bob wrote, "We can remove the teeth one at a time, see what happens. I think one is the French tooth, the other Greek, the other is the mixer. I don't know which is which, but two were put in on my left side, one on the right."

"Jeez, this is like going to a casino. I say, we pull the one on the right!"

Miller nodded, then asked, "But what if that does not work?"

Bob wrote, "Then put it back in and take the one's on the left out one at a time. I am more than willing to put up with the discomfort." Miller leaned back and said, "This sounds like a plan. One thing though. What are these symbols that you keep adding?

Bob shrugged and wrote, "I think it will be a new language. It could be called "Freekenchlish"."

Borders commented, "It looks almost hieroglyphic. However, once we get you sorted with your tooth removals, you can get back to your normal life, whatever that is."

Bob leaned back, grinned and wrote, "Either of you dating anyone?"

The women sighed as Miller said, "Meeting over Bob. Look for a girlfriend somewhere else."

*

Frieda was a happy woman for the first time in a long time. Over the last several days, she and Liz had talked through the issues and events that had led them to where they were now.

She had a few chores to attend to this morning now that Mariam and Danielle were assigned to be part of her team. The two women were hard workers and did their jobs without much supervision. Still, she liked to stay informed. So, she was on her way out the front door of the mansion where she would climb in her golf cart and roll over to where a new palm tree grove was being installed up near the front gates.

To her surprise, when she arrived at the cart, Liz slid into the passenger side. Already sitting in the back were Sally and Billy.

Frieda giggled and climbed into her seat, and they were rolling up the main drive towards the path which would take them directly to the grove.

Waiting for them were Mariam and Danielle. The group walked around and talked about how beautiful this was all going to be in just a few years as the trees settled in.

The palms were already of the more mature variety, as Liz had said she didn't think they should have to wait long to see the grove in all its glory. A crew of workman were running irrigation, digging holes and planting the trees.

It was then that Liz's phone rang. She pulled it out of the back pocket of her shorts and without looking to see who was calling put it on speaker and said, "Liz here."

"Um, yeah, Liz, this is Juanita up at the front gate. Um… we have some visitors."

"Oh, who is it?"

"Um, well, they said to tell you it was Special Agent Miller from the FBI."

Liz nodded and said, "Okay, lead them down and seat them on patio one. We will be there in a few." She looked at the group and said, "let's go."

Nervously, Frieda asked, "The FBI?"

Liz nodded and said, "Yeah, been expecting Miller to show up and try to rattle some info out of us. Not to worry."

Frieda nodded, though she did not feel as reassured as Liz sounded.

*

Once they were all seated on the patio, Liz said, "So, Coffee? Or, whatever you like."

Miller looked at Borders, smiled and said, "Sure, coffee sounds great."

While they were being served, she pulled a wad of documents out of a thick folder she had with her and slid them across the table to Liz. Liz glanced down, then back up and said, "So, what can we help you with Special Agent Miller?"

"Oh, we don't need much, unless you want to confess to the charges in those documents. Also, there is a search warrant in the pile for the FBI to go through this property."

Liz said, "The entire property? You are going to busy for a bit, I can tell you that for sure."

Miller looked confident as she said, "Got all the help I need. But before we start, what about Bob?"

"Bob?"

"Yeah, Bob Oppenheimer. Your former employee with fucked up implants."

"Ah, that Bob. Well, he did ask to get some of the PhoenixGen teeth to fix some dental issues he was having."

"The ones that made him unable to speak coherently?"

"I have no idea what you are referring to Special Agent Miller."

"I see. Well, one thing you overlooked in your little scheme. Bob could still write."

Liz nodded but said nothing. She decided it was time to enforce the penalty phase of Bob's severance contract. She said, "I am having a hard time with this whole cockamamie story, sorry. Sounds like Bob though."

Miller nodded and said, "Well, let's get him in here to…talk with you. He's doing a lot better all of a sudden." Liz nodded, trying to keep her cool, laying her own phone on the table.

Five minutes later, Bob showed up, under FBI escort and sat down directly across from Liz, smiling. Liz smiled back, noting his smug look—a bit of her rage dragon rose in response, but she subdued it.

She nonchalantly placed her right hand on her phone as she said, "Wow, this is terrible that you think we did something to you Bob. Especially after that generous severance you got, as you might…recall."

Bob said, "Oh you certainly did. And I spilled the beans to the FBI, well sort of, well… His voice trailed off, then he added, "We had to remove the two teeth on the left side for that to happen." Liz went wide eyed and said, "So you took out two of your teeth? And you spilled the beans?"

She rolled her eyes, almost laughing, then continued, "Mister, you really make me wonder why I gave you a severance after what you did to Mariam and Danielle?"

Without looking down, she then opened the app on her phone, knowing exactly where it was and subtly tapped it to activate one of the customized Wi-Fi emitters located on the underside of their table. Bob suddenly stopped smiling and said, "Uh, I feel…bizarre!"

Liz said, "Bizarre? Isn't that the French word for weird?"

Miller said, "What the hell is wrong now Oppenheimer?"

He rambled out a sentence, but it was not French, English or Greek. Miller looked alarmed now and said, "Bob, write it down, write it down!" He nodded, though looked alarmed as Liz herself slid a pad and pen over to him. He began writing and it was his new hieroglyph based language.

Miller stared at what he wrote and said, "What the hell did you do to him?"

Liz said, "Special Agent, I am just sitting here. I did nothing, I assure you, absolutely nothing! This is why we had to get rid of him, plus, I bet he failed to mention in his earlier statement that he sexually assaulted two of our employees just a short time back who would love to tell their story to the local police as well as the FBI, especially since you are here! Your witness is a total flake with criminal tendencies in more than one area of his life!"

Billy jumped in at this point and said, "Special Agent, Liz is right! We were on the verge of firing Bob Oppenheimer at work for timecard fraud as well—he literally stole thousands of dollars. I can show you all our books on that if you would like. Liz here hired the twit after we canned him to try and save him from himself."

Sally nodded in confirmation and said, "That is all completely true Special Agent Miller."

Miller was now furious as she got to her feet and spun Bob around in his chair. She hollered, "You left that part out, asshole!" Bob, wild-eyed and clearly distressed, slumped back in his seat and continued his incomprehensibly mutterings.

Liz, doing her best to look concerned, said, "Um, we should get him a doctor. And, from now on, Special Agent Miller, you'll need to talk to my lawyer, because I am tired of this constant investigation that continues to demonstrate we are innocent."

Miller glowered at her but said nothing.

Liz continued, "Now, feel free to search the place as much as you like. I can even get you a guided tour going."

She signaled Nigel, "Show the FBI... everything!"

Nigel grinned and said, "With pleasure!"

Miller, clearly off her game with her witness looking like the criminal idiot and her case in tatters, said, "Fuck me over!"

Liz nodded as she thought to herself, *In that regard, I will assist you in any way that I can!*